Bryson Coventry thrillers by Jim Michael Hansen

NIGHT LAWS
SHADOW LAWS
FATAL LAWS
DEADLY LAWS
BANGKOK LAWS (Upcoming)
IMMORTAL LAWS (Upcoming)

What they're saying about Jim Michael Hansen's
DEADLY LAWS

"[A] chain reaction that keeps the reader glued to 400+ pages of electrifying tension. ... Hansen has once again demonstrated that he is a gifted wordsmith and is able to balance the thriller, crime, romance and violence aspects of writing and develop them into a well written novel. ... The masterful twist at the end is stunning."

—Aldo T. Calcagno (Mystery Dawg)
FUTURES MYSTERY ANTHOLOGY MAGAZINE, FMAM.biz

"Talented author Jim Michael Hansen keeps the many subplots and characters moving in a delicate balancing act . . . I'm pleased to recommend this tale to any thriller or mystery fan. The imaginative departure from the time-tired plotlines will satisfy and have readers looking for other books by this author."

—Anne K. Edwards, NEW MYSTERY READER MAGAZINE
NewMysteryReader.com

"Just as with the previous three books, this one grabbed me from the first page. . . . This author has a great knack for going just deep enough into one area and then shifting to another just at the right time. This technique also helps to build the tension. And believe me – there is tension. Should you read this book? Yes, definitely. I have said this before about this author's other works and it still applies now; turn off your crime thrillers on television and tune-in to this book."

—Kathy Martin, IN THE LIBRARY REVIEWS
InTheLibraryReviews.com

"Jim Hansen is more than an experienced trial lawyer, he is a master of the erotic serial killer mystery. *Deadly Laws* is his latest and best in a series of similar novels set in the Denver area featuring protagonist Bryson Coventry, the 34-year-old head of Denver's Homicide Unit. . . . Jim's plots are hairy, his pace is harried, and his stories are kinky. He is a master of Alfred Hitchcock-like endings which really throw the readers off the track and yet are logically explained eventually. None of his books end like one might expect. For those readers who like to predict endings, be very careful out there.."

—Bob Spear, HEARTLAND REVIEWS
HeartlandReviews.com

"Hansen's plots are masterful and terrifying because they could be real life. His characters are rich, multi-dimensional and deeply flawed. . . [*Deadly Laws*] is a page-turner that leaves you scared, wary of strangers and breathless."

—Andrea Sisco, ARMCHAIR INTERVIEWS
ArmchairInterviews.com

"*Deadly Laws* is Jim Hansen's fourth Bryson Coventry novel, and I'm still on the edge of my seat. . . . The cases are always shocking. Jim Hansen knows how to keep his readers on the edge of their seats, and perhaps a time or two you may find yourself teetering on the edge in the process. Expect a spiraling plot and some seriously deranged characters, they drive the plot along and make you glad you are locked up in your cozy little house

and not in the streets of Bryson Coventry's district!"
—Tracy Farnsworth, ROUNDTABLEREVIEWS
RoundtableReviews.com

"[T]his is one top-notch read. Again, Mr. Hansen adds just the right amount of mystery, suspense, romance, horror and nail-biting adventure to keep you turning the pages. . . . It is a murder mystery that you will never know or even imagine what lies around the next turn; I promise you that. Excellent read!"
—Shirley Johnson, MIDWEST BOOK REVIEW
MidwestBookReview.com

"This is one book you will have trouble putting down from page one. The author has done a fabulous job of pulling the reader in and keeping them there. ... I highly recommend this book!"
—Dawn Dowdle, MYSTERY LOVERS CORNER
MysteryLoversCorner.com

"*Deadly Laws* by Jim Hansen: Fourth in the *Laws* series, drawing us again into the life and work of hard charging, coffee drinking, womanizing, homicide solving Denver detective Bryson Coventry. . . . Crisp as a Rocky Mountain morning and as exciting as a new powder run at Vail, this is the best *Laws* yet."
—Jack Quick, BOOKBITCH REVIEWS
Bookbitch.com

"Jim Michael Hansen has a way of delving deep into the heart and soul of his characters. His ability to bring out their actions, and yes even their very thoughts and feelings, will leave a picturesque scene in the mind long after you, the reader, have put the book down. He is one of today's best thrilling suspense writers."
—Wanda Maynard, SIMEGEN REVIEWS
Simegen.com

NIGHT LAWS
Trade Paperback—ISBN 9780976924302

Denver homicide detective Bryson Coventry is on the hunt for a vicious killer who has warned attorney Kelly Parks, Esq., that she is on his murder list. Something from the beautiful young lawyer's past has come back to haunt her, something involving the dark secrets of Denver's largest law firm. With the elusive killer ever one step away, Kelly Parks frantically searches for answers, not only to save her life but also to find out whether she unwittingly participated in a murder herself.

"A chilling story well told. The pace never slows in this noir thriller, taking readers on a stark trail of fear."
—Carolyn G. Hart, author of the Demand on Demand series and the Henrie O series, carolynhart.com

"*Night Laws* is a terrifying, gripping cross between James Patterson and John Grisham... Hansen has created a truly killer debut."
—J.A. Konrath, author of *Whiskey Sour, Bloody Mary* and *Rusty Nail,* jakonrath.com

SHADOW LAWS

Trade Paperback—ISBN 9780976924340
Unabridged CD Audio Book—ISBN 9780976924395

Denver homicide detective Bryson Coventry, and beautiful young attorney Taylor Sutton, are separately hunting vicious killers but for very different reasons. As the two dangerous chases inadvertently intersect, both of the hunters get pulled deeper and deeper into an edgy world of shifting truths where there is more at stake than either could have imagined, nothing is as it seems, and time is running out.

"As engaging as the debut *Night Laws*, this exciting blend of police procedural and legal thriller recalls the early works of Scott Turow and Lisa Scottoline."

— LIBRARY JOURNAL

"Wow. This is how, in short, I would describe *Shadow Laws*, the second in the line of hard-hitting *Laws* series by attorney Jim Michael Hansen... A page-turner of a read that is, mildly put, spectacular... The suspense in the novel is spine chilling... A fine, fine read and a highly recommended buy."

—Narayan Radhakrishnan
NEW MYSTERY READER MAGAZINE
newmysteryreader.com

"As with *Night Laws*, this is the thriller equivalent of comfort food."

—Russel D. McLean, CRIME SCENE SCOTLAND
crimescenescotland.com

"Hansen's story surges with action like a screaming Ferrari with no brakes. His plot captivates and terrifies, while the characters vault from the page . . ."

—Mark Bouton, author of *Max Conquers the Cosmos* and
Cracks in the Rainbow, markbouton.com

"From the opening scene to the wrap up, *Shadow Laws* is one edgy thriller. Edgy characters, edgy plot, skillful storytelling—a page-turner for sure. … Definitely a recommended read!"

—L.B. Cobb, author of *Splendor Bay* and *Promises Town*,
www.LBCobb.com

"A fast-paced, well-plotted tale by very talented author Jim Michael Hansen… Highly recommended."

—Anne K. Edwards, author of *Death on Delivery* and
Journey into Terror, mysteryfiction.net

"In Jim Hansen's latest legal thriller, *Shadow Laws*, he does it all … the reader hasn't a chance to put the book down…"

—Ann Ripley, author of the *Louise Eldridge*
gardening mysteries

"*Shadow Laws* has everything you could want in a suspense novel—intriguing complex characters, a gripping tension-filled plot, [and] fast-paced action… Jim Michael Hansen has given his fans another winner."

—Nancy Tesler, author of the *Carrie Carline
Other Deadly Things* series, nancytesler.com

FATAL LAWS
Trade Paperback—ISBN 9780976924364

When several women are found buried in shallow graves near one another, each murdered in a brutally different way, Denver homicide detective Bryson Coventry finds himself pulled into the edgy world of Tianca Holland—a woman involved enough to be a prime suspect, vulnerable enough to be the next victim, and beautiful enough to be more than just a distraction.

"[Jim Michael Hansen] builds suspense effectively, and his hero is both likeable and multidimensional. A too-little-known hard-boiled series that deserves attention."

—BOOKLIST

BANGKOK LAWS
Trade Paperback—ISBN 9780976924319
(Early 2008)

As Denver homicide detective Bryson Coventry finds himself entangled in the collateral damage of a killer who uses the entire world as his playground, newly licensed attorney Paige Alexander lands her very first case —a case that could possibly destroy the most powerful law firm in the world; a case involving a deadly, high-stakes international conspiracy of terrible proportions; a case that started in Bangkok but will not end there.

IMMORTAL LAWS
Trade Paperback—ISBN 9780976924358
(Late 2008)

While Denver homicide detective Bryson Coventry investigates the savage murder of a young woman who is killed with a wooden stake through her heart, blues singer Heather Vaughn discovers that she and the dead woman are both bloodline descendents of men reputed to have been vampires. When the evidence suggests that obsessed slayers are roaming the world and eradicating bloodline descendents, both Heather Vaughn and Bryson Coventry find themselves swept into a modern day thriller born of ancient and deadly obsessions.

DEADLY
LAWS

A Bryson Coventry Thriller

JIM MICHAEL HANSEN

Dark Sky Publishing, Inc.
Golden, CO 80401

Dark Sky Publishing, Inc.
Golden, CO 80401
darkskypublishing.com

Copyright © 2008 by Jim Michael Hansen
jimhansenbooks.com
jimhansenlawfirm.com

ISBN 978-0-9769243-3-3

Library Of Congress Control Number: 2007900448

Cover photography / Getty Images

10 9 8 7 6 5 4 3 2 1

Made in the USA

DEDICATED TO
EILEEN

Acknowledgements

The author gratefully thanks and acknowledges the generosity, encouragement and contributions of the following fantastic people—Tania Allen, Paul Anik, Baron R. Birtcher, Rebecca Blackmer, Kathy Boswell, Mark Bouton, Aldo T. Calcagno, Tony M. Cheatham, Angie Cimarolli, L.B. Cobb, James A. Cox, Lisa D'Angelo, Linnea Dodson, Dawn Dowdle, Anne K. Edwards, Geraldine Evans, Tracy Farnsworth, Sgt. Mike Fetrow, Carol Fieger, Denise Fleischer, Barbara Franchi, Norman P. Goldman, Eric L. Harry, Carolyn G. Hart, Joan Hall Hovey, Shirley Priscella Johnson, Harriet Klausner, J.A. Konrath, Katherine Shand Larkin, Andrei V. Lefebvre, Sarah Lovett, Karen L. MacLeod, Kathy Martin, Wanda Maynard, Cheryl McCann, Russel D. McLean, Evan McNamara, Byron Merritt, K. Preston Oade, Jr., Stephanie Padilla, John David Phillips, Sally Powers, Lt. Jon Priest, Jack Quick, Nayaran Radhakrishnan, Patricia A. Rasey, Ann Ripley, Kenneth Sheridan, Shelley Singer, Andrea Sisco, Bob Spear, Mark Terry, Nancy Tesler, Safiya Tremayne and Laurraine Tutihasi; and

My many friends at Barnes & Noble, Borders, Once Upon A Crime (MN), and countless other fine bookstores, and libraries, throughout the country; and

The many wonderful people I have had the pleasure to meet at my author events; and, most importantly,

My readers.

Chapter One

Day One—May 5
Monday Morning

—————————

THIRD-YEAR LAW STUDENT KAYLA BECK was at a scratched wooden desk in the belly of the college, knee deep in editing Professor Miller's insanely dull Law Review article, when her cell phone rang. She circled a sentence, wrote *repetitive* in red ink, and looked at the incoming number. Her phone didn't recognize it. She drained what was left in her coffee cup, almost tossed the phone back in her purse but answered instead.

A man's voice came through.

One she didn't recognize.

Not a normal voice.

More like something filtered through a scrambler.

Very weird.

"I have a very simple proposition for you," the man said. "A woman is in the process of dying as we speak. I'm going to give you the opportunity to save her—correction, *possibly* save her. I'm giving this opportunity to you and you alone. No one else in the universe gets this phone call. You're the chosen one. So the question I have for you is very simple. Do you want to try to save her? If you do, then she has a chance. If you don't, then she doesn't. It's that simple. It's that black and white. You're her god. How's it feel?"

Kayla brought her 24-year-old body to a standing position and pushed long blond hair out of her face.

The chair squeaked.

"Who is this?"

The man laughed. "No time for chitchat," he said. "Just tell me if you're going to do this or not."

She picked up a pencil and snapped it in two.

Pissed that someone had just stolen two minutes of her life and she let him.

"Look," she said, "I don't know which one of my soon-to-be-ex friends put you up to this, but go back and tell them it wasn't funny and I wasn't dumb enough to fall for it."

TEN SECONDS AFTER SHE HUNG UP HE CALLED BACK. "Don't ever do that again," he said. "You think this is a joke? This is as far from a joke as you could ever get."

Even through the scrambler he sounded serious.

"If you're going to do this then you need to tell me right here, right now. If you're not then that's fine too. But if you don't, then the woman dies, make no mistake about that. Nice guy that I am, I'll even call you after the fact and tell you who she was."

"Tell me now," she said. "Let me verify that someone's missing. If it turns out to be true then count me in."

The man chuckled.

"You're going to be a lot of fun, you really are. But right now your time's up. Give me your answer. But before you do, remember one last time, you're her only hope. She has no one else. Only you."

Kayla bit her lower lip and paced.

She couldn't say yes.

But she couldn't say no.

Just in case this was actually real.

She needed time.

"What happens if I say okay?" she asked.

"Good girl," the man said. "I'm going to take that as a yes. Be at the public parking lot at the corner of Broadway and 20th tonight at eight o'clock. Have your cell phone with you. Find a place to park and then sit in your car until I call."

"Broadway and 20th —"

"Right. Eight o'clock sharp. And here's the most important part—don't tell anyone a single thing, don't bring anyone, don't do anything stupid, and above all, don't call the police. If you do, I'll know. I can always tell. Then all bets are off. Do you understand?"

"Yes."

"I hope so. I really do."

"What if I don't show up?"

The line went dead.

THAT EVENING SHE DROVE INTO DENVER a half hour early, still not sure whether she would pull into the parking lot or drive past.

All afternoon she kept her mouth shut and didn't say a word to anyone.

Instead she went to classes and hung out in the Law Review as if everything was normal. Now, in hindsight, she realized how incredibly stupid that had been.

The guy could be luring her to her own death. At a minimum she should have typed out an explanation and set it on her desk in case she never returned.

Too late now.

She circled around the side streets while a nasty rain fell out of an ominous sky. The storm grew even louder as she surprised herself by pulling the junk-heap-of-a-car into the parking lot and killing the engine.

Lightning crackled and twitched overhead.

He was watching her.

She could feel his eyes.

But he wouldn't be able to see the Taurus .357Mag revolver sitting in the passenger seat under a towel, fully loaded with the safety off—just in case. She slid her hand under the cloth and fingered the cold steel of the weapon.

It felt as she remembered it.

She wasn't sure if it made her feel secure or more nervous.

She'd shot it plenty after she got it for her fifteenth birthday; all the way through high school in fact, but hardly at all after she started college.

Better to have it than not.

Still, she wouldn't be totally helpless without it.

She was stronger than she looked. At five-feet-four and in baggy clothes she didn't appear threatening, especially because of her easy white smile and pleasant tanned face. But underneath it all she had a sprinter's thighs, good lungs and a hard stomach.

And knew how to wrestle.

Growing up, on Saturday nights when her parents went out to the movies, her older brother would have his wrestling team buddies over. Out in the backyard they let her hang out with them and then, after they drank enough beer, they'd show her moves on the grass.

Mostly to get an excuse to pin her down and tickle her to death.

She knew that.

But still, she learned.

Suddenly her cell phone rang.

"THERE'S A HUMMER PARKED about six cars down from yours," the man said. "In front of that Hummer there's a yellow post. Sitting on top of that post is a key. Go get that key and then come back to your car."

"You said before that you chose me," she said. "How did you do that? I mean, why me?"

"Just shut up and get the key," the man said.

"Do we know each other?" she asked.

The line went dead.

Not good.

She opened the door, stepped into the storm and looked for the Hummer. There it was, right where he said. The rain beat down with a fury and had her drenched by the time she got to the key. She grabbed it and ran back to the car as fast as her legs would take her. Then she slammed the door and wiped the water out of her eyes.

And waited for him to call.

He didn't.

Come on.

I did what you said.

Minute after minute passed.

Her ponytail dripped water down her back and she didn't care.

Then he called.

"Don't ever screw with me again," he said. "Do you understand?"

She moved her hand over until it touched the gun.

"Yes."

"I sure hope so," he said. "Are you ready for your instructions?"

"Yes."

"Listen carefully because I'm only going to say them once," the man said. "The woman you're going to go to is in a railroad car—a boxcar to be precise—in an abandoned industrial area on the north edge of the city. I'll give you directions in a minute. The door to the car is shut but not locked. You'll have to struggle a little but you'll be able to get it open. The woman is chained inside. She has a steel collar around her neck. That collar is secured by a padlock. The key that you have in your hand fits that padlock. If she's still alive all you have to do is unlock her and then drop her off somewhere where she'll be found, on the side of a street or something. Don't ask her name or ever try to contact her afterwards. And above all don't ever tell anyone about any of this. That's all there is to it. Do you think you can do it?"

She did.

No problem.

"There's one small thing you should know about," he said. "I put her in there three days ago. I told her I'd never come back which, by the way, is technically true. I left her with only two things, a bottle of water and a razorblade. She definitely used the water by now. Whether she used the razorblade, I have no idea. But she might have, so you need to be prepared for that. In fact, to tell you the truth, most of 'em don't last three days."

A chill ran up Kayla's spine and into her brain.

"Give me directions," she said.

You sick freak.

Chapter Two

Day One—May 5
Monday Evening

KAYLA BECK TOOK I-25 NORTH as the worn-out wiper blades
of her older-than-dirt Ford Mustang did a pathetic job of keeping up with the storm. The high-speed setting broke more than
five years ago. The bald tires threatened to hydroplane at any
second. Other drivers wove around her and she knew they were
giving her the finger.

Right now she didn't care.

Darkness approached.

Streetlights would kick on soon.

The wetness of her clothes worked its way into her bones, so
much so that she turned on the heater, which amazingly still
worked. She cut east when she got to I-70, exited at Vasquez
and then wove her way into an industrial area north of the city.

She'd never been in this particular section of the world before.

It was cold and hard and creepy.

She drove deeper and deeper into a darkening terrain. The
buildings became fewer. More and more of them were boarded

up and surrounded by chain-link fences. The asphalt turned to gravel.

One eye in the rearview mirror told her no one followed.

Still, the guy might be waiting for her. Don't forget that. This whole thing could be a setup, in which case she would go down as one of the dumbest people on the face of the earth. The Taurus .357Mag gave her some comfort but not near as much as she thought it would.

She had no idea if she could actually point it at a human being.

Finally, after what seemed like a long time, she saw the designated landmark—a water tower that carved an eerie silhouette against a swirling black sky.

She pulled up to the gate of a chain-link fence and killed the engine, just like she'd been told.

Lightning arced across the sky.

That's when she saw the boxcar—a solitary shape sitting in a field by itself, to the left of an abandoned building.

She picked up the gun and held it in her hands.

Then she studied the surroundings as the storm beat down on the roof.

No one was around.

She double-checked the weapon to be sure the safety was off, then kept it in her right hand and got out of the car. The storm immediately pounded her and fingered its way into her clothes.

THE CHAIN-LINK FENCE RAN PARALLEL to the road. About fifty steps down she found an opening, right where the man said it would be. She bent down, twisted through and walked across a squishy field towards the boxcar.

She kept a good lookout.

It was still light enough that she'd be able to see anyone coming. But no one did and she concentrated more and more on the boxcar.

The man could be hiding inside.

Hidden under a blanket or a pile of hay.

Or even on the roof waiting to drop down.

The thought made her tighten her finger on the trigger.

Wait.

That was weird.

The man said the door would be closed.

But it was open.

Not all the way, but enough for someone to get in or out.

She approached.

One step at a time.

Walking slower now.

Suddenly a woman's voice came from inside, sobbing and desperate.

No!

Please stop!

Kayla climbed a rusty ladder at the side of the door, took a deep breath, and stepped into the black opening.

THERE SHE FOUND A HEAVYSET MAN thrusting wildly between a woman's legs. He still wore a shirt but had his pants all the way off. The fat of his body rippled each time he struck her with his pelvis. The stench of urine and body odor filled the air.

The woman was totally naked.

A steel collar wrapped around her neck, chained to something in the corner. Her arms were tied behind her back. Suddenly she spotted Kayla and shouted, "Help me! Please help me!"

The man started to get up on one elbow and turn.

But before he could get all the way around Kayla closed the gap and hit him as hard as she could with the gun on the side of his head.

He muttered something, then made a strange sound and fell limp on top of the woman.

"Get him off me!"

Kayla grabbed the man's shirt and dragged him off.

The woman immediately scrambled into the corner.

"It's okay," Kayla said.

The woman finally calmed down enough to let Kayla put the key into the padlock. It actually fit and the collar came off. Then Kayla untied her hands.

The man still hadn't moved or made a sound.

As soon as the woman was free she picked up Kayla's gun, stuck the barrel in the man's face and pulled the trigger.

Chapter Three

Day Two—May 6
Tuesday Morning

THE BODY GOT CALLED IN by an anonymous man who sounded like a drifter. At the scene, Bryson Coventry—the 34-year-old head of Denver's homicide unit—raked his thick brown hair back with his fingers and hardly paid any attention to the dead man's fat ass or the mangled mess of flesh that had once been a face. He was a lot more interested in the collar.

The collar attached to the chain.

The collar that no longer held anyone captive.

It was a quarter-inch thick and an inch wide.

Black.

Hinged on one side where it could be opened, with a clasp on the other side to accept a padlock.

Detective Shalifa Netherwood—the newest member of the team and the only female African American detective—held a Kleenex over her nose to fend off the urine and guts as she squatted down to take a look at the padlock.

"This lock has the key in it," she said.

Coventry already knew that and said, "Do you see any fingerprints on it?"

She laughed.

"Two or three."

"Can you tell whose they are?"

"No. They're not any of the ones I have memorized."

"Too bad," he said. "I was hoping we had this all wrapped up so I could get back to doing what I do best."

"Which is?"

"Drinking coffee. I thought you knew that by now."

OUTSIDE, THE CRIME UNIT STILL HADN'T SHOWN UP, so they walked across the field to Coventry's truck to wait. He pulled out a thermos of coffee, filled two disposable cups, handed one to Shalifa and then took a long noisy slurp.

Ah, good stuff.

Still pretty hot.

Last night's storm had given way to a cloudless blue sky. Springtime bugs were everywhere and sparrows darted in zigzag patterns to gobble them up.

"So what's your theory?" Shalifa asked.

He shrugged. "I'd rather be a bird than a bug. That's my theory."

She rolled her eyes. "I'll remember that if I ever get the power to change you," she said. "Which I've been praying for, by the way."

He chuckled and then got serious. "The dead guy's a drifter. He probably stumbled on the boxcar last night and ducked in to get out of the storm. Judging by the fact he had his pants off, I'm guessing a woman was there, in the collar, when he entered."

"Can you imagine?" Shalifa said. "Crawling into a boxcar out in the middle of nowhere and finding a woman chained up inside?"

Coventry grunted.

"It would be like winning the drifter's lottery," he said. "Whoever put the woman there in the first place must have come back when the drifter was having his fun. He didn't take kindly to some stranger humping his property and rearranged his face with a bullet. Then he took the woman somewhere else."

"Meaning she's still alive," Shalifa nodded.

"At least as of that time." Coventry scratched his head. "What I don't understand is why he didn't take all the stuff—the collar and chain and padlock. It's evidence. Why didn't he take it? I would have."

Shalifa made a face.

"I don't know, but I do know that I'm not getting paid enough for all that stench."

Coventry chuckled.

"Toughen up," he said. "I own cologne worse than that."

"Yeah, I know. I've been meaning to talk to you about that."

Chapter Four

Day Two—May 6
Tuesday Morning

LANCE LUNDEEN—TARZAN—OWNED a four-story building next to the BNSF switchyard on the west edge of the city. Back in its heyday it housed a furniture manufacturing company. Now it only housed him. He lived on the top floor in a 6,000 square foot space that he called the loft. The space was just that, space, meaning one large rectangular room with oak plank floors and fourteen foot ceilings. There was only one enclosed area, for the darkroom.

Other than that there were no walls.

Not a one.

Not for the bedroom, or the bathroom, or even the area where the models changed. Of course, he kept a few partitions on rollers around for the faint of heart—one by the toilet and one where the models dressed.

At six-three, 235 pounds, the space fit his frame just fine.

Anything smaller would be a cage.

The west windows looked down on the tops of boxcars and engines and track. The clanging and squeaking of the switching operations were his wind chimes.

He pushed his naked body off the mattress at the usual time, about 11:00 a.m., got the coffee machine going and jumped in the shower, soaking the thick blond mane of hair that hung half-way down his back, a good twelve to eighteen inches past his shoulders. He lathered his face with soap and shaved under the spray. Then did the same with his balls and dick, getting rid of every hair, so Del Rae wouldn't be fighting with distractions when she went down to visit.

He toweled off in front of the mirror.

Tarzan stared back.

All muscle.

Ripped.

Nothing but rugged jungle looks.

WITH A CUP OF COFFEE IN HAND, he checked the answering machine and found twelve messages. One turned out to be from Dexter Vaughn, the VP of Three Streets, which was one of the top ten ad agencies, headquartered in New York. He dialed Dexter's direct number and got him just as he came back from lunch.

"What's this message you left about a new project? How am I supposed to spend my life getting laid if you keep cluttering it up with work?" Lance asked.

Dexter laughed.

"Here's the deal," he said. "And let me tell you right off the bat, this is huge. The client's Sensory Perceptions. In four months they're going to roll out a cologne called Snare, the tar-get market being males between twenty and thirty. They want a seriously edgy image for the product. Whoever wears it is a dangerous bad-boy, that kind of thing. And who does edgy better than you?"

Lance chuckled.

"No one."

"Exactly," Dexter said. "No one. I need you to work up some outrageous concepts for them to look at. The ones they finally choose are going to be everywhere, as in across the nation, on billboards, buses, magazines, the whole bit. They're going to throw seriously stupid money at it."

"So exactly how much of an edge are they looking for?"

"An edge that's fallen over the edge," Dexter said. "The idea is that whoever wears this stuff attracts the most beautiful and dangerous women on the planet. Picture one guy surrounded by five barely-dressed women in heat."

Lance winced.

"Trite," he said. "How soon do they need it?"

"Two weeks, two and a half max."

Fine.

Doable.

"Later today I'm going to wire you thirty grand in seed money," Dexter said. "Just be sure to give me something fresh, something no one's even thought of before, much less seen."

"I already have some ideas," Lance said.

AFTER HE HUNG UP, LANCE SAT DOWN AT THE DRUMS, put "Sweet Child of Mine" on repeat mode, cranked up the volume and played along. A half hour later he had several pretty good ideas for photo shoots.

Then he worked the phone to get things in motion.

Models.

Costumes.

Setup.

Lighting.

An hour later Del Rae Paris called. He pulled up a mental picture of exotic green eyes and a sensuous curvy body, a picture so vivid that his cock tingled.

She had news.

Some very interesting news.

"He actually brought up the idea last night," she said. "All on his own."

She didn't need to define *he*—he was Robert Sharapova, Esq. The target.

"So you actually think he'll do it?" Lance asked.

"Yeah, I really do," she said. "About time, too. I'm sick to death of screwing the guy. I'm coming over tonight so be warned."

He smiled.

"Can't wait."

"Have some coke," she added.

"Done."

"I love to screw on coke."

"Yes you do."

Chapter Five

Day Two—May 6
Tuesday Morning

AFTER THE WOMAN—ASPEN WHITE—BLEW AWAY the fat man's face last night, Kayla Beck brought her back to her one-bedroom apartment at the Silver Reef in Lakewood and gave her a bar of soap, half the refrigerator and the bed. Then, around midnight, Kayla drove alone up Highway 6 west of Golden into Clear Creek Canyon, past the second tunnel where the river forges between rock walls. There she threw the gun into the black turbulent water while the storm beat down.

On the way home she tried to figure out just how much trouble she'd gotten herself into, legally speaking.

She'd struck the man in the head with her gun.

Assume that's what killed him.

In that case she probably wasn't in any trouble. It was an act in the nature of a justifiable defense of another person. The other woman—Aspen White—wouldn't be in any trouble either. Sure, she shot the guy, but if he was already dead then no harm done.

But on the other hand assume that the blow to the head didn't kill him. Assume he was still alive when Aspen White shot him. That bullet wouldn't be a justifiable act of self-defense because no one was in physical danger at that point.

It would be an act of rage.

An act of murder.

And in that event, Kayla would be an accessory to murder, an accessory-after-the-fact to be precise. First, because she harbored Aspen White after the shooting by helping her escape from the scene and then giving her refuge. Second, because she disposed of the murder weapon.

Being an accessory to a murder is a felony offense.

So now she might be a felon.

It all depended on when the man died.

And that's something she might never know.

One thing she did know, however, is that felons can't be lawyers. Meaning that all the brain damage she had endured for the last two years might be for nothing.

If she got caught.

Still, she wouldn't change what she did.

The guy was dead but he brought it on himself.

And neither she nor Aspen White deserved to be punished for it.

ON TUESDAY MORNING SHE GOT UP at her normal time and attended classes, not wanting to break her routine just in case it ever became an issue for some reason. In her two-hour afternoon window, however, instead of heading to the Law Review where she had a million-and-one things waiting to be done, she headed back to the apartment to see how her new guest was doing.

Aspen White didn't just scrub up good, she turned out to be seriously stunning.

Twenty-six years old.

Five-foot-ten.

Bronzed exotic skin and long raven hair.

"I don't know an easy way to say this so I'm just going to come right out and say it," Aspen said. "You're the new me. I was the designated rescuer for a long time. Then, this last time, I just couldn't do it anymore. I didn't go. A woman named Natalie Harwell died as a result. The guy got a lot of pleasure afterwards, calling and telling me her name."

"What a freak."

"That was six months ago," Aspen said. "Then I was opening the refrigerator Friday morning. The next thing I knew, I woke up inside the boxcar. The collar was on my neck and everything was pitch-black. I felt around in the dark and found the razorblade. In a spur of the moment decision I threw it as far as I could. As soon as I did it I wished I hadn't, because now if I wanted to kill myself, I'd have to bang my head on the steel or choke myself or something. I had no idea if he would even send someone to rescue me, much less whether they'd come."

"How horrible," Kayla said.

Aspen nodded.

"So you're in the middle of it now," Aspen said. "You'd have been a lot better off if you hadn't taken the bait."

True.

"But then you'd be dead," Kayla said.

"I'll probably wind up dead anyway. I don't believe for a second that he's going to let me live."

Kayla twisted her hair.

Then she stood up, walked over to the window, pulled the

curtain aside and looked out.

Everything was normal.

By the time she sat back down she'd already made up her mind. "In that case we need to find out who he is."

"How?"

Kayla frowned.

"I don't know, but somehow."

"We need to keep the cops out of it," Aspen said. "I'm not going to prison, period." She paused and looked Kayla in the eyes. "If we do find him, I'll do it."

"Do what?"

"You know, what has to be done."

Chapter Six

Day Two—May 6
Tuesday Afternoon

COVENTRY KNEW THE SILVER REEF APARTMENTS fairly well because he used to have a bed-buddy there named Dawn, who he picked up at a LoDo club one drunken night five or six years ago. They quickly found that they'd never get serious but had an uncanny ability to lust each other up. So over the years, between significant others, they had standing reservations to call each other. Of course that was before she went off to L.A. to be a star and never came back. In any event, he still remembered the apartment complex well and knew right where to go to find the unit he wanted.

He checked his watch.

4:00 p.m.

He found three empty parking spaces, pulled the Tundra into the middle one and stepped out. Overhead, the morning sunshine had, as usual, given way to thick rolling clouds, which were filling their big black bellies with water.

Thunder rumbled over the mountains about five miles to the west.

Rain was coming.

Which was fine.

Coventry never met a rainstorm he didn't like.

When he knocked on the door of the apartment something happened that he didn't expect. A woman answered, a woman so stunning that he actually stopped breathing. Before either of them could say a word he already knew that he had to know all about her.

What she liked.

Where she grew up.

What made her laugh.

If she screamed in bed.

Everything.

She had thick black hair and engaging green eyes that wouldn't let him look away.

"Are you Kayla Beck?" he asked.

The woman shook her head. "No. Kayla's at law school," she said. "You just missed her."

"So who are you?"

"I'm Aspen."

He held out his hand. "Bryson Coventry."

"Bryson," she said. "I like that." Like most people who met him for the first time, she studied his face, trying to figure out what was wrong. Then the corner of her mouth turned up ever so slightly. "Your other green eye's blue."

"Either that or my other blue eye's green," he said. "It's a raging debate. You want to go out somewhere and get a cup of coffee?" As soon as the words came out of his mouth he couldn't believe it. "I'm sorry. Did I say that out loud?"

She laughed.

"Yes," she said. "And yes."

"The second yes is to the coffee question?"

"Yes again," she said.

"Great," he said. "I'll buy."

She chuckled.

THEY ENDED UP AT THE BLUE SKY CAFÉ near Colfax and Indiana, sitting at an outside table under an increasingly threatening sky. So far, on the drive over, he discovered absolutely nothing about her.

She deflected every question about herself.

The only thing he learned is that he wanted her in his life.

He explained that he was with Denver homicide and why he wanted to see Kayla Beck. A drifter had been shot in the face last night in a remote industrial area north of town. By their best guess it happened around dark. One of the buildings about a mile down the road happened to have a security camera that recorded an old Ford Mustang in the area, something in the 1964-1968 range. It didn't pick up the license plate number, because of the rainstorm, but they found out that there weren't that many light-colored first generation Mustangs registered in the Denver area, fifteen to be exact. They were tracking down all the owners to see if they were there and, if so, whether they saw or heard anything.

Aspen wrinkled her forehead.

"All that for a drifter," she said. "I'm impressed."

Coventry shrugged.

"A life's a life," he said. "But I'll admit there's more to it than that."

"Unfortunately, Kayla Beck won't be able to help you," she said. "She was with me last evening."

Coventry raked his hair back with his fingers.

"Did anyone borrow her car last night?"

"No. It was right here the whole time."

"Figures," he said. "That's the way my life works."

"Sorry," she added.

A strong wind suddenly came out of nowhere and pushed swirling black clouds across the sky.

"Going to rain," Coventry said.

Sure enough, a handful of heavy splats fell. They were those big suckers, the kind that give a ten-second warning before the whole sky drops down. One landed in Coventry's cup and splashed coffee over the edge. He grabbed his cup and started to stand up but Aspen didn't.

Instead she cocked her head as if debating something and then said, "How would you like the opportunity to get out of paying for the coffee?"

Coventry grinned.

"You know me already."

"The first person who runs for cover pays," she said.

Coventry eased back in the chair, picked up the cup and took a sip just as a strong drop landed on his face. He wiped it off and said, "I hope you brought money."

THE STORM GOT MEANER. Neither of them flinched. Finally Aspen laughed and said, "Okay, you win."

"So you pay?"

"No, you win me."

Coventry cocked his head.

"What do you mean?"

She stood up, grabbed his arm and led him towards the Tundra.

"What do you think I mean?"

Coventry grinned.

"I didn't know that's what we were playing for."

"Well now you do."

"Wait a minute." He ran back to the table, slipped a ten-dollar bill under his coffee mug and then caught up with her. She locked her arm through his and nestled up.

"How far is your house?"

"Too far," he said, and meant it.

A half mile later they were passing the Jefferson County Fairgrounds. Coventry gave in to a spur-of-the-moment impulse and swung into the muddiest parking lot he had ever seen in his life. He punched the 4WD button and drove to the far end, over by the Cottonwoods, with "Dancing in the Dark" on the radio. The wind kicked up even more and blew the storm as horizontal as it could.

The sky had grown so dark that it might as well have been night.

No one was around.

Aspen had her pants off before Coventry killed the engine.

He couldn't believe her body.

Lightning ripped across the sky.

Then thunder exploded.

So close that Aspen jumped.

Neither of them even looked up.

Chapter Seven

Day Two—May 6
Tuesday Afternoon

SCOTTY MARKS WAS THE BEST GUY in the world to build custom stages for photography shoots, hands down. Lance called him as soon as he had the concept sufficiently solidified in his mind.

"What I'm looking for is a giant spider's web, somewhere in the nature of fifteen feet or so in diameter," Lance said. "It needs to be strong enough to hold three or four people at a time. And here's the most important thing—it needs to look realistic. Go down to Barnes & Noble and get a book on spiders or something. We can't have it looking like a circus net or anything stupid like that."

Scotty chuckled. "Who is this?"

"Funny," Lance said. "I'm really excited about this, so get over here as soon as you can, please and thank you. I want to be sure this is doable."

"Anything's doable."

"That's what I want to hear."

An hour later Scotty showed up with some pictures he pulled

off the Internet and they went down to the second floor. Scotty looked exactly the same as always, a throwback to the sixties right down to the long hair and the red bandana. He may as well have just come back from Woodstock.

And lit a joint to prove it.

Lance shook his head. "You need to get into coke, man, and quit messing with that baby stuff."

"Too expensive," Scotty said.

True.

Lance had to give him that.

The second floor of the building had been gutted of clutter a long time ago and now pretty much looked like the inside of a giant matchbox.

"I was thinking we could build it over there," Lance said, heading that way. "The lighting will be as good as anywhere."

Scotty studied the ceiling.

"Lots of places to anchor it," he said. "The best way to do it is build it as a rectangle rather than trying to mess with a circle or an octagon or whatever it is that spiders do."

Lance had no problem with that.

The edge of the web didn't need to be in the shoot.

"It shouldn't be that hard either," Scotty said. "I can draw it on the floor in chalk and build it right on the ground. We might need a JLG to hang it, though. I'm not sure how heavy it's going to be."

"The service elevator still works," Lance said. "So if we need to get a lift in here, then fine."

Scotty smiled.

"Far out."

Lance slapped him on the back. "And right on."

They talked about the schedule, which was ASAP or sooner.

And then talked about money until they reached an agreement.

WHEN SCOTTY MARKS LEFT, Lance called Suzanne Clark, a 25-year-old Greek bombshell who was extraordinarily talented in the bedroom and also happened to own MOD-ELLES, one of the best modeling agencies this side of the Mississippi—California excluded, of course.

"I need five or six of your sexiest ladies, early twenties," Lance said. "They need to have absolutely killer legs. I'm talking about the kind of legs that guys want wrapped around their faces for three hours straight." She promised to make some calls and have a crew of lovelies show up at his place tomorrow at noon.

All in sleeveless summer dresses that hung above the knee.

Like he wanted.

"By the way," she added, "If that woman you're seeing, what's her name—?"

"—Del Rae."

"—Right, Del Rae. If she ever puts your feet to sleep, pencil me in for another ride through the jungle."

Lance chuckled.

"You're too much," he said.

HE CHECKED HIS WATCH, found it was only 2:37 p.m., and decided he had enough time to get started on the Del Rae Paris project.

The one that would put millions in his pocket.

And Del Rae's.

If they could actually pull it off.

He took the stairs down to the first floor where he parked his cars—a red BMW convertible, a white 4Runner, a Chevy Silverado pickup truck and, his personal favorite, a black 1982 Ferrari 328 with collector plates.

He hopped in the 4Runner and took I-25 to I-76, then exited on Highway 85 and headed north into the flatlands. There he drove around aimlessly down gravel roads under an increasingly stormy sky. He came to a turnoff with a faded sign that said "No Outlet" and headed in that direction.

The road dead-ended two miles later at a small river.

An old wooden bridge sat abandoned in place. Four or five thick posts with faded yellow paint stuck up in front of it to prevent crossing. Lance stopped the 4Runner, killed the engine and stepped out. A steady breeze pushed heavy clouds across the sky.

Several sparrows flew into the wind.

Hardly moving in relation to the ground.

Snatching insects out of the air.

He walked across the bridge to stretch his legs and on the way back he spotted an old rickety house a mile or so away. He hiked over and found it abandoned. It had two small bedrooms, an old bathroom, and a great room with a kitchen. Everything of value had long since been stripped off. Surprisingly, all the windows were still intact and there wasn't much dust or debris inside.

Outside, he followed the weed-infested dirt driveway for fifteen minutes, where it met up with the gravel road, not more than a quarter-mile from the bridge. The vegetation left little trace of the old drive.

A black-and-white magpie flew overhead.

He threw a rock at it and missed by a mile.

45

No one had been in this neck of the woods in recent history.
Perfect.
Better than perfect.
Now all he had to do is remember how to get here.

Chapter Eight

Day Two—May 6
Tuesday Evening

BY THE TIME KAYLA BECK GOT HOME from her afternoon classes, Aspen had eaten just about everything in the kitchen, so for supper they drove to the McDonald's on Alameda, at the base of Green Mountain, and then motored down the road to find a quiet place to talk and eat.

On the way Kayla had a crazy idea.

"How's your strength? Do you have it back yet?"

"Pretty much."

"Okay then," she said. "I'm going to show you a part of Denver that no one knows about. It's called the Hatchet Lady's Cave. We can talk there."

Aspen laughed.

"You're kidding, right?"

"There is no kidding when you're talking about the Hatchet Lady," she said.

They snaked up one side of the Dinosaur Hogback, down the other, and then winded into Red Rocks Park, eating on the way. They parked not far from the amphitheater and then headed over to the base of a mountain of bald red rock. A sign said, "No Climbing on Rocks."

Kayla led Aspen past it and said, "Be careful. We're going through a few places where you don't want to fall."

Then they climbed.

Sometimes out in the open.

And sometimes through hidden passages.

Some of it was easy.

Some of it was hard.

Some of it was downright scary.

A half hour later and twenty stories higher they entered the Hatchet Lady's Cave. It was a large opening in the side of the mountain that hung over the amphitheater. To the east, fifteen miles away, lay the Denver skyline and beyond that stretched the wide-open Colorado plains.

"This is where the Hatchet Lady lives," Kayla said. "If you sit on the thirteenth row of the amphitheater at midnight, she can see you from here and comes to get you."

Aspen made a scared face.

"The high school boys used to bring us here after it got dark and the rangers left. We'd sit on the thirteenth row and drink beer. The guys had this story that the only thing that could keep the Hatchet Lady away was if they were getting blowjobs exactly at midnight."

Aspen laughed.

"Did it work?"

Kayla nodded.

"I think so because we never had an actual sighting."

Aspen laughed.

"No use taking a chance."

"Exactly," Kayla agreed. "Anyway, during concerts people

used to sneak up here and watch for free. Then they'd kill themselves trying to get back down in the dark, all drunk and stoned and stupid and everything. So the rangers got pretty tough about keeping people out of here, even during the day. So tough that most people don't even know the place exists anymore."

"Did you ever see a concert from up here?"

Kayla nodded. "Just one, the Eagles. It was totally awesome, until afterwards when I slid down about thirty feet and broke my arm."

"Ouch."

"No problem. That's why we have two. I told my mom I fell down my girlfriend's steps. She kept talking about suing them and then one day actually went out and consulted a lawyer. I had to tell her the truth. Then she grounded me for a month."

She picked up a rock and threw it.

"I don't want to die all alone in a boxcar," she said. "I know I sound fine and I'm rambling on and everything, but deep down inside I'm scared."

"I'VE RACKED MY BRAIN a million different ways and still have no idea how he chose me," Aspen said. "The best I can figure is that he saw me somewhere and thought I'd be someone fun to bring into his little games."

Kayla frowned.

"Were there others before you?" she asked. "Rescuers, I mean."

Aspen shrugged.

"Good question. I wish I knew."

"So how many so-called rescues were you sent on in all?"

"Four," Aspen said. "The first one was about two years ago,

a 23-year-old woman by the name of Misty Garbarek—an airline stewardess—who lived in Oregon."

"Oregon?"

"Right."

"So you actually had to travel?"

"Yes, every time in fact," Aspen said.

"Wow. So you were pretty convinced right off the bat that this guy was for real."

Aspen nodded.

"He put her in this hidden rocky area on the Oregon coast, south of a town called Waldport, not much higher than where the tide came in," Aspen said. "She was naked and had a steel collar around her neck, chained to a big rock." She exhaled. "When I first saw her and knew it was real, I ran to her as fast as I could. She looked alive. I can't even begin to tell you how happy I was. But it turned out I was wrong. She'd already slit her wrists."

"How terrible."

"I sat there for a long time and held her hand," Aspen said. "She was so fresh. I still think to this day that if I'd gotten there ten minutes earlier she'd be alive right now."

Kayla said nothing.

Picturing it.

"Then what'd you do?"

"I found the key where the guy said it would be, in a blue plastic box about twenty yards away from her," she said. "I took her out of the collar because she didn't deserve to be in anything like that, even dead. Then I covered her with my jacket and went back to Santa Fe."

"Did you ever contact the police?"

Aspen looked at her as if she was crazy.

"No. That's the rule. I'm glad I didn't, too. Because the next time he called everything turned out different."

"You saved someone?"

Aspen nodded.

"A waitress from Memphis by the name of Sarah Young."

"Is she still alive?"

"I don't know."

"Did you try to talk to her, afterwards?"

"Not at first because of the rules," Aspen said. "Then I tried to contact her late last year. I couldn't locate her, but not for lack of trying."

"So she disappeared again?"

"It seems that way," Aspen said. "Maybe she went underground so the guy would never be able to find her again."

"Or maybe something worse happened," Kayla suggested.

Aspen nodded.

"Right. I just don't know."

Chapter Nine

Day Two—May 6
Tuesday Night

IT WAS ALMOST NIGHTFALL when dispatch called Bryson
Coventry at home and told him that the body of a young
woman had been found near the railroad tracks next to Santa Fe
Boulevard, south of downtown, almost near Evans. Because of
the timing his first thought was that this was the woman who
had been collared in the boxcar.

Another spring storm moved in.

He hopped in the Tundra, set the wipers to medium, swung
by a gas station on Simms to fill a thermos with coffee, and then
splashed his way through the darkening city as he slurped the
so-called coffee from a disposable cup.

It tasted like old shoes.

Better than nothing but not by much.

He turned on the radio, flicked the channels for a few moments and finally let the dial rest on a country-western station.
Five songs later—three of 'em about cheating hearts—he arrived at the scene.

Sergeant Kate Katona, who had duty tonight, was already

there, hunkered under an umbrella over by the body. Coventry checked in with the scribe, said "Lovely night," put on his gloves and headed over.

He scooted under Katona's umbrella and gave her a quick hug as lightning ripped across the sky. Katona was a catcher of things since her tomboy days. She had an easy smile and short drenched hair that dripped water on her face. Her rain-soaked shirt clung to a chest that could only be described as world-class.

Coventry didn't know a man in the department who wouldn't lay down a twenty for a ten-second peek.

His eyes must have lingered there longer than they should have because she punched him in the arm, said "Pay attention," and jiggled her flashlight on the dead woman's face.

He looked down.

Unprepared for what he saw.

THE VICTIM—A YOUNG WOMAN—WAS NAKED and her arms were tied behind her back.

Her feet were tethered with a three-foot rope, long enough to walk but too short to run. Another piece of rope had been worked into a knot, gagged into her mouth and tied behind her head.

All the rope was blue.

But the bondage wasn't what bothered Coventry the most.

What bothered him the most was the way she died.

Someone pushed or pounded a screwdriver into her left ear.

All the way up to the handle.

"I need a different job," he said.

Coventry put his index finger under the victim's elbow and

lifted her arm to get a feel for how stiff she was.

"I'm guessing she's been dead less than an hour," he said. "Who found her?"

"One of the train guys."

They worked the scene until almost two in the morning and found nothing of interest. Freight trains rumbled past, one after the other, so close that the puddles shook. Now totally soaked, they walked through the water instead of around it. Kate said at one point, "I swear that webs are starting to grow between my toes."

As soon as they wrapped up, Coventry realized he had been running on fumes.

On the drive home he kept the window open and stuck his head out every few minutes to keep from falling asleep at the wheel.

And thought about Aspen White.

Chapter Ten

Day Three—May 7
Wednesday Morning

LANCE LUNDEEN'S ALARM CLOCK jerked him out of a deep sleep with all the subtleness of a cattle prod. His first instinct was to slap it across the room but instead he jabbed at it until he hit the snooze button, then rolled on his back and wondered why he'd set it at all, much less at the ungodly hour of 9:00 a.m.

Then he remembered and smiled.

Today would be a good day.

He took a long heaven-sent piss, threw on a pair of sweatpants and headed outside shirtless for a wakeup jog. The guys at the railroad yard didn't appreciate that he ran down the middle of the tracks but tolerated it as long as he stayed clear of the cars.

He liked the roughness of the rails and the timbers and the gravel.

They'd been put there by men.

Back when men were men.

Not today's shriveled wimps who spent all their time hunched over computers and staring at TVs.

He ran north out of the yard for miles, until he got tired, then turned around and did what it took to maintain the same pace all the way back—slightly uphill. Then, outside on the asphalt parking lot, he muscled through a high-impact routine that he developed several years ago. After that he dropped to the ground and pumped out pushups until he didn't have a single one left; then took a three-minute rest and did it again.

He showered and ate breakfast while the coffee pot gurgled. By the time the models showed up he was wide-awake and ready to make magic.

THERE WERE EIGHT WOMEN ALL TOLD, the best MOD-ELLE had to offer. They all wore short, sexy sundresses as requested. Lance gave them a brief tour of the loft area and then packed them into the freight elevator for a trip down to the second floor.

Scotty Marks was working on the spider's web. Early Stones—"The Last Time"—spilled out of a boombox.

Sixties.

When Scotty saw the women he couldn't help but come over, introduce himself as the President of the Whole Freaking Universe, and give each one a giant bear hug.

He was cute enough that they let him.

Lance watched with amusement.

And waited patiently.

Knowing that Scotty wouldn't calm down until he got it out of his horny little system.

"Okay," he told the group. "Here's the deal. I'm not sure how many of you I'm going to use yet, maybe half of you, maybe all of you, we'll see. We're doing a shoot to launch a new men's fragrance called Snare. The client's targeting men aged twenty to thirty. He's looking for a seriously edgy image. Right now, here's the concept. Mr. Hugger, who you just met, is building a giant spider's web. When he's done, which should be—?"

"—later this afternoon—"

"—later this afternoon, we're going to hang it. You guys are going to be caught in the web. The concept is that the web has been sprayed with Snare. Sexy women can't help but get drawn into it and captured. The cologne is that powerful."

"Awesome."

Lance bowed, "Thank you. What I'm saying is, you guys are going to have to get up on the web. If anyone has a problem with heights, now is the time to talk."

They all looked at one another.

No one backed out.

"Good," Lance said. "Once you get stuck in the web, it's going to be a windy day. Your skirts are going to blow. We'll do some shots where they're way up with your thongs showing as well as some others not quite so explicit. We'll also do some with your legs spread pretty wide and some where they're more closed. That way the client will have a range of stuff to choose from. My guess is that he's going to want the whole spectrum so he can match a variety of magazines."

"Yummy."

"What we're going to do today is put you up on chairs, have you pretend you're tangled up in the web, then blow your dresses up and take some pictures. Is everyone in?"

They all nodded.

"When will you choose?"

Lance thought about it and said, "You know what? I'm just going to use all of you and then let the client choose. So you all have a decent shot. Is that fair?"

Yes.

Absolutely it was.

AFTER THE SHOOT, DEL RAE PARIS CAME OVER. They drank Jack and snorted coke. Then Lance beat his Tarzan chest, flung her over his shoulder and carried her across the room.

They wrestled on the mattress.

And planned their next move.

Chapter Eleven

Day Three—May 7
Wednesday Morning

KAYLA BECK DROVE ASPEN TO THE BUS STATION early Wednesday morning and bought her a one-way ticket to Santa Fe. Right now Aspen was a ghost-woman who carried no identification, driver's license, credit cards, money, clothes or evidence of existence. She would round all that up this afternoon and then drive back to Denver.

To hunt.

Bus fumes permeated the air.

"I didn't tell you something last night that I should have," Aspen said.

Kayla raised an eyebrow.

"Oh?"

"A homicide detective by the name of Bryson Coventry showed up at your apartment yesterday afternoon."

Kayla's stomach dropped.

"A detective?"

Aspen told her the story of how a security camera down the road picked up an old Ford Mustang on the night in question and the cops were trying to locate the owner to see if he or she saw anything. Kayla must have had a worried expression because Aspen added, "It's nothing to be concerned about. I told Coventry that you and I were together all evening."

"Did he buy it?"

"Sure, why wouldn't he? Plus the camera didn't pick up a license plate number, or the driver's face—your face—on account of the rain and the camera angle, so it wouldn't matter much even if he didn't."

Kayla exhaled as a layer of stress peeled off.

"He took me out for coffee," Aspen added.

"He did?"

"Yep."

"And you let him?"

"I had to—he has one green eye and one blue one."

Aspen's voice had a flutter in it, so much so that Kayla said, "You're in lust."

"Maybe a little," Aspen said, "which isn't necessarily a bad thing because he'll be a good source of information. He already told me that there's more to the case than just the drifter. Although he didn't come right out and say it, it's pretty clear that what he's really interested in is the collar and chain. He wants to know who was in it and why and, more important, who put them there. So he's after the same guy we are. And he'll end up getting information that you and I wouldn't be able to dig up in a million years."

"Which he'll then share with you?"

Aspen nodded.

"It's called pillow talk."

Kayla swallowed.

"You need to be careful," Kayla said. "You need to be sure

you don't give us away."

Aspen hugged her.

"I won't. I have a lot more to lose than you do, remember."

FROM THE BUS STATION, Kayla headed straight to the University of Denver College of Law and parked her body in a worn leather chair in the Law Review room.

She got invited to join the Law Review—the law school's journal that published articles on legal topics—by ranking in the top 10 percent of her class after the first year of school. During her second year—last year—she served as an Associate Editor, primarily responsible for minor text editing and for ensuring that all citations and references were in compliance with the Harvard Citator.

At the end of the second year she got elected to be the Articles Editor, meaning that this year she was responsible for choosing the articles that would be published.

Quite the challenge.

Law school professors around the country were dancing to the publish-or-perish beat and scrambling to get their articles inked in any law review journal that would have them. Meaning she received daily knocks on the door in the form of letters, phone messages and emails.

Every knock needed to be answered.

Most knockers needed to be turned away.

Some of them didn't take too kindly to it.

Who was *she* to say no to *them*?

Wasn't she smart enough to recognize their brilliance? And how their stuff was so much better than all the other crap being published?

Noise.

Noise.

Noise.

Still, today she welcomed it. It was familiar and normal. It was sand to stick her head in and make the rest of the world disappear.

The secret to being a good law student is to not waste an hour of time. The secret to being a good law student who also worked on the Law Review is to not waste a minute of time. She'd wasted plenty of both this week.

Which only amped-up the stress.

She kept her nose to the grindstone to recapture lost ground, getting up only to get and get rid of coffee, as the buzz and hustle inside the room steadily increased.

Someone brought in a box of Krispy Kremes.

She kept them in her peripheral vision for ten minutes and then grabbed the last one before someone else did.

SHE NOTICED A COPY of the Rocky Mountain News sitting on the desk next to the coffee pot. The front page had a small teaser about a woman who had been found dead last night.

Kayla turned to the article.

Apparently the body of a young woman had been discovered last night near the railroad tracks next to Santa Fe, close to Evans. Police were in the process of identifying the victim. The article had a picture of a body covered by a sheet.

The victim's foot stuck out.

The ankle of that foot had a tattoo.

A tattoo that Kayla recognized.

She dropped the paper as she pulled up a mental picture of

Marilyn Poppenberg, a third-year law student who parked on the same street as Kayla.

AT THAT MOMENT HER CELL PHONE RANG. She almost didn't answer but did. A man's electronically scrambled voice came through.

Him.

"I underestimated you," he said. "I didn't take you for the kind to bring a gun. Be sure that never happens again. I already warned you once not to screw with me."

"I'm out," she said.

"There is no out. What you need to do is be real sure that you and your new friend Aspen White don't do anything stupid. Don't underestimate me."

Then the line went dead.

Chapter Twelve

Day Three—May 7
Wednesday Morning

BRYSON COVENTRY WOKE TO THE RINGING of his cell phone. Light crept into the room around the edges of the blinds meaning the day had started without him. He looked at the clock and couldn't believe the time. Then he remembered shivering down at the railroad tracks until two in the morning. He flipped open the cell as he headed for the bathroom.

The voice of Dr. Leanne Sanders, the FBI profiler, came through. He pulled up an image of a classy woman, about fifty, with shapely StairMaster legs.

"Let me put you on hold for ten seconds," he said. "Otherwise you're going to hear something you'd rather not." He muted the phone, pissed like a madman and brought her back up.

"I'm heading to Denver this afternoon," she said. "So be warned."

That was good.

He left her a message yesterday to see if she'd tap her resources and find out if there had been any other reported cases around the country involving women chained with black collars. He also emailed her photos of the collar.

Now she was headed to Denver.

And sounded excited.

"I've been hunting this guy for years," she said.

"You have?"

She had.

"I've been dead in the water for the last six months, waiting for fresh blood," she added. "I never pictured getting it in Denver."

Coventry pumped her for details.

Then he shaved in the shower, popped in his contacts and hopped in the Tundra. He wound out of South DeFrame Way to the 6th Avenue freeway and headed east, steering with his knees while he ate cereal.

Duran Duran's "Rio" came from the radio.

One of his favorite songs.

He hardly paid attention to it.

AT HEADQUARTERS HE HEADED STRAIGHT for the coffee.

Shalifa Netherwood walked over, looked at her watch and then at him.

"Late night," he said. "Leanne Sanders is flying into Denver this afternoon. It turns out that our collar friend's been on her radar screen for some time. Unfortunately, I think she's excited about finding someone who actually survived. I didn't have the heart to tell her about the body last night."

"What body?"

He told her about the woman at the railroad tracks with a screwdriver in her ear.

"Two bodies in one day," she said. "I'm impressed. You earned your keep yesterday."

He grunted.

"So you think she's the woman who was in the collar? That's your theory?"

He shrugged. "That's my guess, based on the timing. Plus they both have connections to trains. We need to check her DNA against what we found at the boxcar and see if there's a match. Can you run with that? Do you have time?"

She made a sour face.

"No."

He hugged her on the shoulders and said, "Expedite it, please and thank you. If anyone gives you any pushback let me know."

She laughed.

"What?" he asked.

"Coventry, no one's scared of you, in case you don't know."

HE CHECKED THE MISSING PERSON REPORTS and found a possible match to the woman they found last night, based on age, weight and hair color—namely one Marilyn Poppenberg, a D.U. law student. Poppenberg reportedly had a tattoo on her right ankle, some sort of Asian design that meant blessed.

Coventry pulled out the yellow pages, called a tattoo shop, explained the situation and asked if they'd fax over whatever designs they had that matched that description.

Five minutes later the fax gurgled a picture of the exact tattoo on the dead woman's ankle.

Bingo.

A match.

He'd verify it later with dental records but had no doubts.

The dead woman was Marilyn Poppenberg.

Then he realized that he'd been working for over a half hour with only one cup of coffee in the gut.

He headed over to the pot.

Time to correct that little oversight.

Right this second.

DENVER HAD GOTTEN SOME RAINY MAYS BEFORE, but nothing like this. Clouds were already moving in from the mountains, even this early in the morning, meaning another thunderstorm this afternoon.

Guaranteed.

Coventry didn't mind the rain.

But he didn't mind the sun either.

He drove east on 6th Avenue with "Surfer Girl" coming from the radio. That was the same song that had been playing at the eighth grade school prom when he slow-danced with Mary Winters and rubbed an erection on her stomach.

Wondering if she noticed.

She did.

But still grabbed his hand and dragged him to the floor every time a slow song came on.

Two weeks later they made love down by the river on a Saturday night.

His first.

Her second.

He crossed Colorado Boulevard and sipped coffee as stately mansions on oversized lots slipped by, owned by people who definitely didn't work as detectives.

Ten minutes later he arrived at the University of Denver.

He got twisted around with all the one-way streets and maniac drivers, but finally spotted the car he was looking for, a 1985 Camero, parked three blocks north of campus.

It had two tickets under the wiper blade.

He found a place for the Tundra a block away and then doubled back on foot with a disposable cup of coffee in hand. A peek through the driver's window of the Camero showed nothing of interest, so he sat down on the curb to wait.

Ten minutes later a young woman walked up.

She wore a long-sleeve green cotton shirt that hung over faded jeans. Long thick red hair cascaded down around pale skin and freckles. He liked her immediately and for some strange reason pictured her in a juice commercial. She muscled out of a backpack, lowered it to the ground and extended her hand.

"You're Detective Coventry, right?"

He nodded.

"Which means you're Samantha Oakenfold."

She smiled. "Just Sam."

She was the woman who filed the missing person report on Marilyn Poppenberg, who they found down by the tracks last night.

"Thanks for coming, Just Sam."

She laughed and said, "Whatever I can do to help find Marilyn. She still hasn't shown up for classes."

Coventry frowned.

She must have read the expression on his face because her forehead tightened. "What?"

He reached out and held her hand. "I think we already found her."

Then he explained.

And showed her a picture.

"That's her," she confirmed.

"I need to ask you some questions," he said. "You want to go somewhere?"

She nodded.

And he picked up her backpack.

Chapter Thirteen

Day Three—May 7
Wednesday Afternoon

LANCE LUNDEEN DROVE DOWN BROADWAY past the "Buy Here Pay Here" car dealerships, antique stores and greasy spoons. A half hour later he spotted a ragged Jeep Wrangler with a For Sale sign sitting in an RTD Park-N-Ride. It was an older model with square headlights. The plastic windows in the soft top were brittle and yellow. The springs showed rust.

He called the number on the sign and talked to a man named Dick Zipp—no joke—who swore up and down that the vehicle was mechanically sound and well maintained. He only wanted two thousand for it, which was a "screaming-banshee steal for whoever gets lucky enough to buy it."

"Can you leave the plates on it until I get my own?"

"Keep 'em," Zipp said. "I don't have any use for 'em."

"Do you have the title?"

He did.

Lundeen explained that he wanted the car but was pressed for time and couldn't turn it into a multi-trip project. "Here's what I can do," he said. "I'll put two thousand cash right now under the carpet by the back seat. You pick it up and then leave the title and registration in the same place. Will that work?"

"Sure, as long as the cash is really there, like you say."

"It'll be there," Lundeen said. "Go ahead and sign the title but leave everything else blank. I'll fill it all in later so you don't have to bother."

"I'll be down around five," Zipp said. "Where do you want me to leave the keys?"

"Same place as the title."

"Okay," Zipp said. "Just be sure no one sees the money. If it disappears between now and five that's your problem, not mine."

"The money will be there."

"In that case treat it good. That little fellow and me have been through a lot."

TARZAN RETURNED LATER BY CAB AND WATCHED as Zipp exchanged the papers for the money. The man, unbelievably, had a solid build and stood about six-one, just two inches shorter than Lundeen. He had black rimmed glasses, shaggy brown hair, and clothes befitting the jeep—namely ragged jeans, a flannel shirt and dirty tennis shoes.

After Zipp kissed the vehicle's mirror and disappeared down the road on foot, Lundeen went over to see if the piece of crap ran. It fired right up and actually handled pretty good.

Perfect.

For two thousand dollars Lundeen got himself a pretty good vehicle.

And—by incredible blind luck—an identity.

Dick Zipp.

He couldn't believe the name.

The guy's parents must have been nuts.

"Hey, Mrs. Zipp, what should we call our new baby?"

"I don't know, Mr. Zipp. How about Richard?"

"Yeah. I've always liked that name."

"It has a classy ring to it."

Yeah, right.

Real classy.

Dick Zipp

ON THE WAY HOME Lundeen picked up a cheap shaggy-brown wig, a pair of black rimmed glasses, two pairs of cheap jeans and two flannel shirts—paying cash. Back at the loft he clipped the wig until it was the right length and popped the lenses out of the glasses.

Outside he rubbed the jeans and shirts on the asphalt until they got greasy and dirty, then washed them and smiled when the stains stayed.

A few well placed rips made them look ten years old.

Yeah, baby.

Perfect.

Chapter Fourteen

Day Three—May 7
Wednesday Afternoon

———————————

KAYLA BECK KNEW IN HER HEART that Marilyn Poppenberg's death was somehow connected to the man behind the scrambled voice. It was too much of a coincidence that Poppenberg got killed and Kayla got chosen at almost exactly the same point in time. She and Poppenberg parked on the same street and often walked together.

Maybe he picked one of them, then saw the other one and picked her too. Maybe Poppenberg had been the chosen one but refused to cooperate, so the guy killed her.

Suddenly Kayla's cell phone rang.

The incoming number had a private number.

When she answered, Aspen's voice came through.

"I'm pulling out of the driveway right now," Aspen said. "I should be there in six hours, give or take."

Kayla told her about Marilyn Poppenberg, the fact that Coventry was involved in the investigation according to the newspaper, and her theory that the woman's death was somehow connected to the man they were looking for.

Aspen agreed a hundred percent.

But she also had a concern.

"Coventry will be showing up at the school to talk to people," she said. "Be real sure he doesn't see you or hear your name, because if you get on his radar screen a second time he's going to want to know why."

Kayla agreed.

"Get up here and keep an eye on him," she said.

"I'm on my way."

THE NEWS OF POPPENBERG'S DEATH spread quickly through the law school. It turned out that she'd been bound with blue rope. And the death wasn't just an ordinary death; it was a murder. And not just an ordinary murder, either; some sicko had pounded a screwdriver through her eardrum into her brain.

Everyone had questions.

A boyfriend?

A stranger?

Wrong place, wrong time?

Revenge?

Jealousy?

Drugs?

The first of a series?

To Kayla, Poppenberg had always been too wild to be a friend but had grown to be a fairly strong acquaintance. Kayla had seen her around during the first year of school, with her outlandish fashion and wild hair, and wondered about her from a distance. But they never spoke and didn't have any classes together.

Then last year they ended up in the same Evidence class.

They talked occasionally and walked to their cars together if they both happened to be heading that way at the same time. On one of those occasions, Poppenberg had a flat and had no idea what to do.

So Kayla changed it for her.

Poppenberg gave her a joint for her trouble.

Kayla said, "Thanks," then flushed it the first chance she got.

In spite of her wild streak, Poppenberg had a good sense of justice. In Evidence they learned about the exclusionary rule. It was a principle holding that evidence obtained by the police in violation of a person's Constitutional rights couldn't be introduced at trial, but instead got excluded, hence the name. The theory was that if the police couldn't benefit in court from trampling on the Constitutional privileges of people, then they'd be less inclined to trample in the first place.

Poppenberg hadn't disagreed with the rule.

But she did take issue with the fact that after guilty people escaped justice the police didn't keep an eye on them.

Especially murderers.

She even told Kayla once, "I have half a mind to do it myself."

"What do you mean, monitor them or something?"

"Right. Be there when they screw up the next time. Then tell the cops."

Kayla laughed.

"You're nuts."

"Yeah but that's beside the point."

SUDDENLY KAYLA REMEMBERED SOMETHING and stopped breathing. One of the Evidence cases involved a man who had abducted a woman and had her tied up in the trunk of his car. The police pulled him over for a burned out taillight. During that stop the man acted nervous. The police asked if they could search his car. He said no but they searched it anyway and found the woman in the trunk.

At an evidentiary hearing, the trial court ruled that the search had been in violation of the Fourth Amendment and that all evidence resulting from it was non-admissible.

Without that evidence, the police had no case.

So they had to let him go.

The woman in the trunk had been bound.

With blue rope.

Chapter Fifteen

Day Three—May 7
Wednesday Morning

AS USUAL, BRYSON COVENTRY NEEDED TO DO ten things and had time for two, so he ended up letting Just Sam tag along in the Tundra as he drove back to the railroad tracks to check the crime scene by the light of day. Just Sam flicked the radio stations until she landed on Madonna's "Burning Up," then turned up the volume.

They took 8th Avenue west to I-25 and then headed south. He had a thermos of coffee but only one cup, which they passed back and forth.

"This is good," she said.

"It's just cheap stuff," Coventry said. "I can afford quality or quantity but not both. So I go for quantity."

"You just rent it anyway."

He chuckled.

"Exactly."

It turned out that Just Sam wasn't just a law student. She was also a bartender at Shotgun Willies and lived in the apartment across the hall from Poppenberg. At least three or four nights a week they ate supper together, usually sending out for pizza or Chinese.

They also did some clubbing together.

"The only weird thing that I can think of is that she was doing some kind of surveillance every once in a while," she said.

Coventry heard the comment but was more interested in not being killed by an 18-wheeler merging from the Alameda ramp and trying to squeeze in front of him.

He tapped the brakes and let the guy in.

"What kind of surveillance?"

"I don't know exactly," Just Sam said. "I always pictured it as something out of an old black-and-white TV show—stakeouts in the rain, following people around in the shadows, that kind of thing."

Coventry raised an eyebrow.

"Well that's weird," he said.

She chuckled. "Actually, it's not that weird if you know Marilyn. She pretty much did what she wanted."

Coventry frowned.

"Who was she following?"

Just Sam didn't know.

Didn't have a clue in fact, even when Coventry pressed her.

Marilyn really never talked about it much.

"Was she moonlighting for a P.I. or something?"

"Not that I know of."

"Would you know if she was?"

She considered it. "I think so. We talked a lot about money since neither of us had any. If she had some coming in she would have mentioned it."

Coventry cut off I-25 onto Santa Fe southbound.

"So is that why she's dead? Because of these people she was

following?" Coventry asked. "Are they the ones who killed her?"

"How would I know?"

"You got to have a gut feeling."

She did.

And the feeling was negative.

"If she was in danger, she would have known it and would have said something," Just Sam said. "She had a sixth sense about people."

Coventry turned left on a gravel road, stopped a couple of hundred yards down and killed the engine.

"We found her over there," he said, pointing. "I'm going to ask you to stay in the truck if you don't mind."

"Sure."

Coventry scouted the scene, found nothing new of interest except a cigarette butt that he put into an evidence bag, and came back to the Tundra.

"Do you have the key to her apartment?"

She did.

"She allows you to go in?"

She did.

Meaning she could let him in without a search warrant.

"Mind if we go take a look?"

Chapter Sixteen

Day Three—May 7
Wednesday Evening

THE MOUNTAIN VIEW TRAILER PARK, to its credit, technically did have a view of the mountains. But it had a better view of the junkyard to the right, and the thousands of cars rushing down I-70 about a quarter-mile to the left. Lance Lundeen pulled Dick Zipp's Wrangler into the gravel entryway just before dusk and decided the place was a dive even by trailer court standards.

Unit 15, a thirty foot blue trailer, sat on cinder blocks in the back corner, surrounded by junk. It had a For Rent sign in the window. Lance pulled in front of it, killed the engine and stepped out.

He wore his Dick Zipp suit.

Jeans, flannel shirt, black glasses and wig.

He even improvised a little and added a baseball cap, which disguised the wig better.

When he knocked no one answered.

He tried the doorknob.

It was unlocked.

"Hello?"

No answer.

He stepped inside, got greeted by a musty smell, and pictured the roof and walls leaking for the last ten years. Dark fake wood, tattered cushions and scratched vinyl made up the interior. The floor of the toilet sagged under his weight, no doubt the victim of rotting wood.

Perfect.

The person he was supposed to meet—John Frickey—pulled up ten minutes later in a rusty Oldsmobile with a missing front fender. A black lab sat in the passenger seat.

"Stay here," Frickey told the dog. He looked like another Zipp, except shrunken, and smelled like a forest fire. "You the guy I came here to meet?" Frickey asked.

Lance shook his hand.

"That's me," he said. "Thanks for coming."

Frickey chuckled. "Yeah. I had to cancel my speech to be here, but what the heck."

Lance laughed and said, "I already took a look around. I hope you don't mind."

"Naw. She's a beauty, huh?"

"Actually, she'll do," he said.

He explained that it was his brother who would be staying there. He was coming into town from Atlanta to look for work. Five minutes later he handed Frickey three hundred dollars in cash and got the key for a month.

Frickey fired up a Camel, coughed, and drove off.

He never even asked Lance his name.

DEL RAE PARIS OOZED SEX. Her five-feet-six-inch body was

perfectly curved in all the right places, taut and smooth, with small pointy nipples that always showed no matter what she wore. There wasn't a color in the rainbow that didn't go with her flawless, golden skin. Her face was that of a woman, not the girl next door, seriously feminine and disturbingly hypnotic.

She could meet a man for the first time and have him buy her a car ten minutes later.

And had as a matter of fact.

But that was before.

Back in the smalltime days.

Before Lance Lundeen, a total stranger, cast his Tarzan eyes upon her in a crowded nightclub one Saturday night eight months ago, pulled her stomach to his and kissed her like he owned her.

He kept her in heat for eight long days and nights before he took her.

WHEN LUNDEEN GOT BACK from the Mountain View Trailer Park, he took a shower, got a call from Del Rae Paris saying she'd be over in a half hour, and then headed down to the second floor to study the spider's web and figure out how to do tomorrow's shoot.

The sun dresses weren't working the way he wanted.

It was too hard to get them to blow up just the right height.

And getting two of them to coordinate was impossible.

The background wasn't right either.

It needed to be a soft blue to bring out the harshness of the web.

When Del Rae showed up, Tarzan met her in the loft and told her what he'd gotten done today, namely buying Dick

Zipp's Wrangler and renting the trailer.

"Dick Zipp?" she said. "You're kidding, right?"

Lance chuckled.

"He's a pretty big guy," he said. "I doubt that he got ribbed about it that much."

"Maybe not to his face," she said.

He grabbed her hand, walked her over to wardrobe and told her to strip out of her clothes.

She did.

He riffled through the hangers and finally came upon a silk dress, pale green, that just might do the trick. He had her put it on, decided it was too long and cut it with a jagged line about six inches above her knees. Then he cut a slit up her left leg so it would open up when the wind blew.

"This doesn't come free," she warned him.

He laughed.

Then took her down to the second floor and had her get up on the web, as if caught in a spread-eagle position, while he adjusted the fan.

Different speeds.

Different angles.

All good.

The dress opened perfectly.

She hadn't put panties on so he had to imagine what it would look like with them.

"Do you still want to go through with this?" he asked.

"Are you talking about the lawyer?"

"Right."

"You better believe it."

"Because once we start there's no going back," he said.

"I know that."

"I know you know," he said. "I just want to be sure you're not having second thoughts. If you are, no big deal. You're my woman either way."

"I haven't been screwing him for three months for nothing," she said. "Don't even ask me again. By the way, does that bother you? That I'm screwing him?"

"What do you think? Stay exactly where you are. Don't move a muscle."

He walked over to the wall switch, killed the lights, and then climbed up the web like an animal and took her.

Chapter Seventeen

Day Three—May 7
Wednesday Afternoon

THE LAW SCHOOL BUZZED with energy—learning energy, stress energy, life energy. Ordinarily Kayla Beck fed off it but this afternoon, even in the Law Review room, she couldn't shake the darkness. An image kept popping up. An image of her alone and forgotten in some dark corner of the world where nice people never went, collared, growing increasingly desperate with a razorblade as her only friend.

She couldn't let that happen.

No matter what.

Maybe she should disappear, forget Denver, get in the car this minute and drive until either it broke down or she did.

Get a job as a waitress.

Change her name.

She pushed the thought aside, filled her coffee cup and went to the library. There she found a copy of the textbook from her Evidence class last year. The chapter that covered the exclusionary rule summarized six cases in the text and listed another twenty-two in footnotes. It didn't take her long to find the case involving the blue rope, which was a trial court decision out of California. Clearly the court understood that the defendant—Gordon J. Andrews—would be found guilty if the case was allowed to proceed to trial. The pain of letting him go was evident in the tenor of the decision. But the judge was "constrained to" exclude the evidence after finding that it had clearly been obtained in violation of the defendant's Fourth Amendment rights.

Did Marilyn Poppenberg investigate Gordon J. Andrews to find out what he was up to after escaping justice?

Was Andrews the one putting the women in collars?

Did he find out about Poppenberg's investigation?

And then kill her?

Kayla had her doubts, primarily because the defendant was from California. Poppenberg would be more likely to investigate someone who lived in the Denver area.

One of the references cited in the footnotes involved a man named Todd Underdown and a crime committed in Cheyenne, Wyoming—somewhat close to Denver, but not close enough that Poppenberg would have been investigating him.

Then, bingo!

One of the footnotes cited a Denver case. She pulled the full decision from the stacks. It involved a man named Ryan Tasker.

A very bad man.

When Kayla finally closed the book her hands shook.

She headed back to the Law Review room and Googled both defendants. Neither showed up so she refined her search and tapped into a variety of databases.

What she found she could hardly believe.

The blue rope defendant, Gordon J. Andrews, had changed his name to Lance Lundeen, and now lived in Denver.

Unbelievable.

He was even listed in the local white pages.

The other defendant, Ryan Tasker, also changed his name. Now he was Mitch Mitchell, also listed in the Denver white pages.

Bingo.

AT HER APARTMENT, JUST BEFORE DARK, Kayla's cell phone rang and an electronically scrambled voice came through. "Listen carefully because I'm only going to say this once. You are to never, ever talk to Aspen White again. You are to never, ever see her again. If you do I'll kill you both. And not in a pleasant way."

The line went dead before she could say a word.

She almost threw the phone at the wall.

Instead she remembered having a bottle of bourbon buried deep in the cabinet above the fridge. She muscled onto the counter, dug until she got it, then broke the seal and took a hit from the bottle.

Her mouth burned.

And tried to reject it.

But she swallowed it before she could spit it out.

Aspen White called ten minutes later and said she had just turned off I-25 onto I-70 west and should be arriving at Kayla's apartment in fifteen or twenty minutes.

"No!" Kayla said.

And told her about the threat.

No, not the threat, the promise.

Aspen stayed quiet for a few moments and then said, "He's going to kill us anyway, so screw him. Our only chance is to get him before he gets us."

Kayla paced.

Too rattled to get her thoughts in a straight line.

"Pack up everything you can't live without and be ready to leave by the time I get there," Aspen said.

Lightning crackled outside.

Rain thundered on the windows.

THEY ENDED UP AT A CHEAP HOTEL near 6th and 40 in unincorporated Jefferson County, getting the last room, a single bed unit. Aspen found a vending machine near the front office, out in the rain, and braved the weather long enough to buy a couple of cans of Coke to cut the bourbon.

"Freaking hurricane out there," she said.

"I can't get drunk," Kayla said. "I got classes in the morning."

Aspen laughed.

"Honey, you're already drunk."

Kayla fell back on the bed and watched the ceiling swirl. Then she leaned up on her elbows and said, "I did some research today."

"What on?"

"Our hunt."

"Really?"

"Yeah. Do you know a guy named Mitch Mitchell, formerly known as Ryan Tasker?"

No, she didn't.

Neither did she know Lance Lundeen, formerly Gordon Andrews.

"Too bad."

"Why?"

"Because then we'd know which one of them to focus on."

Chapter Eighteen

Day Three—May 7
Wednesday Afternoon

WHEN DR. LEANNE SANDERS, THE FBI PROFILER, walked into headquarters mid-afternoon, she barely had time to set down a briefcase before Bryson Coventry put her in a bear hug and spun her around full circle. She felt lighter and stronger than he remembered.

She stepped back and looked him over.

"You're still jogging I see," she said.

"True but not as fast," he said. "You lost weight." As soon as the words came out of his mouth he wanted to suck them back and swallow them.

There were two subjects that should never be broached with a woman.

The first was age.

The second was weight.

Both were train wrecks waiting to happen.

"Yeah, a couple of pounds," she said.

He exhaled.

A near miss instead of an actual crash.

"I want to see the boxcar," she added.

ON THE WAY TO THE CRIME SCENE they talked about the woman down by the railroad tracks, bound in blue rope, and Coventry's initial theory that she might have been the woman who got held in the boxcar. But now he was backing off that concept since none of the fingerprints found at the boxcar matched hers.

"We're still waiting on DNA," he said.

She nodded and said, "I want to see the razorblade when we get back to your office."

"What razorblade?"

She looked at him as if trying to figure out if he was messing with her. His face must have said he wasn't because she said, "You didn't find a razorblade?"

"No. Why? Should we?"

Then she told him something he didn't know. The woman always got a razorblade. In fact, that was the point of the whole thing, to slowly drive her to suicide.

"Now do you see why this bastard's high on my list?" she asked.

He did.

He did indeed.

WHEN THEY ARRIVED AT THE BOXCAR, the door was shut and padlocked as they had left it. Coventry had forgotten about the lock and couldn't remember what he did with the key.

"Wait here a minute," he said.

Then, back at the Tundra, he miraculously found the key

sitting innocently in one of the cup holders. When he got back to Dr. Sanders he said, "Left the key in the truck."

Dark clouds pushed across the sky.

"What's with that?" Leanne asked. "I thought this was Denver."

"We've been a little under the weather."

She grimaced.

"Not funny."

"I wasn't going for funny. I was only going for clever."

He got the lock off and pushed the door open. Inside it was darker than he expected, so he ran back to the Tundra and got a couple of flashlights.

Then they stepped inside.

They meticulously searched the area where the collar and the drifter's body had been found.

No razorblade.

"Strange."

Then they worked their way across the floor.

"Bingo," Leanne said.

Coventry went to where she was, almost at the far end, and looked.

Sure enough, a shinny new razorblade lay half hidden in the dirt. Leanne had a weird look on her face.

"What?" he asked.

"She threw it over here so she couldn't use it. I don't think I could have done that," she said.

Coventry pictured it.

"That little act may have saved her life," he said.

Chapter Nineteen

Day Three—May 7
Wednesday Night

RAIN ST. JOHN ARRIVED at Lance Lundeen's building a few minutes before midnight wearing an expensive long-sleeve shirt tucked into a short black skirt.

No bra.

No panties.

High heels.

Mildly drunk.

Seriously sexy.

Smoke from the club hung in her clothes.

She looked over her shoulder to be sure no one had followed and ran from her car to the entry. She rang the bell, got buzzed in, and took the elevator to the fourth floor. A few candles provided the only light. Lance waved to her from a bed at the opposite end of the room, not much more than a silhouette in the darkness. An exotic naked woman who Rain had never seen before muscled up from a lying position and studied her as she walked over.

The storm pounded on the roof and windows.

She unbuttoned her shirt on the way and had it off by the time she got to the bed. She twirled it in a circle and threw it over her shoulder, not watching where it landed.

Keeping her eyes locked on the woman.

Almost the way a predator studies its prey.

Then she pushed the woman down on her back, straddled her and pinned her arms above her head.

"Who's this?" she asked Lundeen.

Lance chuckled.

"This is Del Rae," he said. "Your co-conspirator."

"Del Rae my co-conspirator, huh?"

She kissed the woman on the mouth, released her grip on the woman's wrists and ran her fingers teasingly down her arms. She traced circles on her captive's nipples until they got hard. Del Rae bit her lower lip, shut her eyes and stretched her arms higher above her head.

"I like her," Rain said. "She's cute."

"Yeah, she's not bad."

She moved farther up on Del Rae's chest, grabbed her wrists and pulled her arms even tighter above her head. Then she wiggled up until her crotch was almost on Del Rae's mouth.

"Does she eat?" Rain asked.

Lance raised an eyebrow.

"I don't know," he said. Then to Del Rae: "Do you?"

"I do if she does," Del Rae said.

Rain lifted her skirt up and off, over her head. Then she sank her weight down until she was on Del Rae's mouth.

"You first," she said.

AFTER THE WOMEN PLEASURED ONE ANOTHER they gave

Lance a two-for-the-price-of-one blowjob. Then the three of them laid back on the bed, watched the candlelight flicker on the ceiling and talked about how things would work.

Tomorrow would be the day.

When Rain finally got around to leaving, Lance handed her a shoebox full of hundred dollar bills.

"Don't deposit that anywhere," he said. "We can't have anything happen out of the ordinary. Put it in a safe deposit box if you're worried about it."

She lifted up her skirt and flashed as she headed for the elevator.

"Don't worry about it," she said. "I know what I'm doing."

Chapter Twenty

KAYLA BECK FORCED HERSELF OUT OF BED when the first rays of light hit the hotel windows, unsure where she was. Her mouth felt like someone had stuffed cotton in it and taped her lips shut. In the bathroom she turned on the cold water, found no cups, bent over and put her mouth under the flow.

Lapping at it with her tongue.

Then she turned on the shower, waited for the temperature to adjust and looked around to see if the hotel supplied shampoo.

No.

Of course not.

It wasn't quite that kind of place.

It did supply one bar of soap, though, so her hair got that. By the time she soaped up and toweled down, the alcohol haze around her brain had almost dissipated. Her legs needed shaving but she had no razor or time.

That was the least of her worries.

The immediate problem, other than staying alive, was to not

tank her Secured Transactions exam this afternoon. That would be hard even if she jammed information in her brain all morning.

Starting this second.

As soon as she opened the bathroom door Aspen pushed through and said, "Got to go like a madman." She must not have been kidding, because she headed straight for the seat without even slowing down to swing the door closed.

When she came out Kayla said, "I have a huge test at two o'clock that I absolutely, positively have to get ready for."

Aspen had no problem with that.

"Go for it," she said. "I'm going to shower and then I'll head out and get us some breakfast. I saw a McDonald's down the road. What do you want?"

"Whatever—as long as it comes with three gallons of coffee."

"One Whatever with Coffee, coming up."

Kayla knew she should smile.

But couldn't.

Instead she pulled out her notes, spread 'em on the table and tried to get her arms around the best way to shoehorn ten pounds of information into a two pound brain.

A half hour later Aspen fetched breakfast and coffee, lots of coffee, three larges for each of them to be precise.

Then she wrote down the addresses of the two defendants Kayla came across during her research yesterday—the men Poppenberg may have been investigating.

Mitch Mitchell—formerly Ryan Tasker.

And Lance Lundeen—formerly Gordon Andrews.

The blue-rope-in-the-trunk guy.

She picked up her keys and said, "I'm going to swing by their places and see if I can at least get a look at them."

Kayla brought her head out of the notes.

"I thought you never got a look at the guy," she said. "You said he wore a mask."

Aspen nodded.

"That's true," she said. "I want to get a look at 'em so we know who to follow."

"Be careful."

"I will."

"I'm serious," Kayla added. "Stay out of sight until we can come up with a game plan."

"I'll be fine. Just worry about your test. I'll be back at 12:30 to take you to class."

"I really wish you'd wait until I can go with you."

"We don't have that luxury," Aspen said. "Time's already running out."

TRUE TO HER WORD, ASPEN RETURNED just before 12:30 and said, "I think we're still safe here, so I paid for another night. Come on, I have food in the car."

They wound over to I-70 and headed east, eating Arby's roast beef sandwiches and fries.

With diet Cokes.

"How'd the studying go? Did you get it all crammed in?"

Kayla swallowed a fry and said, "Good enough to fake it."

"I thought it was a law test?"

"It is."

"Sounds more like an orgasm test."

Kayla laughed.

"God I hope not," she said. "I haven't picked up that book

98

in over three months."

"No boyfriend?"

"No time."

"Well at least get a vibrator," Aspen said.

"No time."

"Honey, you got your priorities all mixed up. You know that, don't you?"

Then Aspen told her what she'd found out this morning.

The address for Lance Lundeen turned out to be an old four -story building in a ratty industrial area on the west edge of downtown, close enough to the 6th Avenue freeway to pick up plenty of noise, and next to a switchyard to get even more. All the windows were on the west side of the building, meaning they'd have to get into the track area to see inside. That had been impossible this morning with all the train workers around.

"The place gave me the creeps," she added. "Even in day-light."

"Why?"

"I don't know. Maybe because you could do all kinds of in-sane things in there and no one would ever know."

"What about the other guy?"

"Mitch Mitchell?"

"Right."

"That's weird too," she said. "He doesn't live that far from here, actually, on a dead-end street off South Golden Road, next to something that looks like an old armory."

"I know where you're talking about. It has an old canon out front."

Aspen nodded.

"He has a dilapidated house, not more than a thousand square feet. It couldn't pass a code inspection in a thousand years. It's the last house on the left."

Kayla laughed.

"Just like the movie."

Aspen looked confused but didn't press it. "I drove down, not knowing it was a dead-end, and actually had to turn around in his driveway. There was no car in the yard and the front door was shut just like you'd think if no one was home. I didn't see any signs of life, but felt eyes on me."

Kayla studied her.

"It really bothered me that there was only one way out," Aspen added.

Chapter Twenty-One

Day Four—May 8
Thursday Morning

COVENTRY WOKE UP BECAUSE SOMETHING WAS WRONG. A recessed survival gene pounded on warning drums deep inside his brain and made his heart beat faster. He opened his eyes and concentrated. For a brief moment he thought he heard a noise, but it disappeared as quickly as it came and he couldn't be sure.

He was in his bedroom.

It was dark.

He turned his head and looked at the red digits of the clock. 4:57 a.m.

The alarm would go off in three minutes.

The strange sound came again, unmistakable this time, definitely not his imagination. He slowly got out of bed, realized he was naked and concluded just as quickly that he had no time for clothes. He pulled his gun out of the holster, took off the safety and walked as quietly as he could towards the sound.

It came from the kitchen.

He held the gun with both hands, in firing mode, and twisted around the corner as fast as he could. Someone was there. He pointed the barrel at the person's heart and almost pulled the trigger before he recognized who it was.

Dr. Leanne Sanders.

Then he remembered that she spent the night in the down-stairs bedroom. A look of terror gripped her face. Then, as she realized he wasn't going to fire, it washed off.

"I knew I'd see you in the morning," she said. "I just didn't realize it would be this much of you."

He winced.

"I am so sorry—"

She laughed.

"Don't shower, we're going to jog. Remember?"

He disappeared around the corner.

"Right."

"I thought I'd get up early and make coffee," she hollered.

"Good idea."

"You got anything to stir it with?" she shouted.

"Not funny," he shouted back.

HE WASHED HIS FACE, popped in his contacts and slipped into gray sweatpants and a T-shirt. Five minutes later they were jogging down the street, clicking off the streetlights.

"I'm going to say something, but if you ever repeat it I'll deny it," she said.

He dreaded what was coming but asked anyway.

"What?"

"Nice."

He thought he knew what she was talking about but wasn't positive.

"What's nice?"

"Don't press it Coventry," she warned. "You were lucky to get it once."

He laughed.

"Oh, that."

"Right, that."

"Glad you approve."

"At least now I know the rumors are true."

"What rumors?"

"About the size of your feet."

Coventry lived in a green split-level ranch near the top of Green Mountain on South DeFrame Way. It was the third house from the end of the street and backed to open space. None of the neighborhood roads were level. They all went up or down, depending on which way you were going. That made jogging problematic.

Coventry hated running uphill.

And didn't like downhill much better.

But Leanne Sanders didn't seem to mind.

"I've been thinking about the case," she said. "And the more I think about it the more it bothers me."

"What bothers you?"

"The dissimilarities."

"What do you mean?"

"This scene is too different from the other ones," she said. "The collar looks similar but it's different. The razorblades from the other scenes are identical, from the same manufacturer in fact, maybe even the same box. This one's similar, but different. Then we have the padlocks. The prior scenes all had identical Master locks. This one has a Master lock too, I admit, but it's bigger. Same thing with the chain, close but not quite."

Coventry sucked in enough breath to talk.

"So what?" he said. "Different stores sell different things. There's no magic in one padlock versus another or one razor-blade versus another. They're all the same for what this guy does. He buys what he needs wherever he finds it. That's all there is to it."

"I don't think it's that simple."

"Of course it is," he said.

"There's something here, some kind of a clue or something and I'm not smart enough to figure out what it is."

"Here's your clue," he said. "No one ever does the same thing the exact same way twice. For example, I had a girlfriend once who was a great lover, and yet—"

She pushed him.

"What?" he asked.

"Spare me the details. I catch your drift."

"Okay."

"But there's more to it, trust me."

Coventry laughed and said, "You're too stubborn. Does your husband ever tell you that?"

"All the time," she said. "It doesn't do him any good."

Chapter Twenty-Two

Day Four—May 8
Thursday Morning

RAIN ST. JOHN LOOKED APPREHENSIVE as she walked down Bannock and got closer to the Wrangler. Lance Lundeen could see it—no, could *feel* it—in the way she cast her eyes and clutched her purse.

He didn't blame her.

Not a bit.

He'd be nervous too if he was about to go through what she was.

But he didn't feel sorry for her.

She was being paid well, win lose or draw.

Money or no money, though, she had guts.

He had to give her that.

He sat behind the wheel wearing his Dick Zipp suit, right down to the stupid black glasses. Rain halted next to the vehicle and scrunched her face as if trying to be sure it was him. He looked around, saw no one and told her to get in.

She slipped in and immediately ducked down.

"You ready?" Lance asked.

She exhaled.

"I hope so."

"Okay. Get in the back."

She crawled into the back, curled up and covered herself with a blanket.

"I need your purse," Lance reminded her.

"Sorry, I forgot."

When she handed it up, he scooped a pencil under the strap to avoid fingerprints. Then he waited. When a teenager in a backpack walked past, Lance brought his hand to his face and looked the other way. Same thing when a drifter shuffled by. Then two middle-aged women walked up the sidewalk, still a half block away. They looked like the types who would take a lost purse to the police. When they weren't looking he tossed it on the sidewalk and then drove off.

"Everything needs to be real," he reminded her.

"I know."

"*Everything*," he emphasized.

"I said I know."

"Okay. I just want to be sure."

They took I-25 to I-76 to Highway 85, heading north into farmland. As soon as civilization sufficiently disappeared, Lance pulled over to the side of the road. He poured liquid on a white rag and held it over her mouth.

"This will knock you out but won't hurt you," he said. "Go ahead and struggle if you want. After you're out I'm going to inject you with something that'll keep you out longer."

She stared at him through wide eyes.

Not moving.

Cooperating.

Then she struggled.

He held her in a Tarzan grip and said, "Go ahead and fight if you need to. It's okay."

She kicked and twisted.

Suddenly desperate to escape.

Finally her eyes rolled back in her head and she went limp. Lance felt a pressure in his pants and realized that Mr. Dick had sprung to life. He covered her and headed for the hideaway, steering with one hand and rubbing his crotch with the other.

WHEN HE GOT TO THE DEAD-END ROAD he took it all the way to the bridge and stopped just short of the faded yellow posts. He got out and surveyed the structure as well as he could without binoculars.

It looked just as abandoned as he remembered it.

Good.

He made a mental note to bring the binoculars next time, then turned the Wrangler around and drove to where the weed-infested driveway met the road. He put the Jeep in four-wheel drive and headed for the house, trying to stay on what he thought was the road. He pulled to the back side of the structure and killed the engine. As soon as he stepped out he pulled off the wig and scraped his fingernails over a sweaty scalp. The stupid glasses came off next.

Then, after putting on latex gloves, he carried Rain St. John inside and laid her in front of the fireplace.

Okay.

So far so good.

A torn mattress lay abandoned on the floor of the largest bedroom. It was a lumpy piece of crap but would still be a lot more comfortable than the wood. A quick inspection found no bugs or mice.

He pulled the mattress to the side of the room and then went outside to look for something to stand on. Five minutes later he muscled an old log into the room.

He stood on it and punched a hole in the ceiling. Then he pulled the plaster away and exposed two solid joists. Around them he wrapped a chain and locked it in place with a Master padlock. The tail of the chain dangled down almost to the floor.

He carried the log outside and moved the mattress back into the middle of the room, directly under the chain.

Rain wore white shorts, a green tank top, white ankle socks and yellow Skechers.

All that came off.

Then he carried her into the bedroom, laid her unconscious body on the mattress, and padlocked her ankle to the chain. No matter how far she pulled she wouldn't be able to reach the window.

He stuck a syringe in her ass and pushed the plunger.

That would keep her out for a good eight hours.

From the Jeep, he brought in the Porta-Potty, food and water and set everything next to the mattress. Then he took eight Polaroid snapshots of her.

THE RULES WERE CAREFULLY SET OUT on a sheet of paper, which he folded in half and set on top of the groceries.

Do not scream for help.

Do not talk or make noises.

Do not attempt to escape.

When you wake up you may stay awake for one hour. Then take one of the pills.

Do not speak to me until and unless I permit it.

Always look down when in my presence.

Refer to me as Master.

Do everything I tell you without protest.

If and only if you obey all the rules at all times, then at the end we will flip a coin. If it's heads you will be released. If it's tails you will die, but it will be quickly. You have a 50-50 chance.

If you do not obey the rules, then you forfeit your right to a coin toss. What happens then will not be pleasant.

WITH EVERYTHING IN PLACE, Lance Lundeen surveyed his handiwork and couldn't think of anything he'd missed. She looked lovely, so lovely in fact that he actually looked forward to what was coming next.

To prove it he put on a condom.

And screwed her good and hard.

Then left.

Chapter Twenty-Three

Day Four—May 8
Thursday Afternoon

KAYLA BECK FELT WEIRD. Maybe it was because the seat she sat on, namely the leather passenger seat in Aspen's silver Audi, cost more than Kayla's entire car. But more likely it was because they were parked behind a dumpster a quarter-mile from Lance Lundeen's building, watching it through Bushnell auto-focus binoculars, and debating whether it would be smart or stupid to break in.

"We're getting nowhere fast," Aspen said.

Kayla agreed.

But still balked.

"Assume worst case scenario," Aspen said. "Assume he actually does live here and comes home exactly when we're inside, which is unlikely. The place is huge. There's going to be a million places to hide."

True.

But still—

"We need to find out if he lives here or not," Aspen added. "I'm guessing the place is empty. The sooner we confirm that

the sooner we can move on." She must have felt a toehold because she added, "We go in and stay quiet. If anyone comes
we'll hear him. Haven't you ever broken into someone's house
before?"

Actually she had, but didn't feel like getting into it.

"We're worse off if we sit on our hands and do nothing,"
Aspen said.

Kayla rolled her eyes.

"I can't believe you're actually talking me into this."

THE GROUND LEVEL PROVED TO BE SECURE. It wasn't until
they got to the third floor, up the fire escape on the north side,
that they found an unlocked window.

The guts of the structure were deathly quiet.

After climbing in, they took a stairwell down to the ground
level to be sure the door opened from the inside, just in case.
Good thing, too, because they found it chained shut.

A wall divided the lower level. A door in that wall took them
to an area being used as a garage. Inside were a number of vehicles.

"Look at this," Aspen said.

The glove box of one of the vehicles—a GM truck—held a
registration belonging to Lance Lundeen.

"Bingo," Kayla said.

Aspen nodded.

"Our boy."

THE FIRST THREE FLOORS were basically empty shells, except
for the garage area on the ground level and some kind of web

contraption on the second. The doors leading to the fire escape from the second and third floors were chained shut from the inside, meaning they couldn't get out that way if the need arose. There were two elevators, a smaller one for people and a larger one for freight. They didn't dare use either and had no idea if they functioned.

A stairwell connected all four floors, nestled against the north wall.

They took it to the top level, opened a steel door and found a living area.

They paused.

No sounds emerged.

No movement came.

"Oh yeah," Aspen said, stepping inside.

Kayla chewed her lip.

"There's nowhere to hide," she said. "If he comes back we're screwed." Aspen ignored her and headed towards a small office area. A flat-panel screen sat on a beat-up pine desk. On the floor was a Dell computer. The only visible external drive was for a CD. Several blank discs were in a plastic case on a bookshelf.

Aspen pushed the power button and then grabbed a blank CD while the computer booted up.

"What are you doing?"

"Copying his files."

"Why?"

"Because computers tell secrets."

"We don't have time."

Aspen ignored her and said, "Keep looking around."

She surveyed the space, searching for the most likely spot to hold something incriminating, and discounted the kitchen, bathroom, bed, drums, lighting equipment and wardrobes. She headed over to the one and only enclosed area.

It turned out to be a darkroom.

A couple of dozen large black-and-white photos hung from clotheslines. They all depicted the same woman, an alluring woman even more captivating than Aspen. She was in a large spider's web, seemingly caught in a spread-eagle position, as a wind blew her flimsy dress.

Incredibly erotic.

She wore no panties.

ANOTHER DOOR AT THE BACK OF THE ROOM looked like it led to a closet. She opened it and found herself in a second room, at least as big if not bigger than the first.

A storage area.

It had hundreds of built-in drawers, running from the floor almost all the way to the ceiling. An eight-foot stepladder leaned against the back wall. White handwritten labels kept things organized. She grabbed one of the drawers at elbow level and pulled it out.

It was stuffed with color photographs.

They depicted a crowded city street.

Not Denver, though.

Someplace trendier.

She sensed L.A.

Men in tuxedos and women in elegant evening dresses waited in a line that spilled down the sidewalk, for a play or opera or some such thing. They all faced the same way. All except one man, whose eyes followed a young black woman in a $10.00 sundress walking in the opposite direction.

The message was clear.

We're animals.

Our lust is always turning its head.

Watching.

She shut the drawer. There had to be thousands of photographs here; tens of thousands. Clearly the man lived for the darkroom. If he was also the one putting the women in collars, then he would have snapped the shutter at them.

The moment would be too important to not capture.

And where would he keep them?

Somewhere in this room.

Secretly hidden in one of these drawers.

Suddenly Aspen bolted into the room, shut the door and turned off the light.

"We have company!"

Chapter Twenty-Four

Day Four—May 8
Thursday Morning

COVENTRY KNEW HE SHOULD TAKE Leanne Sanders somewhere nicer than Denny's, particularly after he let Mr. Happy scare her this morning, but that's where he took her anyway—the one at 6th and Simms. Every penny saved was another one to throw at the '67 Corvette loan.

His baby.

All original.

Numbers matching.

They sat in a corner booth with coffee in hand waiting for food. When "This Bird Can Sing" dropped from ceiling speakers, Coventry waved at the waitress.

She grabbed the coffee pot and headed over, already knowing the drill. As she topped him off he said, "Actually, I was hoping you could turn that song up."

She put an expression on her face.

"Only the manager's supposed to mess with the controls," she said.

Coventry flashed his badge, smiled his best smile, and said,

"This is official police business."

She walked off and said over her shoulder, "Well that's different."

Ten seconds later the song came on stronger.

The way it was supposed to.

Leanne cocked her head and looked at him.

"What?" he asked.

"That's your problem, right there."

"What? That I like the Beatles?"

"No," she said. "Women come too easy to you. My brother was the same way."

"First," he said, "that's not true. And second, even if it was, how would it be a problem?"

"Because it's too easy to move on."

"What do you mean—if the going gets tough?"

She nodded.

"That's why you're still single," she added.

He pulled up images of some of the women in his life.

Kelly Parks.

Darien Jade.

Tianca Holland.

Ja'Von Deveraux.

London Fontelle.

When held up against them, Leanne's comment wasn't fair. He was just about to say so when Kate Katona called and told him that the DNA reports came in. The woman bound with blue rope by the railroad tracks was not—repeat *not*—the same person from the boxcar. Coventry wasn't surprised since none of the fingerprints matched.

"Thanks," he said. "You're the best."

He was just about to tell Leanne the news when the waitress

set plates in front of them—pancakes smothered with strawberries and whipped cream.

"Thanks."

She smiled. "The manager's not here, so I could put a Beatles CD on if you want."

"Awesome," Coventry said. "You got any of their early stuff? The first three or four albums?"

"I'll check."

"That's their best stuff."

"I'll check. But we're not a music store."

He chuckled.

"Understood."

Leanne rolled her eyes. Then Coventry filled her in on Katona's news.

"That means our boxcar woman may still be alive," Leanne said. "This is the closest I've ever been to catching this guy, much less to saving one of his captives."

FROM DENNY'S THEY TOOK A QUICK DETOUR to the Silver Reef Apartments, where Coventry knocked on Kayla Beck's door but got no response, which was strange because her Ford Mustang was parked ten feet away. He knocked again, louder, and still got nothing. Then he pulled a business card out of his wallet and scribbled a note on the back—*Aspen, I'll buy dinner if you'll be the dessert*—and jammed it in the door crack.

Back in the car Leanne asked, "What was that all about?"

"The woman who lives there owns that 1967 Mustang," he said, pointing. "She's not the one we're looking for though."

She looked at him. "Which brings us back to my question. Why are we here?"

"Oh," Coventry said. "Because she has a roommate."

"And?"

"And the roommate kind of took a shining to me."

Leanne shook her head and asked, "Does Mr. Happy ever wake up and say, *You know what? I think I'll just take the day off.*"

Coventry chuckled.

"Not often."

She grew serious.

"So how many of those Mustangs do we need to still run down?"

"Most of them, unfortunately," Coventry said.

Then he remembered something.

Something bad.

He paid for breakfast with a credit card and didn't write in a tip, intending to leave cash on the table so the waitress wouldn't have to pay taxes.

Except he forgot to leave the cash.

"We need to swing by Denny's."

"Why?"

"Major brain fart. I stiffed our waitress."

When they got there he ran in, found only two dollars in his wallet and ran back out.

"Can I borrow ten dollars?" he asked.

She made a face of disbelief and reached into her purse.

"You know, I have to admit something. One of the reasons I came to Denver was to see if I could talk you into joining the bureau. But now, after seeing you in action again, I'm not so sure."

He grabbed the ten.

"Be right back," he said. "Then we have work to do."

Chapter Twenty-Five

Day Four—May 8
Thursday Afternoon

AS SOON AS LANCE LUNDEEN GOT HOME from taking Rain St. John to the hideaway, he stripped naked, downed a Bud Light in one long swallow, and stuck his head under the shower until the Dick Zipp wig itch disappeared.

Ah, better.

Much better.

Ten minutes later Del Rae Paris called with bad news, very bad news. "Megan backed out," she said.

Unbelievable.

"Why?"

"It's just too much for her."

"She's crucial and she knows it."

"So what do we do?"

Good question.

The timing couldn't have been worse.

"Go talk to her and get her back in," he said. "Offer her more money or whatever—tell her we won't do the hair thing if that's freaking her out. For her sake she better be smart enough

119

to make the right decision. Between you and me, *in* is the only place we can afford to have her. This is too important to have a loose cannon running around."

Del Rae understood.

And agreed.

"Talk her back into it for her own sake," Lance added.

Chapter Twenty-Six

Day Four—May 8
Thursday Afternoon

KAYLA BECK FELT LIKE A FROG in a snake pit. The darkness of the room couldn't have been more absolute if they were a thousand feet under ground and wore blindfolds. She felt around, found Aspen's hand and held it.

Aspen gripped back with a sweaty palm.

Neither of them spoke.

There was no need to. They understood the situation. The man would either walk in for whatever reason or he wouldn't. If he did, then that was that. If he didn't, they'd either have to wait for him to leave or try to sneak out tonight after he went to bed.

She had to relieve herself like crazy.

They listened to every sound that came from the main room.

Trying to figure out what he was doing.

Hoping against hope to hear something to indicate he was on the way out.

Instead, cabinets opened and closed. The shower ran for a few minutes and then cut off. A phone rang and words mumbled, too muted to understand, but loud enough to tell when he was talking and when he wasn't. Judging by the volume, Kayla figured it would probably be safe to whisper if she barely used any breath.

"Can you hear me?" she asked.

"Yes," Aspen said.

"There's a ladder against the back wall."

"I saw it."

"I'm going to hold it steady," she said. "See if you can get on top of the drawers."

They felt their way over to it—a stepladder, folded shut and leaning against the wall. Kayla felt the angle and pulled the feet out a little farther.

"Go ahead," she said.

Aspen climbed, feeling her way up, one careful step at a time. Then she stopped and Kayla heard her fingering the wood.

"It's solid up here," she said. "I think it'll hold us."

"How much room is there?"

"About the same as a coffin."

Great.

Still better than nothing.

"It's going to be a little tricky swinging up," Aspen said.

Kayla gripped the ladder and took a firm stance. "Whenever you're ready," she said.

Two seconds later the ladder pushed away from the wall, so hard that Kayla had to put all her weight into it. Aspen grunted and struggled for what seemed like a long time. Then she said, "Whew," and exhaled.

"You up?"

"Yeah, but it was harder than I thought."

A lot harder.

"You're going to need to open the ladder," Aspen added.

"Otherwise it's going to buck off the wall."

Kayla chewed her lip.

Once up, she wouldn't be able to close it.

And if the man came in he'd notice.

"I'll make it," she said.

When she got to the top of the ladder she understood what Aspen was talking about. She got as good a grip as she could on the top of the drawers, then pushed off and swung her leg up.

The ladder jerked away from the wall and sounded like thunder when it slammed to the floor.

Kayla muscled up and held her breath.

Her heart raced.

Ten seconds later a light came from under the door.

Meaning the man was in the darkroom.

Heading here next.

If he came in and saw no one here, he'd look on top of the drawers.

And find *both* of them.

Kayla jumped down and landed on her side just before the door opened.

A HAND WENT TO THE LIGHT SWITCH and the room suddenly sprang to life. The man wore no shirt and towered over her. His body was massive and muscled beyond belief. He had a lion's mane of thick blond hair.

"Who are you?" he asked.

The tone gripped her so hard that she didn't talk.

She'd heard it before.

It meant violence.

"Answer me!" he said.

123

Before she could say anything he slapped her across the face, with an open palm, but still strong enough to make colors flash. Aspen suddenly appeared in her peripheral vision, getting ready to jump on him.

"No!" Kayla shouted.

"No? Come here," the man said.

Then he jerked her up, scooped her under his left arm and slammed the door shut as he carried her out of the room.

HE THREW HER ON THE MATTRESS, roughly, not caring if she broke her neck.

She could only think of one thing.

He didn't recognize her.

He truly didn't know who she was.

Meaning he wasn't the man behind the scrambled voice.

"Don't move!" he said.

She watched him walk across the floor, moving like a wild animal. He returned with a pair of scissors and rope. Then he hogtied her, tighter than tight, and cut her clothes off.

Every stitch of them.

"I think I made some kind of mistake—"

"No kidding."

He smacked her on the side of the head.

Colors flashed as he gagged her.

Chapter Twenty-Seven

Day Four—May 8
Thursday Afternoon

NOW THAT MARILYN POPPENBERG wasn't the woman from the boxcar, Coventry intercepted Kate Katona at the coffee pot and told her he was getting out of her way so she could run with the case.

She made a face.

"Finally, something to do."

"It's all part of my evil plan to keep you from having a life," he said.

"Such a guy."

He headed to his desk which was over by the snake plant, out in the main room with everyone else. As the head of the homicide unit he had every right to occupy the office down the hall, the one with four walls and a door that actually closed. When he got promoted into the position three years ago he actually sat in that room for a couple of days before he realized it was too close to the chief's office.

And too far from the coffee.

And too much like an elevator.

Dr. Leanne Sanders disappeared early in the morning with a list of Ford Mustang owners. Ten of them were men. She wanted to talk to each of them, face to face, to get a personal feel for whether they were the one behind the collar.

She showed up at headquarters mid-afternoon, poured a cup of decaf and slumped in the chair in front of Coventry's desk.

"I talked to all the men but two," she said. "None of 'em got me excited."

Coventry frowned.

"Not even a little?"

She shrugged.

"If we had endless resources, maybe one or two," she said. "But none I could justify throwing money at today."

Suddenly Shalifa Netherwood appeared, gave Leanne a quick hug, and sat down in the other chair looking excited. She ignored Coventry and focused on the profiler.

"You wanted to know if any women disappeared who fit the guy's profile," she said.

Meaning young and attractive.

Leanne perked up.

"Right. You got someone?"

"Maybe—"

ACCORDING TO SHALIFA, a woman by the name of Rain St. John may have vanished this morning. A couple of old ladies found her purse lying in the middle of the sidewalk on Bannock around ten o'clock. Nothing appeared to be missing. Her keys, wallet and cell phone were all safe and sound inside. The wallet still had everything in it, including her driver's license, two credit cards and $126 in cold hard cash.

"They turned in cash?" Coventry asked.

"Yeah. It happens all the time."

"Not on the planet Denver it doesn't."

Apparently Rain St. John was on her way to a girlfriend's by the name of Megan Foster. They were going to get their hair done and Megan was going to drive. Rain called her and said she was parking her car and would be there in five minutes.

But she didn't show up.

Not in five minutes.

Or ten.

Or thirty.

"Megan kept calling the Rain woman on her cell phone," Shalifa said. "When she never answered, Megan walked down the street and found her car. That's when she decided things were weird enough that she should make a report."

Her car was two blocks away.

The old ladies found the purse between the car and Megan Foster's house.

She hadn't shown up at any of the metro hospitals. Nor did she have a history of medical problems.

"What does she look like?" Leanne asked.

"Let's just say no one would kick her out of bed."

Leanne nodded.

Then looked at Coventry.

"Sounds like it's worth a look," she said.

Coventry looked at Shalifa.

"Does the woman live alone or with someone?"

Shalifa shrugged.

"Don't know. Why?"

"Do me a favor and find out," he said. "If she lives with someone, then get a consent to enter. If you can't get consent or if she lives by herself then work up a search warrant. Either way I want to be walking through her door in two hours."

Shalifa rolled her eyes.

"Bryson, I was just relaying information, not volunteering for work," she said.

Coventry cocked his head.

"That's the problem with being the messenger," he said. "You can get killed."

AN HOUR AND A HALF LATER, Coventry and Leanne knocked on the door of Rain St. John's brick bungalow on Grant Street and got no answer. One of the keys from the missing woman's purse fit the door.

Coventry opened it and stuck his head in.

"Police. We have a search warrant."

No response.

Leanne pushed through and said, "Let's see what we have."

Chapter Twenty-Eight

Day Four—May 8
Thursday Afternoon

WHEN TARZAN FINALLY REMOVED THE GAG, Kayla Beck immediately sucked air and didn't make a sound. She didn't scream, mostly because more than anything in the world she didn't want him to shove the gag in her face again; but also because she didn't want Aspen thinking she needed to run out and save her. Their only chance at getting out of this alive was if Aspen had enough smarts to bide her time and escape.

From her hogtied position, she twisted her head up to gauge the man's anger.

He was visibly calmer now.

"The ropes hurt," she said.

"Shut up," he said.

Ten minutes later he untied her and walked over to the fridge for another beer. She sat up, rubbed the circulation back into her wrists and looked for a weapon.

Scissors.

An ashtray.

Whatever.

About the best she could see was a sharpened pencil on the computer desk more than ten steps away.

If she attacked him she'd better kill him.

A pencil would only get him mad.

He took a long swallow of beer, about a third of the bottle, and said, "Lay down on the floor in front of the drums, on your back."

She did.

Still naked.

With her legs pressed together and her hands covering her breasts.

"Put your arms above your head," he said.

She obeyed.

"Now spread your legs."

She did.

"Wider."

She chewed on her lower lip, almost got up and ran, but then remembered Aspen and did as she was told.

"Now don't move a muscle. Do you understand?"

"Yes."

"After I relax a little we're going to talk," he said. "You're going to tell me what you're doing here and why you were trying to copy my computer files. Then I'm going to decide the appropriate punishment. Do you understand?"

"Yes."

"Don't you think that's fair?"

She knew better than to give him the wrong answer.

"Yes."

SUDDENLY "SWEET CHILD OF MINE" filled the room, incredibly loud and extremely clear, pounding out of very expensive speakers. He walked over and stood above her, one foot on each side of her stomach.

"What's your name?"

Her first instinct was to lie.

But she didn't know how much trouble that would get her in if he found out.

"Kayla," she said.

"Kayla what?"

She bit her lip.

And made a split-second decision.

"Kayla Black."

"Are you telling me the truth, Kayla Black?"

She nodded.

"Yes."

"Because we're going to find out and if you're lying the punishment's going to be severe," he said. "Do you like this song?"

She didn't.

But said, "Yes."

"Me too."

He sat down, drained the beer bottle and set it on the floor. Then he twirled a pair of drumsticks, hit the snare three times and played along. Her immediate instinct was to put her hands over her ears but she dared not move. When the song finally ended he didn't get up, but instead sat there and twirled the sticks. Ten seconds later the song started over again.

Then again.

He was halfway through the song for the third time when Kayla saw Aspen sneaking up behind him.

The woman held nothing in her hand.

Not a weapon of any kind.

What was she thinking?

He'd snap her like a stick doll.

She stopped not more than two feet behind him. Then she squatted down ever so slowly and reached for the beer bottle. Tarzan must have seen her because he twisted and struck at the exact moment that she swung the glass at his head.

Chapter Twenty-Nine

Day Four—May 8
Thursday Afternoon

IF RAIN ST. JOHN'S HOUSE HELD ANY SECRETS regarding her disappearance, it wasn't giving them up without a fight. To Coventry's eye everything looked normal. Their primary goal was to find whether the woman had been threatened or had encountered any strange bumps in the night prior to her disappearance. No messages suggesting that showed up on her answering machine. Her emails, old and new, told them nothing.

Other than she had an extraordinary sex life.

"This girl gets horizontal more than you do," Leanne said at one point.

"It's not a fair comparison," he said. "She's obviously bi, meaning she has twice the chances."

"Actually," she said, "she still wins even if you take only half."

He chuckled.

Beaten.

"She even gets more women than you do," Leanne added.

"See, that's where you have me wrong," Coventry said. "You

think I'm after women all the time. Actually—and don't you dare repeat this because I'll deny it—all I really want is one. One good one."

She rolled her eyes.

"And you'll go through dozens to find her if you have to."

He nodded.

"We're all forced to do things we don't particularly enjoy."

"*Please.*"

"Actually," he said, "I'm going through one right now. Or she's going through me. I'm not sure which."

"And?"

"What do you mean—*and?*"

"*And* is she promising?"

"That's what I'm trying to figure out. That's what I'm always trying to figure out."

"What's her name?"

"Aspen."

"Aspen what?"

He shrugged.

He didn't know.

"You don't know her last name?"

"Not yet."

"Did you ask?"

"Not yet. Haven't had a chance."

They found a shoebox full of hundred dollar bills in the bedroom closet behind a barricade of photo albums. Coventry counted it.

"Fifty grand exactly," he said.

"Well that's interesting, isn't it?"

He stood on his tiptoes, stretched up and put it back.

"Very," he said.

THE FRONT AND BACK DOORS got crime scene tape. Then, as long as they were in the area, they knocked at the neighbors and talked to the ones who were home.

No one had anything of interest to say.

Apparently the Rain woman was a night owl, usually sleeping until noon and then going out-and-about until the wee hours of the morning.

The guy across the street, a scrawny man with a pervert's face by the name of Bob Sorensen said, "I don't know much about her. To tell you the truth, I never paid that much attention to her."

His eyes darted nervously.

Coventry spotted a pair of binoculars on the man's coffee table. He would have a clear shot of the woman's bedroom from just about any window in his house.

"Okay, thanks," Coventry said.

IT TURNED OUT THAT LEANNE was the keynote luncheon speaker at a criminal law seminar in Las Vegas tomorrow, meaning she needed to head to the airport tonight or first thing in the morning.

"Stay over tonight," Coventry said. "I still need to take you for a ride in the '67."

"You mean that fiberglass deathtrap of yours?"

"*Red* fiberglass deathtrap," he corrected her. "We can head up to the Little Bear and get a burger."

"I'm more in the mood for a shot and a beer."

"They got those too."

135

She looked at him funny.

"What?" he asked, curious.

"Mr. Happy's not going to come out and visit me again in the morning is he?"

Coventry chuckled.

"No," he said. "Mr. Happy and I had a long talk." He paused, smiled and almost added, *Maybe you two want to shake hands. Just to be sure there are no hard feelings.*

But he didn't.

Chapter Thirty

Day Four—May 8
Thursday Afternoon

———————

AS SOON AS THE BEER BOTTLE SMASHED against his skull, Lance Lundeen knew he'd been hurt bad. Blood immediately gushed down his forehead and into his eyes. His vision blurred but he managed to grab a fistful of his attacker's hair. Hands pounded on his face but they couldn't get his fingers to open.

Then something terrible happened.

A pain.

In his back.

Deep and serious.

He immediately let go and twisted around.

But he couldn't reach the source.

He ran to the mirror to see what had happened. A pencil stuck out of his back, close to his spine, buried deep. He couldn't reach it.

Then tried again.

Straining even harder this time.

A door slammed.

The women were escaping and he couldn't do a thing about

it. He ran to the elevator, stumbled into the wall, and then hit the button for the ground level. As it descended he squeezed blood out of his eyes. When the doors opened he staggered towards the north wall. The toolbox was there on the bench exactly where it should be. He rifled through it until he found the pliers. He gripped them in his right hand, twisted his arm around and pulled the pencil out.

The pain didn't stop but a major layer of stress peeled off.

The thing was out.

He headed back to the loft and looked at the wound in the mirror. Surprisingly it wasn't bleeding that much. He grabbed a towel and pressed it against the opening in his head. The stream of blood immediately tapered off.

Then he laid down on the shower floor and closed his eyes.

Keeping the towel against his head.

He felt faint.

And nauseous.

IT TOOK A LONG TIME but the bleeding eventually slowed to a trickle and then stopped altogether. He brought the kitchen faucet to a lukewarm trickle and stuck his head underneath, being as careful as he could to not open the wound further.

After all the blood came out of his hair he surveyed the damage with a hand mirror. The split was about three inches long.

A good candidate for ten or twelve stitches.

He cleaned it with antibacterial soap, determined that no glass splinters were inside, and wrapped gauze around his head. Then he stepped into the shower and let the stream of water clean the hole in his back.

It took a good hour to scrub the blood off the floor and

drums and elevator and garage. He didn't do a perfect job by any stretch of the imagination but did enough to get by.

Del Rae called just as he finished up.

"Bad news," she said. "I can't get Megan back in."

"You tried?"

"Trust me."

"Then screw her," he said. "She's dead."

"Unfortunately she already thought of that," Del Rae said. "She said she typed out some notes and stuck 'em in a safe deposit box for the cops to find, just in case you and me were thinking about doing something stupid."

Lance threw a book called *Fatal Laws* at the drums.

The snare crashed to the floor.

"Now she's really dead," he said.

WHEN HE TOLD HER WHAT HAPPENED this afternoon she asked, "What did they want?"

"I don't have a clue," he said. "It's a total mystery. And the one who said her name was Kayla Black lied, at least I'm pretty sure she did. There's no such person listed in the phonebook." He exhaled and added, "Maybe we should cool it with everything for a while."

"You mean the lawyer?"

"Right."

"No way," she said. "I haven't been screwing his brains out so we can cool it."

He said nothing.

"I'm going to come over and stitch you up," she added.

"I'm fine."

She grunted.

"This is no time for egos. I'll be there in a half hour."

Chapter Thirty-One

Day Four—May 8
Thursday Night

MITCH MITCHELL HAD A SHAVED HEAD and a lean, no-nonsense skin-and-muscle body with a barbwire tattoo that wrapped around his chest three times. At five-feet-eight he'd never be the biggest dog in the pack, but he looked like the one most likely to die fighting. He wore a pair of loose jeans and nothing else—no shirt, no shoes, no socks. He paced back and forth in the living room, talking intently into a phone and taking swallows out of a bottle of whiskey when he wasn't waving it angrily in the air.

Kayla and Aspen watched him through binoculars.

It was 10:32 at night.

A thick blanket of clouds kept the sky darker than dark.

Even though they were dressed in all things black and hidden in a clump of trees out in the field more than fifty yards from Mitchell's house, the creepiness of the guy still reached them.

Even there.

Kayla handed the binoculars to Aspen and said, "This guy

141

scares me to death."

Aspen grunted.

"Somewhere in that rat hole of a house is a voice scrambler and a half-dozen black steel collars. I can smell 'em," she said. "Ouch!"

"What?"

"He just threw the phone against the wall."

Kayla frowned.

"I guess that's one way to hang up."

Mitchell scribbled something on a piece of paper, folded it in half and dropped it on the coffee table. He threw on socks and shoes. Two seconds later the screen door slammed open and he stormed out, pulling a black T-shirt over his head. He got in an old pickup, pulled the door shut as hard as he could and squealed out of the driveway. Fifteen seconds later his taillights hit South Golden Road and disappeared to the left.

Aspen grabbed Kayla's elbow and squeezed.

"I'm going in," she said. "Stay here and call me if he comes back."

Kayla swallowed.

That was the plan they'd discussed, in the event the opportunity presented itself.

Still she didn't like it.

It didn't feel right.

Something was off.

Wrong.

Something she couldn't put her finger on.

"Be careful," she said.

"If any headlights at all come up the street, call right away. Don't wait to try and figure out if they're his or not. Just assume they are."

"I will."

"If you call I'll probably end up going out the back," Aspen said. "Don't try to figure out where I am. Just get to the car and wait for me."

"I know."

"I know you know. I'm just being sure one last time."

They hugged and then Aspen disappeared into the darkness. Ten seconds later she returned and handed Kayla the car keys. "Hold these," she said. "They're jamming into my leg."

Then she disappeared again.

KAYLA CHEWED HER LOWER LIP, feeling guilty that she wasn't sharing the risk but knowing that one of them needed to be the lookout. They'd flipped a coin earlier. Aspen won and chose to go in.

It had been a long day.

Kayla had mixed emotions about stabbing Tarzan in the back with the pencil this afternoon. He truly had no idea who she was, meaning he wasn't the man behind the collar. So in hindsight they were after someone else, not him. But still, he was violent and weird, and clearly would have done her a lot more harm than he did if she hadn't escaped.

Of that she was certain.

He might have even killed her.

That was clear.

So screw him.

He'd left her no choice.

THUNDER CRACKLED IN THE DISTANCE and then it started

to rain. She nestled up against the tree trunk, picked up the binoculars and pointed them at Mitchell's house just in time to see Aspen walk up the front steps. Mitchell must have left the front door unlocked because Aspen nudged it open and stepped inside.

She spent a few moments in the living room and apparently saw nothing of interest because she disappeared into the back of the house.

The rain intensified.

Water fingered its way through Kayla's hair to her scalp.

Headlights flickered behind her, way back by the rock quarry where the Audi was parked, and then disappeared.

Three more minutes passed.

No sign of Aspen.

Kayla got nervous and dialed Aspen's number.

The connection went through and before she could say anything Aspen asked, "Is he coming?"

"No. I just wanted to be sure you're okay."

"I am. No problem."

"What are you finding?"

"Lot's of bondage stuff," she said. "This guy's definitely way off the charts."

"Did you find a collar?"

"Yeah, but it's leather," Aspen said. "Nothing steel yet. I know it's here though. Just give me another five minutes."

"What did that note say?"

"What note?"

"Whatever it was he wrote right before he stormed out."

"I don't know. I didn't read it."

SUDDENLY SOMETHING GRABBED Kayla's peripheral vision, namely an ever-so-slight movement in the window of the house across the street from Mitchell's. Just for grins she pointed the binoculars that way.

What she saw startled her so much that she dropped the binoculars.

A man was watching her.

Through binoculars.

Looking directly at her.

He had a phone, too.

Talking animatedly.

Suddenly Aspen's voice snagged her attention. She sounded panicked. "The note says, *You're dead*," she said. "I think it's for us. Get out of there right now and meet me at the car!"

Kayla turned.

Just in time to see a dark shape lunge at her.

Chapter Thirty-Two

Day Four—May 8
Thursday Night

—————————

BY ELEVEN O'CLOCK AT NIGHT BRYSON COVENTRY still hadn't fallen asleep. Outside a gusty wind pushed a heavy rain against the windows, wild enough to keep a drunken sailor awake, but that wasn't the problem. The problem was that Aspen hadn't called all day.

Not for supper.

Not for dessert.

Not for nothing.

He got out of bed, put in his contacts, threw on sweatpants and then bounded out the front door, determined to jog three miles no matter how drenched or battered he got.

He ran a mile.

Then came to his senses and turned around.

Back home he stood under a hot shower for thirty seconds, towel-dried his hair just enough so that it didn't drip, and then drove straight to Kayla Beck's apartment, with the radio playing "Paint it Black." He needed to know if Aspen got his note and needed to know now.

He needed to know if he'd misread her.

He needed to know if he was wasting his time.

When he arrived, the Mustang was parked in the exact same spot as before. Kayla's apartment was dark. His business card, with the note on the back, was still stuck in the door jam.

He knocked on the door.

No one answered.

The corner of his mouth turned up ever so slightly.

She hadn't blown him off after all.

When he got back home he fell asleep as soon as his head hit the pillow.

Chapter Thirty-Three

Day Five—May 9
Friday

THE SPIDER WEB SHOOT took most of the day but couldn't have gone better. Scotty Marks' web worked perfectly, the women had attitude and, most importantly of all, Lance felt brand new. The pencil in his back hadn't punctured any organs. As for the gash in his head, it itched like a madman but stayed closed thanks to Del Rae's needlework.

After the shoot, two of the models hung around, thinking they could coax him into a threesome. Eight months ago he would have thrown them on the mattress and rocked their little worlds until they couldn't see straight.

And still have energy to spare.

Back in the pre-Del Rae days.

But not now.

The minute they left, he tuned the satellite radio to a rock station and headed for the darkroom. He was still there hours later when Del Rae showed up with Chinese takeout.

He suddenly realized he hadn't stopped for food all day.

They ate on the roof, under a wide Colorado sky, sitting in

chaise lounges and passing eight-by-ten color prints back and forth.

Del Rae was impressed with the shoot.

She said so.

And then took him to the mattress to prove it.

Afterwards they planned the upcoming evening, going over every little detail until there were none left. So far Lance couldn't see any problems, other than the obvious risk of the cops coming along at the exact wrong time. Del Rae got the toggle switch installed yesterday, the one that would mysteriously kill her engine on demand and bring the vehicle to a breakdown wherever and whenever she chose. It worked fine. The lawyer—Robert Sharapova, Esq.—had already fed his naïve little wife a story about having to go out of town for depositions this weekend. Wifey-poo would drop him off at the airport and wave goodbye with that sweet, innocent little hand of hers.

Del Rae would pick him up fifteen minutes later wearing a short white dress and a black thong.

He'd hop in.

She'd move his hand to her leg and purr as they drove off.

LUNDEEN GOT TO THE HIDEAWAY JUST BEFORE DARK and parked the Wrangler in the back. A three-fourths moon hung in the east, bright enough to cast shadows.

Crickets chirped.

Otherwise the night sat coffin quiet.

Inside the house he found Rain St. John exactly where he left her yesterday morning, naked and chained on the mattress, awake but groggy.

"Lance?" she asked.

The words dripped with nervousness.

He wore his Dick Zipp suit. He wanted her to see him that way at all times so she'd be able to describe him confidently to the police.

"Yeah, it's me," he said.

"Get me out of here," she said. "I can't take any more of this."

He kneeled down and unlocked the chain, surprised to find her ankle raw and bloody. She'd obviously been pulling on it.

"What happened here?"

"I freaked out," she said.

"I'd say so."

He smiled.

Actually, that was a nice touch.

A very nice touch.

It added a lot of unexpected authenticity.

She hugged him.

Tight.

He hugged her back and then rubbed her shoulders.

"I couldn't take another night here," she said. "There was a whole pack of coyotes right outside the door last night. They kept howling and circling the house. I was afraid they'd jump through the window."

"Coyotes won't hurt you," he said. Then he held her at arms length and looked her in the eyes. "Are you ready for the grand finale?"

"No but let's do it."

"Are you sure?"

She nodded.

"We've gone this far," she said.

They had sex.

He wore a condom and took her roughly.

Technically she should be unconscious but he let her stay awake.

She came twice.

Then he injected her and let her walk the stiffness out of her legs while the drug took effect. After she fell unconscious, he cut her hair off with a pair of scissors and threw it in the corner.

Then he carried her nude body outside to the Wrangler, put her in the back and covered her with a blanket.

Game time.

THE CAMEL'S BREATH IS A SEEDY BAR with cheap beer and bad bands that can easily hold three hundred drunks on a Friday night. It sits in that industrial no man's land north of downtown not far from the South Platte River. At the end of a drunken night, the road to the south is the way out. North is nothing more than a mile stretch of lonely road that leads to a dead-end. The more the beer flows, the more cars there are that get to figure that out.

Lance Lundeen parked on the shoulder three-fourths of the way up that dead-end road with the lights out.

Waiting in the dark.

Finally headlights headed his way. As the car passed he slumped down as far as his oversized frame would go and watched.

A woman drove.

A woman by herself.

Perfect.

He tapped the brake lights twice and then threw a bucket full of roofing nails on the road about thirty yards up. When the car came back it came fast.

Lance could read her mind.

She was pissed for going the wrong way.

Trying to make up lost time.

He chuckled.

That isn't the worst of your luck, honey.

Both front tires blew exactly as they were supposed to. The woman screamed and muscled the car to a stop just before running into the back end of the Wrangler.

Lance—make that Dick Zipp—hopped out immediately.

"Watch it, woman, you almost hit me," he said.

She didn't get out.

So he bent down to inspect the damage, looking as normal and helpful as he could.

"You got a flat," he shouted.

"What?"

She powered the window down.

"I said you got a flat."

"Oh."

"You got a spare in the trunk, or what?"

"I don't know."

"Well we better check," Lance said.

She opened the door, slowly, still deciding.

Lance could read her mind.

This guy's huge.

And dressed like trailer-trash.

Out here in the middle of the night.

She finally stepped out and walked up front to see the damage. In the headlights now, Lance got his first good look at her.

Young and pretty.

Insanely drunk.

Perfect.

"Oh, man, they're *both* flat," she said.

She must have sensed danger because she abruptly turned just as Lance grabbed her. He locked her up with one arm and then brought a saturated cloth to her mouth. She kicked helplessly for a few seconds and then went limp.

He laid her on the ground.

Then he put Rain St. John's body in the front seat of the woman's car, put the woman in the back of the Wrangler, and got out of there.

Chapter Thirty-Four

Day Five—May 9
Friday

THE HOTEL HAD AN ALARM CLOCK but the alarm part of it didn't work, so Kayla Beck got up at the first light of dawn to be absolutely certain she didn't oversleep and miss any of her classes. Above all else, she needed to hold her studies together. If that part of her life unraveled, then she was done, plain and simple.

She studied her face in the mirror as the shower warmed up. Her right eye opened fully now but looked terrible.

And probably would for a week.

She needed to come up with a story.

"What happened to you?" would be the first words out of everyone's mouth.

"I fell down," didn't seem quite convincing enough.

Luckily the little freak Mitch Mitchell had been sloppy drunk, otherwise she'd be dead right now, guaranteed. She was pretty sure of what happened last night. Mitchell's neighbor must have seen Kayla and Aspen out in the field and called Mitchell. That was the conversation they saw, when Mitchell threw the phone

154

into the wall.

He didn't want to scare them off.

He wanted to hurt 'em.

Or capture 'em.

That's why he didn't bolt out the front door and charge. They would have seen him and been long gone by the time he got there.

So he left and circled around behind them.

Probably hoping that one or both of them would be stupid enough to be lured into the house; in fact, even making it easy for them by leaving the front door unlocked.

And they fell for it.

He must have felt like he won the lottery when he found that they actually split up.

And that one of them was still out there in the dark.

Alone.

Not even looking in his direction as he crept up.

He was definitely a smart little toad. Too bad he wasn't smart enough to realize how drunk he was.

Or how strong Kayla was.

Or how fast she could run after she got out from under him.

LAW SCHOOL FELT LIKE A COCOON, normal and safe, the way her life was supposed to be. She spent the entire day looking, acting and even feeling like a law student. It wasn't until classes were over, when she realized that she couldn't go back to her apartment, that the reality of her life reentered her thoughts.

Aspen picked her up at six o'clock.

"Anyone notice your eye?" she asked.

Kayla chuckled.

"Let me put it this way, it's the first time some of the guys looked at my face first, if you catch my drift."

"Consider the drift caught."

"Not that my drift is even that big," Kayla added.

"Size means nothing," Aspen said. "It's all about attitude."

"Easy for you to say."

They zigzagged through the city streets until they felt comfortable that no psycho weirdo killer was on their tail and then drove to Kayla's apartment to pick up fresh clothes and her checkbook. Kayla found a card stuffed in the door jam, read it and handed it to Aspen as they walked inside.

"Apparently you're dessert."

Aspen looked like she was uncertain what to do.

"Go ahead and go," Kayla said. "You don't need to baby-sit me."

Aspen shook her head and said, "First of all, I think this is from yesterday, judging by how wrinkled it is. Second of all, we have work to do tonight."

THEY ENDED UP IN GOLDEN FOR SUPPER at a jam-packed watering hole called Woody's, sitting in a corner booth eating salads and keeping one eye on the door. The crowd was an eclectic mix of Colorado School of Mines students and older locals. All-you-can-eat pizza was the main draw, that and pitchers of beer.

Aspen told Kayla what she'd found out today.

Namely that Mitch Mitchell was in and out of his house randomly all day. Sometimes he'd disappear for a few hours. Other times he'd show back up in five minutes.

She saw him walking across the living room with a shotgun

at one point. For some reason she sensed he was setting a booby trap. She pictured a string, one end attached to the doorknob and the other to a trigger.

He came back home around 2:00 p.m. and carried a number of boxes from his car into the house. She wasn't positive but was pretty sure it all had something to do with a security system. She wouldn't doubt it a bit if there were tiny cameras and lasers all over the place now, maybe even tied into some type of transmission device that alerted his cell phone.

"We were so close," Aspen said. "Five more minutes and we would have had him. I know it."

"Well it's too late now," Kayla said.

"Unfortunately you're right. Whatever goodies we could have found last night are gone by now. Either that or hidden where we wouldn't find them in a year."

"So what do we do?" Kayla asked.

Aspen looked as if she had an idea.

But was hesitant to verbalize it.

"What?" Kayla asked.

"Okay," Aspen said, "this is sort of crazy but here it is. We keep him under surveillance as best we can. I'm going to look into buying a GPS tracking device or something for his car, if there is such a thing. But we also turn our attention back to Lance Lundeen."

"Lance Lundeen? Why? He's definitely not the guy."

"I know that," Aspen said. "But once we confirm that Mitch Mitchell is, it would be nice if we had someone else to kill him besides us."

Kayla stopped chewing.

Shocked by the idea.

"Lundeen could eat him for breakfast any day of the week

and not even burp," Aspen added. "Our job is to get some dirt on Lundeen so he ends up with enough motivation when the time comes."

"You mean blackmail him?"

"Exactly."

"That's nuts."

Aspen nodded in agreement.

"There's no part of any of this that's sane, honey," she said.

Kayla chewed on the idea and found it simultaneously both crazy and pragmatic.

In fact she felt a sense of relief at the formation of a plan that might actually get her life back to normal once and for all.

"What makes you think there's dirt to get?" she asked.

"You mean on the guy who had you spread out naked on the floor and beat his drums into your ears while he thought of what your punishment should be?" Aspen said. "Give me a break."

Chapter Thirty-Five

BRYSON COVENTRY PAINTED MOSTLY PLEIN AIR. He brought the canvases home and then let them collect dust for a month before looking at them with a fresh eye. Most of them at that point needed a few more brushstrokes, a small dab of just the right color, or some other minor adjustment to bring them up to commercial grade. He usually made those final tweaks to several paintings at once. That's what he was doing Friday night when his cell phone rang. Unfortunately, the ring came from the living room. He almost blew it off, but then ran for it with a paintbrush still in hand.

Good thing too.

It turned out to be call he was waiting for.

Aspen.

She apologized for not getting back to him sooner. "I have some stuff going on this evening, but I'm going to be able to break away at some point," she said. "Do you want to hook up when that happens?"

He did.

"It may be late," she warned. "After midnight."

He didn't care.

He needed to see her.

"Not a problem," he said.

"Okay," she said. "But be warned, I'm bringing dessert. So don't go spoiling your appetite."

HE FINISHED UP IN THE STUDIO, scrubbed the turpentine off his hands and went out for a three-mile jog. Thirty seconds after he got back his phone rang. At first he thought it was Aspen, but it turned out to be Barb Winters from dispatch.

The woman with the new breast implants.

She had news.

Very interesting news.

Rain St. John had been found. She was alive but traumatized. The responding officers were just now securing the scene, about a half mile up a gravel road from a place called the Camel's Breath.

"I'm on my way," Coventry said.

"You need directions?"

"No, I know where it's at."

"You do?"

"That's where our old friend Nathan Wickersham got one of his victims last year," Coventry said. "Jennifer Holland, to be precise."

"Right, I remember that now. Do you think there's a connection?"

"I don't know. I'll check my crystal ball and get back to you."

HE SWUNG BY THE 7-ELEVEN ON SIMMS to get coffee. When he got there and felt around in the back seat of the Tundra for an empty thermos, he remembered taking them out for an all-expenses-paid vacation to the dishwasher. So he bought yet another new one, dumped in five French Vanilla creamers and poured leaded on top. The B-52's "Hot Lava" came from speakers somewhere.

Then he hit the road.

Five minutes later he was back.

For a disposable cup.

The guy behind the counter looked familiar.

"What's your name?" Coventry asked.

"Jim."

"Jim what?"

"Jim Hansen."

"You look familiar. Do I know you?"

The man studied Coventry and shook his head.

"I don't think so."

"It seems like I know you from somewhere."

"Sorry, you don't seem familiar," the man said.

When Coventry got to the scene, Rain St. John had already been taken away by ambulance. One of the responding officers turned out to be Rex Higgins, a wild-man who straddled both sides of the law. The last Coventry heard, Rex had been on a Harley headed for a few days of R&R at Sturgis, the last rider in a pack of ten, and mysteriously went down doing ninety.

That got him a free ride in a flight-for-life helicopter.

One he didn't remember.

Coventry shook his hand and asked, "Did you ever find out what took you down?"

"Nothing concrete," he said. "Just a vague image in my brain every now and then of my ex-wife sticking a needle in a Voodoo doll."

Coventry chuckled.

"I've never had an ex-wife," he said.

"Well I've got two if you want one."

"Thanks, I'll keep that in mind," he said. "If I take one though, it'll need to be the nice one."

"That would be the one with the Voodoo doll."

"Ouch."

Rex told him what he knew so far, namely that a guy and a girl from that white Cougar over there came up the road by mistake, turned around at the dead-end, and then got a flat on the way back. When they got out, they spotted a naked woman in the front seat of that blue Saturn over there. They checked on her and couldn't wake her. They thought she might have OD'ed and called 911."

Coventry looked around and didn't see them.

"Where are they?"

"They were gone when we got here," Rex said.

Coventry nodded.

Understanding.

They didn't want a DWI.

"There's roofing nails all over the road," Rex added. Then, to prove it, he took Coventry over and showed him with his flashlight.

"I'm impressed," Coventry said. "I don't have that many in my whole roof."

THE SATURN WITH THE FLAT TIRES was registered to one

Tracy Patterson. At least according to the wallet in the console between the front seats.

Judging by her driver's license she was cute.

The woman found in the car was Rain St. John.

"So he takes a new victim and leaves the old one," Coventry said. "An exchange of some sort."

Rex scratched his head.

"*Exchange.* That's the word I was trying to think of. Weird, huh?"

Coventry nodded.

"Very."

Chapter Thirty-Six

Day Five—May 9
Friday Night

LANCE LUNDEEN HAD NO IDEA if his new catch was rich or poor, smart or dumb, sinner or saint, or Sue or Amanda—nor did he care. Right now she was nothing more than 110 pounds of bait stashed under a blanket in the back of his Wrangler speeding down the freeway at sixty miles an hour.

Bait.

Bait.

Bait.

Young sweet bait.

She stayed perfectly and wonderfully unconscious until he was able to get sufficiently away from the city lights to pull over and stick a syringe in her ass, an incredibly taut ass, to be precise. Then he took her to the hideaway and got her stripped and chained in the bedroom.

Déjà vu Rain St. John.

Then he sat down on the front steps to be absolutely sure no one followed. The familiar chorus of crickets sang. In the distance a coyote barked, then another, and in the span of a few seconds a whole pack yapped and yelped. He pictured something lower in the food chain scrambling for ten more heartbeats of life.

Definitely not a good way to go.

Eaten alive.

Suddenly the yelping stopped.

Meaning they'd caught it, whatever it was.

Now on to the next hunt. He had to admire them, as hunters. They wore their teeth up front. Their mission was clear. They couldn't trick their prey. And yet they lived on from one generation to the next.

Human hunters had it a lot easier.

They could hide their teeth.

And confuse their prey.

Even pass themselves off as vegetarians if they had half a mind.

THE MOON WASHED THE NIGHTSCAPE with a muted radiance, not unlike a giant nightlight up in the sky. Lundeen studied the lunar craters and nervously pondered the big question, namely whether Robert Sharapova, Esq., the fancy-pants lawyer, witnessed the abduction.

Everything hinged on that.

Everything.

Not knowing was driving him nuts.

He knew that the basic elements of the plan had been in place. He knew, for instance, that Del Rae had taken Sharapova to the Camel's Breath, a seedy and therefore safe place where no one who lived in Sharapova's stratosphere would be caught dead and hence wouldn't see him.

He knew that Del Rae got Sharapova good and sloppy drunk.

He knew that she drove him down the gravel road and parked at the end, under the auspices that she needed his cock in her mouth right now and couldn't possibly wait until they got to her place. Once she got there she'd flip the toggle switch. She'd make an excuse to move her car only to discover it wouldn't start. Sharapova the hero would try, and maybe even check under the hood, but in the end would be baffled. They'd have to walk out when it came time to leave.

But it wouldn't be time yet.

Forget about the stupid car.

First Del Rae had to have his cock in her mouth.

Lundeen knew that Del Rae would have seen him tap the brake lights, meaning that the car headed up the road towards the turnaround would be the target.

What he didn't know is if Del Rae got Sharapova out of the car in time to start walking down the road and get close enough to the abduction in time to witness it.

He was pretty sure she did.

They didn't have to walk that far.

He had taken his good old time on purpose. He did everything in front of the headlights. They could have seen him clearly fifty yards away.

So, all the pieces fit.

Sharapova must have seen it.

But still—

Lundeen knew his mind wouldn't stop spinning until Del Rae called and told him definitely one way or the other.

FIVE MINUTES LATER SHE CALLED.

"Bingo," she said.

"It went okay?" he asked.

"Perfect," she said. "I'll fill you in later. I got to go now. Be ready for tomorrow."

"I will."

"Love you," she said.

"Likewise."

"Get ready to be rich," she said.

"I can't believe we're actually pulling this off."

"Well, believe it," she said, "because we are."

He punched off.

Then beat his Tarzan chest and yelped at the coyotes.

One of them barked back.

Chapter Thirty-Seven

Day Five—May 9
Friday Night

KAYLA BECK AND ASPEN WHITE PARKED THE AUDI on the other side of the railroad yard and then snuck over to Lance Lundeen's on foot through the dark, a solid twenty minute trek. No lights came from inside the building. They circled around to the east where they could see the garage doors and settled into the shadows behind a small electrical shed.

The moon threw a light patina over the world.

They both wore jeans and dark pullover sweatshirts.

Stalking clothes.

Aspen picked up a pebble and flicked it with her thumb. "We need to get into those photograph drawers," she said. "That's where we're going to find our dirt."

Kayla wrinkled her forehead.

There was no way she would ever step foot in that place again.

"Don't even talk about it," she said.

"I'm just saying as a last resort if all this other stuff doesn't work," Aspen said. "I guarantee you he has a picture of Marilyn

Poppenberg, all tied up in his pretty little blue rope with a screwdriver sticking out of her ear. When I close my eyes I can see him jerking off to it."

Kayla didn't disagree.

Namely that Lance Lundeen killed Poppenberg.

"That's what we need to concentrate on, is those pictures," Aspen said. "If we can get our hands on them, we'll have him on a leash. Then we get him to kill Mitch Mitchell after we confirm he's our collar man. Then we'll turn Lundeen in to the cops."

Kayla said nothing.

They'd already talked about it a number of times.

Conceptually it still made sense.

But there was a million ways it could go wrong.

A million ways they never talked about.

Then she had a thought. "The other thing that might help us is if we could get to his tools," she said. "Maybe the screwdriver in Marilyn Poppenberg's head came out of a set. It would be interesting if he had the rest of that set in his garage, minus that one piece."

Aspen slapped her on the back.

"Good thinking, girlfriend."

"Yeah, well—"

"Now I see why you're the up-and-coming lawyer and the rest of us aren't. The only thing I would add is that as long as we're inside getting your tools, we may as well stop upstairs and get my pictures."

Kayla grunted.

"You don't quit, do you?"

No, she didn't.

Blame the boxcar and the razorblade.

KAYLA WAS HALF ASLEEP when Aspen shook her and said, "Company." Sure enough, a lonely pair of headlights cut through the darkness, bouncing up and down as if on a short-framed vehicle.

Flickering lights lit up the side of a building.

—A fire hydrant.

—An old shirt hanging on a chain-link fence.

Thirty seconds later the garage door opened and a dilapidated Jeep Wrangler pulled inside. Lance Lundeen hopped out dressed in ragged jeans and an old flannel shirt, holding something that looked like a wig.

The garage door closed almost immediately.

"Weird," Aspen said.

"Very."

"What's he doing driving that piece of crap on a Friday night when he's got a Ferrari sitting in the garage?"

"And those clothes—I'd go naked first."

There were no windows on this side of the building so they hiked over to the railroad yard. There they climbed a gritty steel ladder to the top of a boxcar, pulled in the scene with binoculars and found Lance Lundeen in the shower.

They couldn't believe his body.

Or his dick.

"Too bad this guy's so weird because I could sign up for that in a heartbeat," Aspen said.

Kayla swallowed.

"Tarzan," Aspen added.

After the shower, he pulled a beer from the fridge and played the drums.

They listened.

He was actually pretty good.

Then he stopped and disappeared into the stairwell.

There was no sign of him for over fifteen minutes.

"Maybe we should get down," Kayla said.

"Why?"

"Because if he spots us here we're trapped."

"Don't worry about it," Aspen said. "There's no way he can see us. *I* can hardly see us."

Suddenly they saw him.

Up on the roof of the building, not much more than a black silhouette against a not-quite-as-black night; barely perceptible but definitely him. His hair was dry now and hung like a lion's mane.

"See, he's still there," Aspen said. "You worry too much."

Kayla exhaled.

True.

Three seconds later a small light flashed from the roof.

Almost immediately a bullet ricocheted off the top of the boxcar.

"I'm hit!" Aspen said.

Chapter Thirty-Eight

Day Six—May 10
Saturday Morning

BRYSON COVENTRY WORKED THE SCENE of Tracy Patterson's abduction, down the road from the Camel's Breath, until two in the morning. Aspen didn't call the entire time and still hadn't by the time he got home. He went to sleep with the cell next to his pillow. When the first rays of dawn fingered their way into the room and pulled him back to consciousness, he checked the phone.

No messages.

No calls.

What was going on?

He didn't want things to end before they started. Well, correction. They *had* started. They had significantly started, in fact, at least from his end of the equation.

He threw water on his face, popped in his contacts and headed out the door for a three-mile jog, reflecting on last night's investigation. Every single roofing nail had been collected. The game plan was to weigh them, find out where they were sold in town and then see if anyone had made a purchase recently in that approximate poundage. He could already hear Shalifa complain that it would be too much work for too little likelihood of success.

She'd have a good point.

But right now he was willing to buy any likelihood of success.

Also, last night, he interviewed the 911 caller—the one who had been driving the white Cougar and found Rain St. John unconscious. He turned out to be a guy named Dave Montgomery. They got his phone number from the 911 incoming log, dialed him up and asked him to come back to the scene for a chat.

"I might be too drunk to drive," he said.

"We'll send a cab."

"But that's because I drank after," he said. "Not before."

"Of course."

"I just don't want any DWI problems, if I come down."

"You won't," Coventry said. "This isn't about you."

"Okay. I just want to be sure."

"If you do know anyone who drinks and drives, though, you might want to tell him to cool it before it bites him big time," Coventry said.

"Point taken."

Montgomery turned out to be an obnoxious carbon lifeform with a greatly exaggerated view of his own relevance to the universe. Coventry tolerated breathing the same air as him for as long as he could, then packed him in a cab and sent him back into the world. In the end, Montgomery didn't add much to the picture other than the fact that the empty Honda parked at the end of the road was already empty when he got to it. For all he knew it had been sitting there for a week.

COVENTRY FINISHED HIS JOG, showered and arrived at the office at 7:22 a.m. At this hour of the morning the place was a morgue even on weekdays. On a Saturday, like now, it was a sub-morgue.

When Shalifa Netherwood showed up at eight o'clock he had a fresh pot of coffee waiting. She carried a white bag in her left hand.

"What's in the bag?" he asked.

She set it on the counter next to the coffee and poured a cup.

"Nothing," she said.

"It looks like a donut bag."

She studied it and said, "Yeah, it kind of does when you look at it from an angle."

"So is it?"

She shrugged.

"I don't know."

"You don't know?"

She left the bag on the counter and took a chair in front of his desk.

"No. I never looked inside."

"So you have no idea what's in there?"

"Not a freaking clue."

He stood up and headed that way.

"You want me to check? Just to be sure it's not a bomb or something?" he asked over his shoulder.

"Go ahead," she said. "Just don't cut the white wire."

He chuckled.

"I thought it was the red one you don't cut."

He opened the bag and found eight donuts—white cake

174

with chocolate frosting—his all-time favorite. He grabbed one, took a step towards his desk, then grabbed another one to save a trip two minutes later, and gave her a hug on the shoulders before he sat down.

"I'm going to marry you someday," he said. "You know that I hope."

She rolled her eyes.

"I'll take that as a threat," she said.

He filled her in on the events of last night and what he'd learned so far, including his theory that although Rain St. John had been dumped back into the world alive, Tracy Patterson might not be as lucky.

"What I need you to do is get a search warrant for Tracy Patterson's house and see if there's anything there that sheds any light on the matter," he said.

"That'll take a good chunk of the day," she warned.

"That's why days come in full lengths," he said. "So you can take chunks out of them."

WITH THREE DONUTS AND A POT OF CAFFEINE in his gut, Bryson Coventry headed over to Denver General to interview Rain St. John, who was now reportedly conscious and able to talk. The first thing he noticed when he walked into her room was that she had one of the sexiest faces he had ever seen, with bright blue eyes perfectly balanced against a golden tan. The second thing he noticed was that her hair was chopped off.

Rex Higgins told him about that last night but he forgot.

What a mess.

She must have read his mind because she said, "It's the new weed-whacker look. Six months from now everyone will have

175

it." Her voice had a soft sensuous intonation.

Very sexy.

He held out his hand. "Bryson Coventry, Denver homicide," he said. "Sorry about the stare."

"Not a problem," she said. "I've been doing it myself."

She held up a hand mirror to prove it.

"There's a nasty rumor going around that you haven't been having that great of a time for the last couple of days," he said.

She chuckled.

"That particular rumor's probably more true than most," she said.

He nodded.

"You want to start at the beginning and walk me through it?"

He expected her to say *Sure* and start right in, but instead she cocked her head and said, "What's in it for me?"

He studied her.

"I don't know. What do you want to be in it for you?"

She retreated in thought.

"Dinner."

"Dinner?"

She nodded.

"Someplace nice. Unless you're too embarrassed to be seen with this hair."

He put on an inquisitive look. "Someplace nice, huh? There are people who will tell you I'm the cheapest guy on the face of the earth," he said.

"Okay. McDonald's then."

"I didn't say they were right," he added.

"So something in the middle then, is that what you're saying?"

He shrugged.

"I guess I am."

She held out her hand and they shook on it.

Then she told him the story.

HE LET HER TELL THE WHOLE THING in her own words without interrupting her. Then, ever the detective, he brought her back to the beginning and asked questions.

She didn't know Tracy Patterson.

She didn't recognize her picture.

She'd never heard the name before.

In the end the rules intrigued Coventry more than anything. He had her recall them in the exact language that was on the paper, as near as she could, while he jotted them down in a little spiral notebook.

Then he made sure he had them listed in the same order that they appeared on the paper.

"So now you owe me dinner," Rain said.

"That's the deal," he said. "When?"

"Tonight."

"Really?"

"Yeah. Is that okay?"

"You'll be out of here by then?"

"I'll be out in an hour." She diverted her eyes and then looked straight into his. "I'm really looking forward to it."

"Me too."

She grabbed his hand, briefly, and squeezed.

"Good."

FORTY-FIVE MINUTES LATER, back at the office, he typed out the rules and faxed them to Leanne Sanders with a short note— "Call me."

Chapter Thirty-Nine

Day Six—May 10
Saturday Morning

AS FAR A LANCE LUNDEEN WAS CONCERNED, last night had been a major pain. The two mystery women showed up again. It was only by incredible blind luck that Lundeen ended up taking an unplanned hike to the roof to snap a few night shots. It was only by even blinder luck that he spotted movement on top of a boxcar out of his peripheral vision.

Two shapes.

Almost invisible.

The telephoto camera lens pulled them in enough that he recognized the left shape as the woman from the darkroom— the one with the flat stomach. The other one wore a baseball hat and moved around so much that he couldn't pull her in for a good look. If he'd been smart he would have taken pictures of them.

Close ups.

But instead of being smart he let anger explode his brain cells.

He let himself be stupid enough to grab a rifle.

And fire.

As soon as he pulled the trigger he realized how incredibly crazy he was. The thought reached his brain before the bullet reached the women.

He already knew he wouldn't fire again.

The women disappeared over the edge of the boxcar almost immediately.

The right one moved weird.

As if she'd been hit.

This was serious.

The big question is whether they'd call the cops. He had to assume they would and knew he couldn't be there if they did. So he ran down the stairwell, grabbed the first camera case he could get his hands on and pulled everything out.

A camera.

Film.

A lens slipped out of his fingers and fell to the floor with an explosion of glass.

He stuffed the case with cash, checkbooks, passports and one special compact disc hidden on top of the kitchen cabinets. Two minutes later he pulled the pickup truck out of the garage and squealed into the darkness while the garage door closed behind him.

If the police showed up he'd disappear forever.

Plain and simple.

He looped to the north and wedged the truck between two buildings where he could see both his place and the railroad yard. If the cops went to either location he'd spot 'em. Then he sat there with the engine off and waited.

Waited all night, to be precise.

The cops never came.

When the first rays of dawn broke he went home, fell into bed and closed his eyes. Ten seconds later the world disappeared.

THE AROMA OF COFFEE and the clanking of glass pulled him back to consciousness at some point later, a point that could have been ten minutes or ten hours.

He squinted and saw Del Rae in the kitchen. The air smelled like scrambled eggs. Water percolated into a half-filled coffee pot.

He twisted to his back, stretched, and said, "Morning."

She walked over and looked down.

He wore nothing.

"You're too gorgeous for your own good," she said. "Don't move." She hustled back to the kitchen, took the frying pan off the burner, and set it to the side. Then she came back and climbed on top.

Afterwards they dressed, sat on barstools at the kitchen island and worked out the details of their next few moves over coffee, eggs and pancakes.

WHEN DEL RAE LEFT, Lance put on his Dick Zipp suit, hopped in the Wrangler and pointed the front end towards the hideaway, just to be sure that nothing weird had happened during the night.

Nothing had.

His little catch, whatever her name was, laid there on the crappy mattress exactly where he left her.

Still unconscious.

Breathing almost undetectably.

He took eight Polaroid snapshots of her, just like he did with Rain St. John.

Then he ran his hands up and down her body, mesmerized by the smoothness of her skin, before shooting fresh drugs into that wonderful little bubble-butt of hers.

Outside he yelped like a coyote.

A startled magpie on the roof flapped away.

From there he drove straight to the piece-of-crap trailer that he rented from Mr. Dog Owner for three hundred bucks. He placed photographs of Rain St. John and the new woman under a box of salt in the simulated-wood cabinet above the fridge.

Then sat back to wait.

Minutes went by.

Then an hour.

Then two.

Finally his cell phone rang.

BUT IT WASN'T DEL RAE. Instead the voice of Dexter Vaughn, the VP of Three Streets, came through. "Dude," he said. "I'm breathing heavy. Can you hear it?"

He could.

"Ask me why I'm breathing heavy?"

He did.

"I'm glad you asked," Vaughn said. "I'm breathing heavy because I just got off the phone with Andrew Guzman, the President of Sensory Perceptions. He went a hundred percent nuts over that spider's web shoot. I mean this guy couldn't stop telling me what a genius you are. I lied and agreed with him, of course. I knew when I saw the pictures that we were definitely going to be in play, but had no idea this guy was going to react anything like what he did."

Lance grinned.

"Cool," he said.

"Not, not cool, *way cool*," Vaughn said.

"So now what?"

"He wants you to get going on a second concept. Something just as good."

"Just as good?" Lance said. "How about something even better?"

Vaughn chuckled.

"Yeah. I think I could get him to settle for that. You got it in you?"

"Let's find out."

FIVE MINUTES LATER THE PHONE RANG AGAIN. This time it was Del Rae. He didn't answer but instead counted the rings.

Four.

Perfect.

That meant that everything was in play.

The game was on.

Thirty minutes later he walked outside, got in the Wrangler and drove off.

Chapter Forty

Day Six—May 10
Saturday Morning

BY THE TIME THEY GOT OFF THE BOXCAR and back to the Audi, Aspen's sweatshirt and pants were drenched in blood. Kayla drove while Aspen held a hand to her side and fought the pain. When Kayla pulled up to a massive building, Aspen saw the *Emergency* sign and said, "What are you doing?"

"What do you mean?"

"No doctors!"

"Why not?"

"Doctors know gunshots," she said. "They got to report 'em to the cops."

"So what?"

"We can't be tied to this guy."

"Fine, we'll make something up."

"No," Aspen said. "It'll unravel. Get out of here."

"But—"

"Now!"

Twenty minutes later they were at the hotel room. Aspen lay on her back on the bed, barely conscious. The best way to remove her clothes would be to cut them off to avoid further injury, but Kayla didn't have scissors. So she pulled the sweatshirt off over Aspen's head.

The source of the blood became obvious.

The bullet had clipped the side of her abdomen, to the left of her bellybutton, just above the hip bone. A four-inch gash at least a quarter-inch deep oozed blood, slowly but steadily.

"This could have been a lot worse," she said. "A little lower and it would have shattered your pelvic bone."

Aspen pushed up to her elbows and looked down.

"Stitch me up," she said.

"With what?"

"I don't know. Go buy something."

"I don't know how to do anything like that," Kayla said.

"You're going to learn—hurry!"

Two seconds later Kayla was almost out the door when Aspen shouted, "Hand me the whiskey bottle before you leave."

THAT WAS LAST NIGHT. They got up early this morning to check on the wound. It must have opened slightly during the night, judging by the new dried blood, but now it seemed well sealed. They cleaned it, went back to bed and didn't wake up until noon.

Kayla hadn't slept that late since she was thirteen.

Ordinarily she'd be upset at wasting so much of the day.

Today she was just glad to wake up at all.

She took a shower, fetched coffee and donuts for breakfast, and then asked, "Now what?"

Aspen sat at the kitchen table, stiff but upright, in clothes that weren't covered in blood. To a stranger she'd look normal.

"Now we need to be more careful," she said.

"I'm serious," Kayla said.

"So am I."

"I'm starting to think it would be easier to just disappear," Kayla said, which was true.

Aspen's response came immediately.

"No, never."

"Just until the cops catch this guy—"

"You can if you want," Aspen said. "In fact, maybe you should. Throw your cell phone away, drive to California and wait on tables under the name Martha. Stay in touch. I'll call you when it's over."

Kayla chewed on the words and said nothing.

"I'm not running, though," Aspen added. "This guy played me like a puppet for years and then stuck me in a boxcar with a razorblade, not to mention what he did to all those other women. The world's going to be better off without him and I'm going to be sure that happens."

Kayla stood up and paced.

"If I die trying then at least I tried," Aspen said. "At this point I don't care. I really don't."

Kayla stopped pacing and looked at her.

"Okay," she said.

"Okay what?"

"Okay I'm in. So back to my question—now what?"

Aspen held her arms out for a hug.

Kayla gave her one.

A long one.

A tight one.

"The first thing we do," Aspen said, "is get our sweet little undead bodies over to Hertz or Avis or somewhere and rent a couple of cars."

"Why?"

Aspen stood up and lifted her shirt to see if the stitches were holding.

They were.

Not a problem.

Nor did she see any indications of infection.

"I'll tell you on the way," she said. "You can thank me later."

"Thank you for what?"

"For fine-tuning your criminal instincts; it's going to make you a better lawyer some day."

Chapter Forty-One

Day Six—May 10
Saturday Morning

COVENTRY PASSED AN EINSTEIN BROS. BAGELS, viewed it as fate since he now had all his six or seven thermoses strategically repositioned in the back seat of the Tundra, and swung in to see if they happened to have Chocolate Macadamia Nut on tap. Not only did they, but there was no waiting line to pay.

Very strange.

First Rain St. John appears from out of nowhere.

Now this.

What's going on?

His life didn't work like this.

He headed to the Camel's Breath, chasing a long shot. Last night a Honda had been parked at the end of the road, at the turnaround, an apparent breakdown. He'd forgotten to get the license plate number, to call the owner and find out if he or she saw anything.

Most likely the bad guy turned around there so his car would be pointing the right way when he made his move. Maybe the people in the Honda saw the type of vehicle he was driving.

Although Coventry doubted it.

He pictured a couple having sweaty sex in the back seat and popping their heads up only long enough to see if the headlights came from a police car.

When he got to the turnaround something bad happened.

The Honda was gone.

Of course.

He killed the engine and then walked back down the road to where the abduction took place.

Studying the ground.

Looking for anything they might have missed last night.

On the way Leanne Sanders called.

"GOT YOUR RULES," SHE SAID. "I never knew you were so kinky. I have to tell you right off the bat I've got issues with a couple of them."

Coventry laughed.

"Oh yeah? Which ones?"

"Well, to start, the one where you want me to call you Master."

"What's wrong with that?" he asked.

"I don't know," she said. "It just seems a little over the top."

He chuckled and said, "Speaking of over the top, I met someone."

"You already told me that."

"No, this is a new one," he said.

"A new one?"

"The other one sort of blew me off."

"This gets back to my point, Coventry."

Oops.

189

Bad subject.

He put a serious tone in his voice and said, "Let me bring you up to speed on a few things." He told her how Rain St. John showed up alive last night. She had been taken to an old house, drugged heavily and raped at least once. The guy used a condom. The house was in the country somewhere because a pack of coyotes tried to get in.

She hadn't been put in a collar.

Or left to rot somewhere with a razorblade.

Meaning their initial thought that she might be the next victim of the collar killer was off base.

"So we're back to square one," Leanne said.

Coventry grunted.

"But this guy bothers me just as much as the collar guy and here's why," he said. "He did a body exchange. He dumped Rain in the car of a young woman named Tracy Patterson and took her. We're treating her as a homicide in progress."

"He wants credit," Leanne said.

"Huh?"

"That's why he marks his new prey with the body of his old one," she said. "He thinks what he's doing is wonderful."

"Okay," Coventry said. "But what I'm really interested in is getting your take on the rules."

"Well, let me ask you one thing," Leanne said. "Did Rain St. John ever see the guy's face?"

"No, never. He wore a mask."

"That's both good and bad," she said.

"What do you mean?"

"It's good, because it means he's actually playing by the rules," she said. "My guess is that he didn't let her see his face because if she fully obeyed, *and* then won the coin toss—

emphasis on the *and*—he would feel constrained to let her go. Which is probably what happened," she said. "Does she remember a coin toss?"

"No."

"That doesn't mean there wasn't one," she said. "She could have been unconscious at the time. The flip side is that if he's actually playing by the rules and feels bound by them, then his captive is just as bound. Meaning if she screws up or loses the coin toss, then she's dead. I've seen variations of that theme before, meaning rules for captives. It's a way for the guy to take the blame off himself when he kills her."

Coventry considered it.

And couldn't disagree.

Leanne added, "It would be interesting to know if this new woman—"

"—Tracy Patterson—"

"—Tracy Patterson, right, if she's the kind of person who can sit back and obey or whether she's going to do something stupid the first chance she gets. That'll be a good litmus test for whether she's eventually going to live or die. What do you know about her so far?"

"Hardly anything," Coventry said. "Young, pretty, got so drunk at a sleazy bar that she ended up driving down the wrong road."

"She sounds a little wild."

"Agreed."

"That's not a good thing, in this case," she said.

Coventry frowned.

"Maybe he'll keep her drugged the whole time and she won't get a chance to be stupid," he said.

Chapter Forty-Two

Day Six—May 10
Saturday Afternoon

WHEN HE HOPPED IN THE RUST-BUCKET OF A JEEP to leave the trailer park, Lance Lundeen didn't turn his Dick Zipp eyes to the left or the right. He wanted to—to see where Del Rae was hiding—but kept his face pointed straight ahead. She was out there somewhere, sitting behind the steering wheel with the engine off, passing the binoculars back and forth to Robert Sharapova.

Watching the trailer.

Watching him.

The lawyer had seen the body switch last night.

Exactly as planned.

He'd seen Rain St. John get dumped in the other woman's car and he'd seen the other woman get driven off in a Wrangler. Del Rae had written down the license plate number of the Jeep and traced it to one Dick Zipp. While the lawyer slept his hangover off this morning, Del Rae took a cab to the Camel's Breath, somehow miraculously got the Honda started, went to Zipp's apartment and ended up following him to this mysterious trailer.

Now Del Rae and the lawyer were sitting out there waiting for Zipp to leave so they could search the trailer.

Lance could picture the lawyer's face.

Tense.

But exhilarated.

Exhilarated at the thought of making wifey-poo deader than dead and, more important, getting away with it; *easily* getting away with it as a matter of fact. Because he wouldn't be the killer—Dick Zipp would. Then he'd sit back and count wifey-poo's money, enough to bring Del Rae solidly into his life.

What a pathetic idiot.

"Shoot yourself if you ever get that stupid," Lundeen muttered. "Even half that stupid."

WHEN LUNDEEN LEFT THE TRAILER PARK, he made sure no one was following—just in case the lawyer came up with a brainstorm and Del Rae couldn't talk him out of it—and headed home. There he peeled off the Dick Zipp suit, exercised, showered, put on normal clothes and called Scotty Marks.

"Dude, where are you?"

"Home, why?"

"I'm coming over," Lundeen said. "I need to talk to you."

"What? Another project?"

"Right. Plus something else."

"Bring some women."

"You got women."

"Bring your leftovers," Scotty said.

Lance laughed.

"I could live happily the rest of my life on just your leftovers," Scotty added.

Del Rae dialed him up, let the phone ring four times and then punched off.

Good.

That meant everything had gone as planned. Del Rae and Sharapova had broken into the trailer after Lance left. They found the pictures of Rain St. John and the other woman hidden in the cabinet. They confirmed beyond any doubt that they had the right man.

Now they needed to find where the woman was hidden.

Then—after they found her—it would just be a matter of whether the lawyer had the guts to go through with the next step.

Hopefully he did.

It all hinged on that.

SCOTTY MARKS HAD SOMEHOW FIGURED OUT A WAY to keep a steady stream of marijuana passing through his lungs and simultaneously own a house. Not a mansion by anyone's standards but still more than enough to keep stray dogs out of his food.

Lance Lundeen parked the Ferrari in the driveway, knocked on the door, shouted "It's me," and entered before getting a response.

Two heartbeats later he stepped into the sixties.

Orange shag carpeting.

Beads.

Beanbag chairs.

Posters galore—Animals, Shadows of Night, Doors, Hendrix, Janis, Jefferson Airplane, Who, Zombies, DC Five,

Paul Revere, and of course the Stones.

Pot emanated from every pore of the structure.

Jefferson Airplane's "Somebody to Love" played from a vinyl turntable with a scratchy edge.

Scotty stepped out of the bathroom, momentarily startled to find someone in the middle of his living room.

"Time warp," Lance said.

"That's jealousy talking," Scotty said. He lit a joint, took a long deep drag and held it out.

Lance waved it off.

Tarzan didn't put that junk in his lungs.

No way.

He talked about his ideas for the next photo shoot for quite some time before finally getting around to the subject most on his mind.

"I got a couple of women tailing me," he said.

Scotty chuckled. "Yeah, I'll bet you do."

"I don't mean like that," he said. "I'm serious. They actually broke into my place Thursday. They tried to copy my computer files before they got away."

"Why? What's on your computer?"

"That's the crazy thing, nothing."

Scotty shrugged.

"So make a copy and leave it by the front door," he said. "Maybe they'll go away."

"Come on, dude," Lance said. "This is serious. Last night they were on top of a boxcar watching me with binoculars."

"That's weird."

"That's what I'm trying to tell you."

"So who are they?"

Lance raised his hands in surrender. "I don't have a clue. But they're serious. When I saw them on the boxcar I got stupid and shot at them. I think I even hit one. But they didn't call the police."

Scotty took another pull from the joint.

"So why are you telling me this?" he asked.

"Because I'm going to catch them," Lance said. "And I need you to help me."

Scotty shrugged.

"Sure, if you want."

Lance put a serious expression on his face.

"If they don't have a good excuse why they're on my case, then I'm probably going to do something I shouldn't," he said. "You need to know that upfront. I won't hold it against you a bit if you don't want to get involved."

"It sounds like we need to do what we need to do," Scotty said. "They really haven't given us a choice."

Lance slapped him on the back and said, "I owe you one, dude."

Chapter Forty-Three

Day Sic—May 10
Saturday Afternoon

LAW SCHOOL CRASHED IN ON KAYLA BECK. She had a Property exam on Wednesday that was going to be a train wreck unless she did something quick. Deadlines at the Law Review loomed, deadlines that couldn't be postponed, argued with or placated with a smile or a promise—queries, editing, galleys, and on and on. Not to mention all the basics like going to class, reading a gazillion Supreme Court decisions with all their intricate concurrences and dissents, and transforming her sloppy-copy class notes into something halfway intelligible. She felt like the last horse in the race.

Staring at a solid sea of tails.

Then to make matters worse, Christina Holiday—a third-year student and one of the Editors on Kayla's team—called. Kayla pulled up an image of a serious young woman intent on getting a job with the biggest firm she possibly could.

Holiday had bad news.

"Have you seen what happened to Professor Brown's article?"

No, Kayla hadn't.

She knew it had been assigned to two Associate Editors more than a month ago for basic editing but hadn't heard much about it since.

"Let's just say it went in looking like a tiger and came out looking like a giraffe," Holiday said. "I mean they hardly left a sentence unscathed."

"A butcher job?"

"Well, no, not really," Holiday said. "I wouldn't say the over-all quality went either up or down. It's more like a lateral move, a huge lateral move—think hundreds of miles."

Kayla frowned.

Professor Brown didn't like anyone tinkering with his words.

Not even a little.

Because no one was as smart as him. If someone changed something it only meant they didn't understand.

To make matters worse, Kayla was supposed to have the proposed edit to Brown next week; and even that would be tight to get it into the next edition.

"Do you have time to fix it?" Kayla asked.

"Negative," Holiday said. "I'm already so slammed it's not even funny. I wish I could but I just absolutely, one hundred percent can't."

"Okay," Kayla said. "Put everything on my desk."

TEN MINUTES LATER ASPEN RETURNED to the hotel with a rental car, a blue Nissan from Hertz. She must have seen a look on Kayla's face because she asked, "What's wrong?"

"Minor emergency at school," Kayla said. "I'm going to have to go in."

That was fine with Aspen.

She didn't expect any action until tonight anyway.

"You can take the Audi," she said. "Just drop me off at an Avis somewhere on the way."

Good.

That would work.

"How's the side?" Kayla asked.

Aspen pulled up her shirt and showed her.

The stitches were holding up fine.

"You done good," Aspen said.

"We better clean it."

THE LAW REVIEW ROOM ON A SATURDAY morning was one of Kayla's favorite places in the world. People were around, yesterday's donut box almost always had a few remnants, and a professor or two usually dropped by for coffee. Most importantly, everything ran at half speed. The stress of having to dart to a class wasn't there.

Today she used the room as a shield.

To block out the rest of her life.

To be normal for a few precious hours.

Professor Brown's original article turned out to have a few awkward spots but overall was in a fairly publishable state. Kayla decided to use the new editing where it made sense and leave the rest of it alone. Three hours later she emailed the revised version to Professor Brown.

There.

Done.

Now what?"

Before she could decide, her cell phone rang. It didn't recognize the incoming number. She almost didn't answer but then did since it could be Aspen. A man's electronically scrambled voice came through.

Him.

"You should wear that T-shirt more often," he said. "The blue goes with your eyes. And I love the way it rides up and shows your bellybutton when you raise your arm. You have a nice stomach, Kayla, you really do, all taut and firm. You should show it off more often. But the fact remains that you've been a bad girl, a very bad girl. That presents problems."

"Leave me alone!"

"I'd like to, Kayla, I really would," he said. "But we're way past that."

She hung up.

Then she resisted the urge to hurl the phone against the wall and instead turned it off.

Of course it didn't ring again.

But she could feel it wanting to.

He was inside.

Trying to get out.

She paced.

Then broke a pencil in two.

And another.

And another.

Then she threw the pieces against the wall, scooped up her books and ran out of the room.

She drove.

Wildly.

Unleashing the power of the Audi.

Rolling through stop signs.

Busting speed limits.

She called Aspen.

No answer.

When she got to the hotel, Aspen wasn't there. She opened her suitcase, tore into the secret compartment and pulled out all her cash.

A half hour later she walked into a gun store on Colfax Avenue.

Chapter Forty-Four

Day Six—May 10
Saturday Afternoon

THE CAMEL'S BREATH HAD A SECURITY CAMERA, ceiling mounted, pointed at the main cash register, but also spilling onto the edge of the crowd. Coventry obtained copies of last night's tapes and talked Paul Kubiak into transferring them to DVDs—to preserve the originals—on an emergency basis.

Five in all.

Then he spent most of the afternoon with a remote in one hand and a cup of coffee in the other, watching for Tracy Patterson, primarily to see who she was with and whether anyone was acting weird around her.

She showed up more than he expected.

She came to the bar eight times in all and each time it was the same—she ordered a screwdriver, drank it at the bar in two to three minutes while the music moved her hips, left the glass on the counter and disappeared again off screen. She paid for her own drinks and never had a guy in tow. Each time she was sweatier than the last.

Clearly she had gone there to dance.

Not to get laid.

One thing for sure, though. By the time she left she was more than inebriated enough to head down the wrong road.

"Should have called a cab," Coventry said.

DR. LEANNE SANDERS CALLED ABOUT FIVE O'CLOCK.

"Okay," she said. "I tapped my resources as far as I can without having to officially owe people blowjobs. We turned up lots of hits with unsolved cases involving men who had rules. I narrowed the search to written rules, an abduction lasting between one and seven days, rape, and most importantly of all, released alive. Guess how many names made that cut?"

Coventry felt energetic.

"One," he said.

"No, eighteen."

"Eighteen? You got to be kidding me."

"Check your email in ten minutes," she said. "You'll have names, faces, and more information than you want."

"Thanks," Coventry said, and meant it. "You're saving my life here."

"Just find the woman."

He dove into the new information. Outside, the day slipped away, the evening came and the office windows turned to mirrors. All the while something nagged at him but he couldn't finger it.

Then his phone rang.

"I've been stood up before, but never on the first date," someone said.

He recognized the voice but couldn't place it.

Then he did.

Rain St. John.

He was supposed to pick her up for dinner at seven.

He looked at his watch.

Eight.

He stood up.

"I'm walking out the door right now," he said. "I got tied up with something. I really apologize for being late, I should have called."

HE DASHED DOWN TO THE LOCKER ROOM, showered, threw on a fresh pair of pants and a long-sleeve cotton shirt—a sea-foam green color—and dried his hair with a towel as he bounded down the stairwell. Ten minutes later he rang her doorbell, straightening his hair as best he could with his fingers.

She opened the door, grabbed him by the shirt, dragged him over to the couch, pushed him down and stood over him.

She wore a short black dress.

Sleeveless.

Lots of cleavage.

A tanned body.

Firm legs with no nylons.

Black high heels.

Her hair was now a uniform length, about two inches long, perfectly straight with a slight fluff. She looked like she just came from a photo shoot for the cover of a fashion magazine.

He tried to appear unaffected.

"I'm going to go with you, but only on one condition," she said.

He raised an eyebrow.

"And what's that?" he asked.

"This is a date, not dinner," she said. "I've been thinking about what you said before, about how I'm a victim and all vulnerable and everything, and how it would be wrong for you to do anything other than take me out to dinner. But I'm fine and that's the truth. I know what I'm doing. The only reason I wanted to have dinner in the first place was so that it would be a date. If I just wanted food I have plenty in the fridge. So, with that said, here's the condition. We either leave here on a date—wherever that leads us—or we don't leave at all."

"A date, huh?"

"Right." She paused, briefly looked vulnerable and said, "I don't want to lose this chance with you just because the timing's bad."

"Well, I did promise you dinner, so I guess if I just left I'd be breaking my promise."

"Yes you would. And you're not the kind of guy to do that."

"No, I guess I'm not."

"So it's a date then?"

He nodded.

She came close to him, hiked up her dress, straddled his lap and then brought her mouth to his. "This is how I like to start my dates," she said.

Coventry inhaled.

Then blew out.

"Seems reasonable," he said.

Then she kissed him.

He was just about to kiss her back when she hopped off and pulled him up. "I'm starved," she said. "Feed me."

THEY ATE LOBSTER AT SIMMS LANDING and then ended up

in a cozy booth in the back of a packed bar on Larimer Street sipping white wine. They sat on the same side of the table, facing a trendy crowd.

She slipped her shoes off.

And put Coventry's hand on her leg.

"If that gets cold, feel free to move it up," she said.

He inched it up as they talked.

Slowly.

Teasingly.

Until she grabbed it and put it between her legs.

When he started to massage her, she kept a straight face and spread her knees. His hand was hidden from view, behind the table, under her dress, *barely* under her dress, the way it had ridden up, but under it nonetheless.

No one could see.

She brought the wine to her lips, took a sip and then whispered in his ear.

"I'll bet you can't make me come."

"I'll bet I can."

"You're on," she said.

"Loser pays for drinks," he said.

"Done."

They locked eyes the entire time.

He felt as if he was looking directly into her soul.

Ten minutes later she closed her eyes, bit her lower lip and trembled. Then she opened her eyes, kissed him deep and long, and pulled two twenties out of her purse. "Come on," she said. "I got a place I want to take you."

Chapter Forty-Five

Day Six—May 10
Saturday Night

AFTER DARK, LANCE LUNDEEN slipped into his Dick Zipp suit and drove the Wrangler to the trailer. There he waited for more than an hour until he finally got four rings from Del Rae. A few minutes later he pushed through the shaky screen door, muscled his Tarzan frame into the Wrangler and headed for the hideaway.

Del Rae and the lawyer followed.

In his lane, four cars back.

He had to admit that if he hadn't known to look for them, he would have never suspected they were there.

He stayed under the speed limit.

The last thing he needed was for either him or them to get pulled over.

The Jeep was like driving around in a tent. The knobby off-road tires whined and the ragtop flapped. The radio was a piece of tinny crap. The windshield, being flat, cracked in the shape of lightning bolts at three locations. In spite of all that, he liked it. There was something satisfying about the fact that he could pull off the pavement and keep going, or leave the vehicle out in the rain with the top off.

Maybe he'd add a new one to his stable when this was all over.

If nothing else, just to show he was still a normal guy.

In spite of his millions.

His *many* millions.

THE MILES CLICKED OFF and the traffic waned. When he turned off Highway 85 and headed into the deeper sticks, Del Rae's lights were the only ones left, hanging a half mile back. Then they disappeared too. She must have flicked them off.

Very clever.

Later he'd have to ask if that was her idea or the lawyer's.

When he arrived at the weed-infested drive for the hideaway, he stopped the Wrangler on the gravel and got out to see if the twine that he'd laid across the vegetation was still in place.

It was.

Meaning no uninvited visitors.

He pulled it to the side, drove to the house with the headlights off and slipped the mask over his face before going in, just in case the woman was conscious. Thirty seconds later he discovered he didn't need it. She was out cold. She'd been awake at some point, though, because she ripped the rules in half and threw them in the corner.

He chuckled.

Feisty.

Unfortunately, she needed to be raped to keep everything consistent. She also needed her hair chopped off.

To be doubly safe, he stuck a syringe in her ass and pushed

the plunger before getting down to business.

He had to remember to take the rubber.

Take the rubber.

Take the rubber.

The cops would be here at some point. Maybe in a week, maybe in a year. Either way it was important that they not find his DNA hanging around.

The woman was tight.

He was smack dab in the middle of that tightness when he heard a rustling of some sort outside.

Chapter Forty-Six

Day Six—May 10
Saturday Night

WHEN LANCE LUNDEEN FINALLY MADE A MOVE shortly after dark, Aspen White followed him west on the 6th Avenue freeway, hanging back as far as she could, driving the blue Nissan rental. Kayla Beck followed both of them more than a half mile behind in a brown Chevy, the second rental, the one from Avis.

The traffic was thick.

The rentals were fresh.

Lundeen wouldn't suspect a thing.

Kayla's stomach had a knot in it. It was that same kind of feeling she got as a little girl when the roller coaster got snagged by the chain and started inching up that first hill. Lundeen was in his weird clothes and driving the Jeep, meaning he was on some kind of a mission. They might actually catch him at something.

And have their dirt.

"You still there?" Aspen asked.

Kayla pushed the cell phone closer to her ear. "Yeah, no

problems."

"Where are you?"

"Just passed the Kipling exit," Kayla said.

"Oops," Aspen said. "We're getting off."

"Where?"

"Union/Simms."

"Got it."

"He's getting in the right lane; looks like we're heading north."

"Okay."

"Come up behind me," Aspen said. "Then I'll drop back and you can take the point."

"Roger, that."

"Roger, that?" Aspen asked. "Is that what you just said?"

Kayla knew she should laugh but couldn't.

"Yeah, I think I did."

"Roger, that," Aspen repeated. "You're too much, girl."

THEY ENDED UP FOLLOWING HIM to a place called the Mountain View Trailer Park. They parked up a gravel road that led to a junkyard and doubled back through the dark on foot. The Wrangler squatted in front of the last trailer in the row. They took a post in the open space behind a boulder and pulled out the binoculars.

"Weird," Aspen said.

"Very."

They watched and time passed.

Nothing happened, other than Lundeen's shadow occasionally moved around inside the trailer. They expected a car to pull up as some sort of secret rendezvous, but none did.

"I got a call from our collar friend today," Kayla said at one point.

"You did?"

"He'd been watching me because he knew what I was wearing," she added. "He said I was a bad girl."

Aspen looked shocked.

"You're just telling me this now?"

"Sorry," Kayla said. "I guess I wanted to spare you."

"Spare me? Girlfriend, all you did was keep me in the dark. Don't do that again. I need all the information all the time. So do you. That's the only way we're going to get through this alive."

Kayla nodded.

The woman was right.

Ignorance wasn't their friend.

Knowledge was.

"So what'd you do?" Aspen asked.

"Hung up," she said. "Then went out and bought a gun."

"You did?"

"Yes."

"You got it with you?"

"No, there's a waiting period. I get it tomorrow. I got the same kind as my old one, the one you used on that guy in the boxcar," she added. "That way if anyone wants to know where it is then I'll have something to show 'em. No one would know the difference unless they somehow checked the serial numbers."

Aspen was impressed.

And said so.

"The guy is probably calling from a public phone," Aspen said. "Next time he calls, after you hang up, call the incoming number a minute or so later. Maybe someone will answer. Then describe Mitch Mitchell and ask if they see him around."

Kayla cocked her head.

Seriously impressed.

"How'd you think of that?" she asked.

Aspen chuckled. "It's called motivation, sweetheart— motivation to not end up in a boxcar again; motivation to not spend the rest of my life in jail for blowing someone's face off."

Suddenly Lundeen came out of the trailer, hopped in the Wrangler and drove off.

Bad news.

They couldn't follow him.

They'd never get to their cars in time.

"Now what?" Kayla asked.

"I don't know about you but I'm going to get my sweet little posterior into that trailer and see what's what," Aspen said.

"Not without my posterior you're not," Kayla said.

"I love it when you talk dirty."

THEY WEREN'T WORRIED ABOUT POSTING A LOOKOUT. If Lundeen came back they'd see his headlights in plenty of time. Plus they'd be in and out in five minutes, ten max. Wherever he went he wouldn't be back that fast.

The doorknob was locked but the door hadn't been pulled shut all the way, allowing them to push it in with no problem.

Neither of them had a flashlight.

They made sure the curtains were closed, in case of nosy neighbors, and flicked on the lights.

The interior was seriously worn.

And just as seriously outdated.

They found pots, pans and silverware in the cabinets but no food in the fridge.

Very strange.

Clearly no one was actually living there on a day-to-day basis.

Overall the place had nothing of interest.

Not a single thing.

Until they came to the cabinet above the fridge.

There, under a box of salt, they found fifteen or twenty photographs, depicting two different women similarly posed. Each was naked, on a raggedy old mattress, chained by the ankle and unconscious. One was attractive and the other was absolutely stunning.

In the same stratosphere as Aspen, if that was possible.

"Now we're talking," Aspen said.

They chose a photo of each woman, the one that showed the face the clearest. Aspen stuffed those in the back pocket of her jeans and then they put the rest back where they found them.

They turned off the lights and closed the door all the way shut. Before they could step to the ground headlights suddenly punched through the darkness, coming out of nowhere, and lit them up.

"Run!"

Chapter Forty-Seven

Day Seven—May 11
Sunday Morning

BRYSON COVENTRY AWOKE IN A STRANGE BEDROOM next to an intoxicatingly beautiful naked woman who breathed deeply and rhythmically. It took him a few seconds to register where he was, and when he did the corner of his mouth turned up ever so slightly. The first rays of dawn washed the walls with a golden patina. He twisted to his side, laid his head on his arm and let his fingers lightly brush the woman's hair.

Rain St. John.

So sensual.

So complicated.

So fragile.

In a perfect world he'd spend every minute of the day with her. Maybe take her for a ride in the 1967 Corvette, put the top down, wind through Bear Creek Canyon and grab an ice-cold beer at the Little Bear. Or go for a hike in the mountains, at Elk Meadows or Lair O' The Bear, a serious hike lasting hours, the kind where you work up a sweat and can't wait to sit down again.

Unfortunately he didn't live in a perfect world.

He lived in a world where people like Tracy Patterson disappeared. So he slipped out of bed without waking Rain, splashed water on his face, popped in his contacts and left a note on the kitchen table before heading for the front door.

Her black dress lay on the floor in front of the couch.

It still carried the scent of her perfume.

He replayed last night and saw it fall off her body.

He walked back into the bedroom, watched her sleep for a few moments and briefly considered finding out if she wakes up horny. Instead he gave her an imperceptible kiss on the cheek and left.

HIS GOAL TODAY WAS TO FIND TRACY PATTERSON. Technically she didn't fall under his jurisdiction since she was a "homicide in the making" instead of an actual homicide. Coventry had used that concept before to justify throwing time at a case.

The chief—Forrest Tanner—didn't buy it.

Coventry pushed back.

And the chief learned a lesson.

Coventry arrived at an empty headquarters shortly before 7:30 a.m. and kick-started the coffee machine. Breakfast turned out to be fruit from the bottom drawer of his desk; that and two stale donuts that softened to perfection when he dunked them.

He continued going through the eighteen files that Leanne Sanders had emailed.

But found nothing that helped.

None of the men had any apparent ties to Denver.

He was two hours into it and starting to tap his pencil on the desk when his cell phone rang.

A voice came through that he didn't expect.

Aspen's.

He pulled up a picture of them together in his Tundra as a black thunderstorm pounded the earth. He saw her body, her incredible physique, once again. The memory was so real that he could smell her skin and taste her mouth.

"Bryson," she said, "I am *so sorry* for not getting back to you Friday night like I said. I ended up having a medical emergency that took me out of commission so bad that I couldn't even call you to let you know."

He didn't expect that.

Not at all.

She hadn't blown him off after all.

"What happened?"

"It's a long story," she said. "What I need now is for you to kiss my stitches and rub my shoulders. Are you free today?"

He almost said "Yes" but didn't.

The hesitation confused him.

She was beautiful.

Passionate.

Warm.

And he'd already fallen in love with her in the back seat of the Tundra. So why didn't he jump on it? Because of Rain St. John.

Also beautiful.

Also passionate.

Also warm.

Five years ago, even five months ago, he would have known exactly what to do, namely not deprive himself of the incredible charms of either of them. Juggle them both and see which one turned out to be the better fit. Why rush to judgment? But now, today, for some reason Leanne Sanders' words rang strong. *Women came too easy to him. It was always easier to move on. That's why he was still single.*

"I said, are you free today?" Aspen repeated.

"Look," he said. "I'm going to hate myself later for saying this, but I got to be honest with you. I met someone."

"You met someone?"

"Yes."

"When?" she asked.

"Yesterday."

"Yesterday?" Her voice sounded as if she couldn't believe it.

"Right."

"And now I'm out?" she asked.

"I thought you blew me off, and then I ended up meeting someone."

"Well I didn't," she said.

"I know that now."

"How can you do that? I thought we were going some-where," she said. "I honestly believed we had a connection. I screwed you in the back of your truck, for crying out loud. I just don't go around doing that with everybody, for your informa-tion."

"I know that," he said.

Silence.

"So what do we do?" she asked. "I don't want to lose you before I even have you."

He pondered it.

"Coventry," she added, "I fell in love with you the minute I saw you. As corny as it sounds, I've been waiting for you for a long time. Just tell this other woman you had a good time and then let's get back on track."

AN HOUR LATER HE CALLED JENA VERNON at Channel 8. Most people along the front range knew her as the roving TV reporter, the charismatic blond with the bright green eyes who wasn't afraid to get into the middle of the mess. Coventry knew her from the old high school days in Fort Collins when she was the ticklish younger sister of his best friend, Matt Vernon.

They caught up on things and then he got around to the reason for the call. "There's a woman missing named Tracy Patterson," he said. "I want to get her picture on the news and see if anyone has any information. Can you grease that for me?"

"How soon do you need it?"

"Let's put it this way—are we done yet?"

She chuckled.

"Let me call you back in ten minutes."

"Thanks. I owe you one."

"Wrong," she said. "You owe me *one more.*"

He laughed.

True.

"You need to take me out and get me drunk," she said.

Chapter Forty-Eight

Day Seven—May 11
Sunday Morning

———————

TARZAN GOT UP EARLY SUNDAY MORNING anxious to hear from Del Rae. When she didn't call for more than an hour he took off his shirt, traded his pants for a pair of shorts, and jogged down the railroad tracks with his cell phone in hand. After a half mile he picked up the pace, letting his lungs burn and his legs stretch, cranking out five-minute miles according to his best guess. He was twenty minutes into it, still headed out, when she called.

He slowed to a walk and said, "Talk to me."

"I don't have much time," she said. "I'm out on a jog and the lawyer's fixing breakfast."

"So how'd it go?"

"Perfect," she said.

He slapped his hand on his leg.

"Details," he said.

"Okay, in a nutshell, we tailed you to the hideout and then went in after you left," she said. "The woman, whatever her name is, was unconscious on the bed. I see you already chopped her hair off."

Right.

He had.

"The lawyer's all set to do it," Del Rae said.

She didn't need to explain what *it* meant. She was talking about the lawyer stealing the woman from the hideaway, dumping her unconscious body in his wife's car, and then bringing the wife to the hideaway.

Where the lawyer would kill her.

And the weirdo would get the blame.

"When?"

"Tonight," she said. "He wants to steal the woman while she's still alive. That's part of the justification he's using to go through with this—that he's saving someone's life. Instead of the woman dying, his wife does. The number of victims stays at one."

Tonight.

"Perfect," Lance said.

Del Rae paused. "Not totally perfect," she said.

"Meaning what?"

"He's got details he's trying to work out."

"Like what?"

"Well, first of all," she said, "he needs to be officially in Denver when it happens instead of out of town."

Lance didn't get it.

That seemed like the opposite of what the guy should do.

"His thought process goes like this," Del Rae said. "He told his wife he was going out of town on business this weekend. She may have told that to other people. If he tells the police he was out of town when his wife disappears, he won't have any plane tickets or concrete proof of business to back it up. The cops will take it for a phony alibi and zero in on him all the more. So he needs to somehow have an excuse to show back up in Denver this afternoon. Once he does that and is actually in town, the police won't have any reason to ask where he was on Friday or Saturday. I have to agree with his reasoning, as strange as it is."

Lance had no problem with it.

In fact he admired the guy's cunning.

"Fine, let him be back," he said. "That's even better for us, actually."

"Yes it is."

A couple of magpies landed on the tracks ahead. Lance picked up a chunk of gravel and threw it at them, missing by a mile but coming close enough to scare them into the sky. The dumb things flew about thirty yards and landed back on the tracks.

What?

They couldn't tell he was headed that way?

"There's one more thing," Del Rae added. "This one is a lot more serious. He wants to have a rock solid alibi when the wife disappears. So he wants to be somewhere public with lots of witnesses. He wants me to do the body exchange. He'll still do the actual killing but wants me to do the exchange."

Lance threw another rock at the magpies.

Hard this time.

"No way," he said.

"I know."

"It's way too risky," he added. "I don't know what kind of shape his wife is in, but we can't have you dancing with her one-on-one. There's a million ways that can go wrong."

"I know."

"He's going to have to do that part of it," Lance said. "Screw the alibi. You can be with him when he does it, and probably should be. That way he'll get a better comfort level knowing you're in it as deep as he is. But you can't do it alone. Screw him."

She agreed.

"There's no compromising on that," he emphasized. "Be sure you talk him out of it."

She paused.

He felt it and asked, "What?"

"Nothing."

"You liar. I can see your nose growing. What is it?"

"I just hope it's not a deal-breaker for him," she said. "Insisting on an alibi."

"It won't be," he said. "When you get back from your jog give him the blowjob of the century. Keep him focused on the rewards."

FORTY-FIVE MINUTES LATER Lance was back home, freshly showered and banging on the skins to Nirvana's "Smells Like Teen Spirit."

Thinking of the lawyer.

The attorney better get off this alibi hang-up.

This was going to end in either one of two ways.

The lawyer would either kill his wife.

Or Lance would personally rip his head off one dark night and piss in the hole.

Either way the lawyer was going down.

Chapter Forty-Nine

Day Seven—May 11
Sunday Morning

ASPEN WAS NOWHERE IN THE HOTEL ROOM when Kayla Beck woke. She yawned, stretched, and realized that it was Sunday morning, meaning she had the whole day free, but also meaning that tomorrow kicked off another week. She pulled the curtains back and found the Nissan gone.

Hopefully on a coffee hunt.

The photographs of the two chained women sat on the table.

Grim reminders.

She rubbed the sleep out of her eyes and studied the Polaroids as the shower warmed up.

When she closed her eyes the women's faces disappeared.

Her face and Aspen's took their places.

She shivered.

She got the shower as hot as she could without melting her skin and stepped in. Ten minutes later she felt brand new. The clock said 8:12 a.m. Aspen still hadn't returned. Kayla turned on the TV for background noise, booted up her Gateway laptop and logged on to the net.

The plan was to search the local newspapers and try to figure out who the women in the pictures were. She typed in a variety of search phrases.

Missing since.

Last seen.

Abducted.

Young woman.

Long brown hair.

None of the searches brought any luck. Maybe she'd have no choice other than to physically go to a library, get the actual newspapers in hand, and leaf through them page by page, starting with today's and heading back one day at a time.

AN HOUR LATER SHE STILL HADN'T HAD ANY LUCK, nor had Aspen shown up, when something strange happened. A man's face appeared on the TV. At first she thought it was a commercial because the guy had that totally sexy GQ look that could sell anything. But he turned out to be a Denver detective by the name of Bryson Coventry, trying to get information on the whereabouts of a missing woman named Tracy Patterson.

Last seen on Friday night.

A female's face filled the screen.

About the same age as Kayla, maybe younger.

Kayla stopped breathing.

It was one of the two women from the pictures.

Anyone with information should call Detective Coventry at the number on the bottom of the screen. Kayla repeated the number out loud until she found a pencil and wrote it down. When Aspen walked in two minutes later carrying coffee and donuts, Kayla gave her the news right away.

"Isn't Coventry the guy who came to my apartment? The one you got all hot about?"

Aspen nodded.

"Now I see why," Kayla said. "I'm major jealous."

Aspen frowned.

"Don't be," she said. "He dumped me this morning."

"He did? Why?"

"He met someone else," she said.

"What a jerk."

Aspen shrugged. "It's partly my fault. I was supposed to call him Friday night, after you and I were done scouting out Tarzan. When I didn't, he thought I blew him off."

"Did you tell him you were busy getting shot?"

"I don't think the word *shot* came up, but I told him enough so he knew I was legit," Aspen said.

"*And?*"

"*And* he said he met this other woman and sort of let her know he was interested in developing something with her. He didn't think it would be right to just yank the rug out from under her the very next day. And he said it wouldn't be fair to anyone including me if he played me on the side," Aspen said. "The stupid thing is, now I like him even more than before."

Kayla understood.

Not many men would be strong enough to pass up mattress time with the likes of Aspen.

"So what are you going to do?"

"I don't know—something, though, I guarantee you that."

"What's the other woman's name?"

"Rain."

"Rain?"

"Right, as in thunder and lightning."

"Her parents must have been hippies."

THEY BROKE OPEN THE DONUT BOX and dug in while they debated the big issue, namely whether to tell Coventry that Lance Lundeen was connected to the disappearance of Tracy Patterson.

Who might still be alive.

"If we tell Coventry," Aspen said, "we lose our dirt on Lundeen. Once we do that, how do we take care of Mitch Mitchell? Are you going to kill him?"

Kayla pictured the act.

And didn't particularly like what she saw.

"Maybe if I have to, but I'd rather not."

"Well, same here," Aspen said. "Look at it this way. Tracy Patterson is either dead or she isn't. If she's already dead, we stay on Lundeen's tail until we find her body. Then we use it to blackmail him. If she's alive, we do the same thing, namely stay on his tail until we find her. Except then we set her free. After she's safe we blackmail him. Even if he doesn't actually murder her, he's done enough bad stuff to the poor woman to go away for a long time."

Kayla twisted a pencil in her fingers.

It made sense.

There was only one potential scenario that bothered her.

"Assume the woman is alive and we don't tell Coventry," she said. "Then assume that we take longer to find her than Coventry would have and because of that she dies."

Aspen responded immediately.

"We won't let that happen," she said. "He either has her

227

somewhere in his building or somewhere off site. We stay on his tail and see if he leads us somewhere off site. If he doesn't, then we go in."

"You mean into the building?"

"Right," Aspen said. "And while we're in there we'll check his toolbox and photo drawers too. So do we have a plan or what?"

Kayla ran through the options one more time.

And didn't see a better one.

"When do we start?" she asked.

"Right now. When do you pick up your gun?"

"Tomorrow."

"I wish you had it now, this could be a long night," Aspen said. "Let's at least stop somewhere and pick up a couple of good knives. Maybe a pair of night vision binoculars too." She stood up, pulled her T-shirt over her head and walked to the bathroom. "I'm taking a quick shower first. Then we're out of here."

Chapter Fifty

Day Seven—May 11
Sunday Afternoon

BRYSON COVENTRY CALLED RAIN and asked her to meet him on Bannock Street at the place where she'd been abducted. She showed up in a light-blue sleeveless blouse that rode a couple of inches above her bellybutton. Incredibly taut stomach muscles disappeared into faded Daisy-Duke jean shorts.

Coventry fidgeted nervously as she walked towards him.

He lit a flame in her last night, no question.

But what did she think of him by the light of day?

A long tight hug and deep kiss answered that question immediately.

"I missed you," she said.

He chuckled.

"Missed me? I didn't even know you threw anything at me."

She punched him on the arm and asked, "Why are we here?"

He put a serious look on his face.

"Show me the exact spot you got taken," he said.

She grabbed his hand and led him north about forty feet.

"Here. Why?"

He didn't answer and instead checked the scene. To their right, east, was a vacant building. To their left, west, was the street. It had metered parking spaces on each side. If his theory was correct, the man who took her had been parked right there and grabbed her when she got next to his car. That's why he parked in front of the vacant building.

Smart guy.

What was he driving?

That was the big question.

"What kind of a car was parked right there?" he asked, pointing to a vacant space.

She shrugged.

"I have no idea."

"How about there?" he asked, indicating the next space down.

"Coventry, I have no idea," she said.

"There were cars on the street, though, you remember that much, right?"

"Yeah, there were cars, but I didn't pay any attention to them. I had no reason to." She paused and then asked, "Is this guy going to come after me again?"

"I don't see why he would," he said.

He grabbed her hand and walked her back to where she had been parked that day.

"Wait here a second," he said.

Then he ran to the Tundra and pulled it into the space where Rain's attacker had been parked.

"Okay, walk," he shouted.

HE PUT HIMSELF IN THE SHOES OF THE OTHER MAN, hiding on the driver's side of the vehicle as Rain walked up the street. As she approached, Coventry looked around and saw no one. He waited for her to pass and then closed in from behind. He swung his right arm around her head and clamped his hand over her mouth—no chloroform saturated cloth in it but close enough. His left arm simultaneously swung around her abdomen and yanked her into him.

Then he let his instincts take over.

He lifted her up in his arms and carried her to the side of the car. There he muscled her to the ground where no one would see her. He covered her with his body as she struggled. Thirty seconds later he got off and pulled her up.

She immediately punched him in the chest.

"You bastard!"

"Stop!" he said. "What did you see? After I grabbed you, what did you see?"

She punched him again.

"This isn't funny."

He ignored her.

"Work with me," he said. "What did you see?"

It turned out that she saw the underside of his truck and the tires. "Now," he said, "when you got taken that day, what did you see?"

She retreated in thought.

"I remember now," she said. "I remember seeing the bottom of his car."

"Was there space underneath, like mine?" he asked. "Or did it sit lower like a car?"

"Space," she said. "It sat higher, like yours."

"What about the tires?"

"They were like yours," she said. "Knobby—mud and snows

or whatever you call them. Not smooth like car tires."

Good.

Very good.

"What else do you remember?"

"Nothing."

"Think."

She did.

She almost gave up but then said, "Only one other thing. I remember rust. Lots of rust."

The corner of Coventry's mouth went up ever so slightly.

THEN HE HAD AN ADDITIONAL THOUGHT.

"When I grabbed you, how did the other guy compare to me?"

"What do you mean?"

"You know, strength-wise."

"You want the truth?"

"I don't know. You tell me."

She put a serious look on her face. "You're strong, Coventry. Don't get me wrong. I love your body. But you're not strong like this other guy."

Coventry didn't expect that.

"Really?"

She nodded.

"If you ever get in a fist fight with him, be sure you bring a gun," she said.

He chuckled.

Then studied her.

Trying to figure out if she was messing with him.

She wasn't.

"Now you owe me lunch for attacking me."

He agreed.

THEY PILED IN THE TUNDRA AND HEADED TO WONG'S.
On the way Coventry called Shalifa Netherwood. Apparently
she was at Washington Park with two nieces, feeding bread to
geese.

"Okay, just wanted to say hello," he said. "See you in the
morning."

"Spit it out," she said. "What are you trying to get me to
do?"

"Nothing, honest," he said.

"It's okay," she said. "I'll help if you need it. I already heard
you were on the TV today."

"Just keep the geese fed," he said. "I'll talk to you tomorrow."

As soon as he hung up he made a series of calls and finally
ended up getting the home phone number of a guy named Dirk
Smith, a higher-up in the streets department.

"How often do you pull quarters out of the meters?" Coventry asked.

"That depends on which meters you're talking about."

"Bannock Street."

"Every Monday," he said. "If my memory serves me."

"Good," Coventry said. "I want to get the coins out of a few
of them."

"Not a problem. Buy why?"

"I want to check them for prints."

Jim Michael Hansen

Chapter Fifty-One

DEL RAE PARIS LIVED in a modest three-bedroom house at the base of Lookout Mountain in Golden, where the aroma of hops and barley hung in the air more often than not, thanks to the Coors brewery. When Lance Lundeen arrived in his pickup truck shortly after two o'clock, she already had one of the garage doors open for him. As soon as he got the vehicle inside, the door went down. He pulled off a baseball cap, shook his hair free and stepped out.

Del Rae looked incredible.

So much so that he threw her over his shoulder, carried her upstairs to the bedroom and pulled her pants off—nothing else, just her pants.

Then he took her.

Hard.

Like an animal.

Until she lost control.

And screamed those little screams that he liked so much.

Afterwards they sipped coffee and went over the details of

the upcoming events. If all went well, tonight would be the night when Tashna Sharapova disappeared. She'd end up dead within twenty-four hours after that.

Suddenly they heard a noise.

Faint but definite.

A car engine.

Sounding as if it came from the driveway.

Del Rae ran to the front window and peeked out the curtain.

"It's him!"

"The lawyer?"

"Yes."

"What's he doing here?"

"I don't know. Get upstairs. Quick!"

He headed that way with his coffee still in hand.

"Hurry!" she said.

FIVE SECONDS LATER KNUCKLES RAPPED hard on the front door. Del Rae made a rapid survey of the kitchen and living room, determined that no evidence of Lance lingered, then calmed her face and opened the door.

"Robert," she said. "Get your sexy self in here."

"I think I got it figured out," he said.

"So it's a go?"

"Oh yeah, it's a major go."

"When?" she asked.

"Tonight."

"Tonight?"

"Tonight."

"I'm so excited," she said.

He picked her up and started walking up the stairs towards

the bedroom.

Lance slipped into the closet and stood there in the dark as still and quiet as he could.

THE LAWYER THREW DEL RAE ON THE BED, straddled her and then pinned her arms above her head. "You want to hear the plan?" he asked.

"It looks like I don't have a choice," she said.

"No you don't."

"I'm your prisoner."

He kissed her.

"That turns you on, doesn't it? Being my prisoner—"

She wiggled her hips.

"I'll never tell," she said.

He kept her pinned as he told her the plan. They'd leave for the hideaway about five o'clock in Del Rae's car. When they got there they'd put the woman in the trunk, assuming she was still there, bring her back to Del Rae's house and park in the garage.

Then Robert would head home.

His wife was scheduled to attend a director's meeting at the Denver Museum of Nature & Science at 8:00 p.m. Those meetings always lasted until about 10:30 or 11:00. She always parked at the far end of the north lot, away from the other cars where she wouldn't get door-dings in her precious little BMW. The main road out of that lot leads to Colorado Boulevard. But there's another way out, too, to the west.

While Tashna was gone, Robert would make a number of phone calls.

From the house phone.

Through about 9:00.

Alibi calls.

Proof he was home.

Then, dressed in all things black, he'd slip out the back door and make his way through the open space to the side streets on the other side, where his car would be parked. That way no one would see headlights leaving his driveway.

He'd meet Del Rae somewhere, maybe at a King Soopers parking lot.

Then they'd take her car to the Museum and park next to the BMW. When Tashna came out they'd snag her, put the other woman in the front seat of her car, and head out the west exit.

Then take Tashna to the hideaway.

And pump her full of drugs.

Just like the weirdo would do.

Afterwards, Del Rae would drop Robert off where she picked him up. He'd sneak back to his house through the open space and go to bed.

At some point, say two in the morning, he'd wake up, realize Tashna hadn't come home yet and call her cell phone to see where she was.

She wouldn't answer.

"It's not risk free," he said. "We just have to hope that no one's around when she gets to her car. That's the key—not being seen at that point. But if someone's around, we simply abort and come up with a Plan B."

"What about security cameras in the parking area?"

"None," he said. "I checked this afternoon. So, are we going to really do this or what?"

She moaned.

"Shut up and screw me."

FROM THE CLOSET, Lance Lundeen took deep breaths and clenched his fists. He listened to the lawyer doing Del Rae and wondered how long he'd be able to fight the urge to jump out and rip the guy's arms off.

Chapter Fifty-Two

Day Seven—May 11
Sunday Night

———————————

KAYLA BECK POSITIONED HERSELF UNDERNEATH a gondola car, flat on her stomach, alone in the dark. She stayed hidden behind the cold steel wheels, not exposing any more of her body than necessary to keep the binoculars trained on Tarzan. He was inside the building, a hundred yards to the east, wearing boxer shorts, beating the drums to "Born to Run."

The drums made her picture herself stretched out on the floor before him.

Naked.

Awaiting her punishment.

A shiver ran up her spine and into her brain. She let her hand reach down to feel the eight-inch serrated knife sheathed on her belt, expecting it to bring a measure of calmness.

It did just the opposite.

It reminded her how desperate everything had become.

The plan was so simple if they could just get it to come together. All they needed to do was get the final proof that Mitch Mitchell was the collar killer, find Tarzan's captive Tracy Patterson alive, release her, anonymously blackmail Tarzan into killing Mitchell, and then rat Tarzan out to the police. At that point Aspen could get out of Denver and Kayla could get back to her life.

The gravel dug into her skin, even through her jeans and sweatshirt, especially on her elbows and forearms. She shifted, not escaping the sharp edges of the stones but at least moving them to fresh parts of her body.

It had been a fairly productive day.

Aspen insisted that Kayla spend the whole day on law school work, so that's exactly what she did. Having done it made it even more apparent how necessary it had been.

Meanwhile, Aspen spent the day tailing Mitch Mitchell. She hoped to catch him at a public phone, talking into a scrambler at the exact same time that either she or Kayla got a call from the collar-killer.

Would it be only circumstantial evidence?

Yes.

Would it be all they needed to move forward with their plan and end the little freak's life?

Yes.

SUDDENLY THE DRUMMING STOPPED.

Kayla swallowed.

Tarzan walked over to the fridge and drank from a gallon jug of milk.

It would be easier if Aspen was here. But Aspen was on the other side of the building, hiding in the darkness somewhere, ready to run to the Nissan and follow Tarzan if he made a move. If that happened then Kayla would have to decide whether to join the tail or sneak inside the building and see if she could find Tracy Patterson.

She already knew what she'd do.

She'd go inside.

She wouldn't like it.

But she had to.

Time was running out.

Suddenly her cell phone vibrated.

WHEN SHE ANSWERED Aspen's voice came through. "What's going on at your end?" she asked.

"He's been playing the drums," Kayla said. "I'll never be able to listen to 'Born to Run' again. He just stopped. Now he's talking on a phone and walking back and forth."

"Maybe getting ready to make a move," Aspen said.

Maybe.

She lit her watch.

10:32.

Still early for a night owl.

Plenty of time left to make moves.

"You okay?" Aspen asked.

"Yeah, why?"

"You sound weird."

"I am weird."

"So, no sign of Tracy Patterson yet, I take it."

"Not a peep," Kayla said. "I'm starting to think that she's either dead or he has her off site somewhere. If she was in the building he'd be checking up on her. But so far he hasn't moved off the top floor."

"You never know," Aspen said. "He could have her there

somewhere but shot full of drugs, meaning he wouldn't check on her that often. You want to come over here and hang with me?"

She did.

But couldn't.

"No," she said. "Let's just stick to the plan. Like you say, he still might drag her out of the woodwork. If that happens, I don't want to miss it. That's all we need, just that one little thing, to know she's alive and where she is."

"Okay."

"If he heads out somewhere I'm going in," Kayla added.

"You are? You made up your mind?"

"We don't have any choice," she said. "Just be sure you don't lose him and call me with plenty of warning if he starts heading back this way."

"Watch for booby traps," Aspen said. "I wouldn't put anything past this guy. Wait a minute. I think I see headlights."

Silence.

"What's going on?"

"I'm not sure," Aspen said. "There were headlights. They're gone now. They must have turned or something."

"Where are you, anyway?"

"Same place we were before," she said.

"By the electrical shed?"

"Right."

Kayla exhaled.

That was a good place.

Aspen would be safe there.

"I'm punching out now," Aspen said.

"I'll check with you in ten minutes," Kayla said.

"Right. Your turn to call."

EIGHT MINUTES LATER SOMETHING WEIRD HAPPENED. All the lights on the top floor of the building went out. Kayla pictured Tarzan sneaking up to the roof with his binoculars and rifle.

She inched back farther under the Gondola.

Then scooted completely to the other side, climbed out and crouched behind the thick steel.

There was no way he could see her.

She looked around.

The moon washed the night with a pale, almost imperceptible, glow.

She saw no one.

She detected no movement.

She heard nothing other than freeway noise.

Far away a dog barked, deep and rough. She pictured a guard dog, maybe a German Shepherd or a Rottweiler.

Suddenly a shape moved.

Something behind her.

She instinctively turned and simultaneously reached for the knife, fumbling at first but finally getting it out of the sheath.

Don't attack immediately.

It could be someone from the railroad.

She stooped down.

Hiding.

Not making a sound.

Waiting.

Then she saw it again.

A cat.

A stupid cat.

243

She chuckled, surprised at how nervous her voice sounded. Her adrenalin stopped pumping and the racing in her heart slowed.

Just a cat.

She kept the knife in her hand until her breath returned to normal and then slipped it back in the sheath.

Two minutes later she called Aspen.

No answer.

She dialed again.

No answer.

She checked the phone signal. It was strong. No problems there. She dialed again, double-checking that she had the right number.

She did.

No answer.

Suddenly a light on the top floor of the building went on. She saw Tarzan's hand pull away from a small table light next to his bed. He climbed out, walked over to the toilet, took a long piss, headed back over to the mattress and turned the light back out.

That was reassuring.

Very reassuring.

He had turned in for the night.

Kayla dialed Aspen again.

No answer.

She chewed her lower lip for a moment and then headed that way on foot.

At first just walking.

Then walking faster.

Finally breaking into a run.

Suddenly she tripped over something and fell hard, landing directly on the bone of her left knee. An unbelievable pain ripped through her body, so intense that it shot vomit into her mouth. She swallowed it down, got up and kept going as fast as she could.

Something was wrong with Aspen.

Otherwise she would have answered her phone.

Chapter Fifty-Three

Day Eight—May 12
Monday Morning

WHEN BRYSON COVENTRY'S CELL PHONE RANG and pulled him out of a deep sleep, he knew it meant trouble. He didn't have to look at his clock to tell it was the middle of the night. He twisted and checked anyway. Sure enough—2:55 a.m. Few things in life are certain, but one of them is that no one ever calls with good news at 2:55 in the morning.

Someone in the bed moaned and shifted.

Rain.

Coventry answered the phone, listened for a few minutes and then fell on his back and stretched.

"Who was that?" Rain asked.

"Work," he said. "I got to go."

"Work? It's the middle of the night."

"Yeah, I know."

He tried to get up but his body pleaded for just another few minutes of rest. Then Rain climbed on top of him, laid flat and wiggled.

"I don't want you to go," she said.

As if he could now.

He took her.

And realized that no moment in his life had ever been this perfect.

Afterwards, he slapped her on the ass, climbed out of bed, took a five-minute shower, popped in his contacts and headed to the Tundra with his hair dripping.

A cool night greeted him.

He took 6th Avenue to Colorado Boulevard and then turned north.

The entire way he could feel Rain pressed against him.

He could hear her moaning.

And taste her mouth.

And feel her sweat.

A COUPLE OF MILES LATER he came to the Denver Museum of Nature & Science. He turned into the grounds, saw the light-bars at the north side of the building and headed that way. Three squad cars and an ambulance had beaten him there. Hopefully at least one of them was experienced enough to keep the scene from getting contaminated to death.

He walked straight to the ambulance.

There he found a woman lying on her back.

Covered in a white sheet except for her head, arms and feet.

Conscious.

But dazed.

Her hair had been chopped off, just like Rain's.

Considerable bruising showed on her left ankle. Again, just like Rain's. No doubt from pulling at a chain.

Two EMTs were checking her out, but not with any obvious

sense of urgency. He pulled one of them outside and learned that the woman was still under the influence of some type of narcotic, but otherwise all her vitals were normal. There were no obvious signs of physical trauma other than to her ankle and bruising around her private area. When they found her she was naked.

"I want a rape kit," Coventry said.

"Already in the works."

"You guys are always one step ahead of me," Coventry said. "I like that. Can I talk to her?"

"Sure."

HE CLIMBED INTO THE AMBULANCE, sat down next to the woman and held her hand. "You're Tracy Patterson," he said. "I'm Bryson Coventry, a Denver detective. I've been looking for you."

The corner of her mouth went up ever so slightly.

"I'm right here," she said.

"Figures," he said.

"What do you mean?"

He chuckled. "That's how my life works," he said. "Every time I look for something I always find it in the very last place I look."

She laughed.

"How you feeling?" he asked.

"Fuzzy."

"Too fuzzy to talk?"

"No. Just don't use any big words."

"I don't know any big words," he said.

She studied him.

"Your eyes are two different colors," she said.

He stood up and looked at his reflection on a strip of stainless steel.

"So that's what's wrong."

She laughed again.

THEN HE GOT THE BASIC STORY. She left the Camel's Breath pretty drunk on Friday night and ended up going down the wrong road. On the way back she got a flat tire. A man was parked on the side of the road. She couldn't remember what kind of car he had. He offered to help change her tire. He was big—with jeans, a flannel shirt, a baseball cap and black glasses. She remembered that because he looked like he had nothing to lose, which made her have second thoughts about getting out. Other than that she didn't remember much about him.

"Was he someone from the bar?" Coventry asked.

"Not that I know of."

"So he wasn't someone you talked to in the bar?"

"No. I would have recognized him."

"Would you recognize him now?"

"I kind of doubt it," she said. "I was busy freaking out about my car and trying to not trip over my own drunk feet."

"I'm going to have you look at some videotape from inside the bar that night," Coventry said.

"Sure, if you want, but it'll be a waste of time. I don't remember him being in the bar."

"That doesn't mean he wasn't there," Coventry said.

SHE CONTINUED THE STORY. She got out of the car to look

at the flat. When she turned, the man grabbed her from behind and held a wet cloth over her mouth, saturated with some kind of chemical.

"Would you recognize the smell?"

She nodded.

"You better believe it."

"We'll do a few tests later if you're up to it," Coventry said. "Try to identify what he used on you."

"Good," she said. "I want to know what it was anyway and find out if there are any long-term side effects."

She woke up in some kind of an old house. It was dark outside and she was all alone. Coyotes barked outside, lots of them. She was on a mattress and chained by her ankle. She tore at it as hard as she could but couldn't get away. She stayed awake all night, cold, expecting someone to show up at any minute and do something to her.

In the morning she found a piece of paper with rules on it. She tore it in half and threw it in the corner. There was a bag of food.

She ate.

There was a bottle of pills. She assumed they were sleeping pills of some sort. She didn't want to be awake anymore anyway so she took one.

She had a nasty dream about being raped.

The next thing she remembered was waking up in the car.

"What car?" Coventry asked.

"The one in the parking lot," she said.

"You mean this parking lot?"

"Right."

"Okay."

She woke up in the front seat and had no idea where she

was. She thought the car belonged to the man who took her so she got out and ran towards the traffic.

She was naked but didn't care.

She ran right into the middle of the street and waved her hands for someone to stop. A woman pulled over and let her in; then called the police.

THE CAR TURNED OUT TO BELONG to one Tashna Sharapova. Victim number three. When Coventry closed his eyes he could see her on the mattress.

He could feel the cold steel on her ankle.

And hear the coyotes.

The first two women had won the coin toss.

What were the chances of three in a row?

Coventry didn't know, but this time—unlike with Tracy Patterson—he smelled death.

Chapter Fifty-Four

Day Eight—May 12
Monday Morning

TARZAN WOKE UP MONDAY MORNING to the sound of Del Rae in the kitchen making pancakes and coffee. He opened his eyes just enough to take a quick peek. She wore a dark green T-shirt that barely covered her cheeks. He closed his eyes and let the image play while he debated whether he wanted to wake up yet.

Everything had gone perfect last night.

By midnight tonight, or tomorrow at the latest, Robert Sharapova would murder his wife.

He'd do it for greed.

He'd do it for lust.

Whatever the reason, the important thing was that Lance would have the whole dirty little deed on videotape.

The lawyer would get a copy in the mail a week later.

Together with a demand for money.

The rest, as they say, would be history.

Very rich history.

Del Rae looked over. "Hey there, sleepyhead."

"Hey there back."

"Today's the day," she said.

"I know."

"I know you know," she said. "I just like saying it."

"Say it again."

"Today's the day."

Yeah.

Oh yeah.

And it had been a long time coming.

LANCE HAD DONE A LOT OF RESEARCH on the fancy-pants attorney, Robert Sharapova, Esq. He and wifey-poo—Tashna Sharapova—held about five million in joint accounts, most of which was in banks, CDs and stocks—beautifully liquid. But that was the baby money. The *real* money, about twenty-seven million worth, was owned solely by Tashna, being premarital property. But Robert was the sole beneficiary, meaning his life would be pretty sweet if wifey-poo ever woke up dead.

Dead.

Dead.

Dead.

The beauty of the last few days was that the lawyer was fully, irrevocably entangled now. As of last night, to be precise. Even if he chickened out today and didn't go through with the murder, he had already kidnapped her—with intent to kill.

He was screwed.

At a minimum, Lance and Del Rae already had enough dirt to convince him to fork over the five million that he had his hands on even with wifey-poo alive. Once he actually killed her, though, he wouldn't just be screwed, he'd be screwed to the wall.

Plus, he *had* to kill her.

What else could he possibly do?

Once he did that he'd end up coughing up the lion's share of everything. Of course it would take time, plus they'd let him keep some of it, maybe three or four million, just so he didn't do something stupid.

Like put a bullet in his head.

And leave a note for the police.

AFTER BREAKFAST TARZAN GOT THE SHOWER temperature perfect, then picked Del Rae up, put her against the wall and made love to her under the spray.

Not releasing her until she screamed.

Then they headed outside for a walk.

They opened a garage door and stepped outside. The day couldn't have been more perfect.

Warm.

Sunny.

Classic Colorado.

Suddenly, without warning, Del Rae screamed.

Lance looked at her and followed her eyes to the left. There on the ground lay Scotty Marks.

Face down.

Covered in blood.

Not moving.

Looking dead.

Chapter Fifty-Five

Day Eight—May 12
Monday Morning

KAYLA BECK SAT IN THE THIRD ROW of her Environmental Law class, safe for the moment, but not knowing how much longer she could handle the stress. An image of getting on a Greyhound bus and stepping off at the other end as Susan Smith or Janet Jones kept popping into her head.

Run.

Run.

Run.

Last night didn't help. She'd been stupid and that stupidity almost got her killed, not to mention Aspen. When Aspen hadn't answered her cell phone four times in a row, Kayla knew something was wrong and headed over on foot. What she didn't know at the time is that a man had taken a position in the dark not more than thirty feet from Aspen.

Unaware she was there.

But Aspen knew he was and dared not answer the vibration in her pocket.

Kayla came around a corner and walked right into the man.

At first she thought it was Aspen and started to say, "What's going on?"

But before she could get the words out, the shape knocked her to the ground and forced her into a tight submission hold.

"Don't fight me!"

The voice was rough.

The man wasn't overly big but was incredibly strong. He smelled like marijuana.

She struggled.

Desperate.

Wham!

Colors flashed.

"Stop moving! You hear me?"

He pounded her head.

Wham!

Wham!

She couldn't get enough air in her lungs and her muscles lost their strength. She kept fighting but knew she had already lost. In a matter of seconds she'd be in total submission.

Then she heard Aspen's voice.

Directly above them.

Screaming.

Then the strength suddenly went out of the man's body and he shouted something unintelligible. Aspen had done something to him, something drastic, something that hurt him bad.

Kayla twisted out from underneath him.

Then they ran.

Later Aspen told her that she'd stuck her knife in the guy's back.

"How many times?" Kayla asked.

"Just once."

"How far?"

Aspen shrugged. "I don't know—a ways. Enough that he got off you."

That was last night.

Now it was morning.

KAYLA WAS IN THE LAW REVIEW ROOM with her umpteenth cup of coffee, doing her best to jam the endless technical nuances of Property Law into her brain, when Aspen called.

"Here's where we're at," Aspen said. "I went back to the electrical shed about ten minutes after you left this morning."

"Aspen—"

"Don't worry, I was careful. The guy from last night was gone. Then I headed over to where I saw the headlights last night. I found a car there, sitting by itself without any particular reason."

"Probably his," Kayla said.

"Exactly," Aspen agreed. "I did a license plate search. It belongs to a guy named Scott Marks. He's got a house in Lakewood. I drove past it and didn't see any activity. I Googled him but didn't find much other than he posted a couple of comments on a blog about Woodstock."

Woodstock.

The guy from last night was a hippy.

Kayla lowered her voice and said, "So do we know if he's alive?"

"Not a clue," Aspen said. "I don't know if he's in a morgue or a hospital or vacationing in Bermuda."

Kayla exhaled.

"I'm not betting on Bermuda. This is the second time you

saved me," she said.

Aspen chuckled. "Now I'm one up on you."

"Yes you are."

"You didn't know I was keeping score, did you?"

"I was hoping you weren't."

"Now you owe me one," Aspen added.

Kayla put a serious tone in her voice. "I don't know how much longer I can keep up with all this," she said.

Silence.

Then Aspen said, "We're getting close to the end. I don't know exactly what that end is going to be, but we're getting close to it. Just hold on."

Chapter Fifty-Six

Day Eight—May 12
Monday Morning

BRYSON COVENTRY DIDN'T WRAP UP the Tashna Sharapova
crime scene at the museum until the first rays of dawn crept into
the sky. There were still lots of people he needed to talk to, including the board members, but they'd be friendlier if he didn't
jerk them out of bed. So he hopped in the Tundra and headed
west on 8th Avenue while Meat Loaf's "Two Out Of Three Ain't
Bad" spilled out of the radio, not knowing if he would head
home for a nap or go straight to work and start injecting coffee
into his veins.

Time was ticking.

That was the problem.

So he decided to go the injection route and headed to the
office. Shalifa Netherwood showed up early, around 7:30, and
said, "You look like you got dragged behind an 18-wheeler all
night. You want my advice?"

"No."

"Good, because here it is," she said. "Go home and get
some sleep."

"I'll sleep in my next life," he said.

"Did you eat breakfast?"

"No, why?"

She pulled him up by the arm. "Come on," she said, "before you collapse or something."

He pulled his wallet out.

It didn't look good.

Nor had it since he took out that loan to buy the '67. Not that he would undo that deal, of course.

"Put that away," Shalifa said. "This is my treat."

"Really?" he said. "In that case I'm thinking Brown Palace."

"Too bad because I'm thinking Denny's," she said.

She grinned as if she just heard a joke.

"What?" he asked.

"Let's just hope they don't have your picture up for stiffing that waitress," she said.

"Hey, that was a total accident," he said. "Plus I went back."

AS THE SUN GOT HIGHER and the pancakes dropped into his stomach, Coventry started to feel more and more like a human being. Now he was glad he hadn't wasted time on a nap.

He must have had a puzzled look on his face because Shalifa asked, "What?"

"There's a few pieces of this thing that are bugging me," he said.

"Like what?"

"Like the fact that Tashna Sharapova doesn't fit the mold," he said. "Rain St. John and Tracy Patterson were both younger. Tashna's thirty-two."

"A good thirty-two or a bad one?"

"Meaning what?"

"Meaning is she a MILF?"

Coventry chuckled.

"Yeah, I suppose."

"You know that that means? MILF?" she asked.

He leaned forward.

"Actually," he said, "for your information, I'm a lot smarter than you think. In fact, between me and my brother, we know the answer to every single question in the world. If you don't believe me, just go ahead and ask something."

She cocked her head.

"Okay," she said. "What's the capital of Costa Rica?"

"That's one my brother knows," he said. "Go ahead and ask another one."

She punched him in the arm.

"Got me," she said.

"Yes I did."

She slurped coffee and said, "Nothing personal, but I'm not too impressed with your mold."

"My mold *theory*," he corrected her. "Tashna Sharapova doesn't fit the mold."

"That either."

"But it's more than just the fact that she's older," he said. "The first two—Rain and Tracy—were taken from places where there would be choices. In Rain's case, people would be walking down the street. In Tracy's case, people would get drunk and head the wrong way after they left the Camel's Breath—not a lot of people, granted, but some. In this latest case, there wouldn't be any traffic at all in that parking lot at that time of night."

She agreed.

"It's almost as if the first two were random," he said, "but

Tashna Sharapova was specifically targeted."

Shalifa shrugged.

"She could be just as random," she said. "He spots the car and decides to hang out for a while and see who walks over to it. By chance it turns out to be a female. Maybe, since it's his third time, he decides he needs to be more careful. Hence the dark parking lot option."

"Maybe," Coventry said.

"Plus there's nothing to say that the guy can't be both random and have targets," she said. "You've done that yourself with women."

He nodded.

True.

"She's filthy rich, you know," Shalifa said.

"So I hear."

"She donated half the stuff in the museum," she added. "That's why she's on the board." She smiled. "And why you're not."

ON THE DRIVE BACK TO HEADQUARTERS Shalifa asked, "What's the husband's take on all this? I picture him as some know-it-all who's going to be calling the chief every five minutes and asking why everyone on the case is such an idiot."

Coventry processed the question but put it on the shelf for a second while he gave his attention to a minivan on his tail, driven by a woman with one eye on the road, one on a makeup mirror and the other on her cell phone.

Wait.

That's three eyes.

The point remains nonetheless.

"I'm going to get killed by lipstick some day," he said. "The husband's take on this? Is that your question?"

"Right."

"I don't know yet," he said. "I talked to him a few times over the last couple of hours. He's staying as calm as he can and trying to be optimistic."

"Good for him."

"By the way, here's what I want you to do today. Talk to everyone who was at the board meeting last night. See if they saw anything in the parking lot, a car parked there, someone walking around, whatever. Find out what kind of security the museum has. If there are any videotapes, get them and make DVDs. Any prints from Tashna's car that don't belong to the victim or to Tracy Patterson need to be run to ground."

"What are you going to do while I'm doing all the work?" she asked. "Repeat: *all the work.*"

"Me? I'll be drinking coffee," he said.

She gave him a mean look.

"And having a talk with the husband."

Chapter Fifty-Seven

Day Eight—May 12
Monday Morning

LANCE LUNDEEN DRAGGED SCOTTY MARKS' bloody body into the garage, closed the door and checked to see if he was alive. He was still breathing but didn't respond to shouting or shaking.

"Those women did this," he said. "And they're going to pay for it, big time."

Del Rae stared at the body.

"We can't let this screw everything up," she said.

"What does that mean?"

"It means we can't get connected to it," she said. "The last thing we need right now is to be rubbing elbows with the cops."

Lance agreed.

"We need to get him to a hospital," he said.

"How? We can't exactly just drive up and dump him on the front steps. All those places have security cameras."

They found Scotty's car keys in his pants pocket. Then they drove around until they spotted his car and brought it into the garage. Lance lifted the man up and set him in the back seat.

Then he cranked over the engine and headed west on the 6th Avenue freeway while Del Rae followed in her car. They pulled into a small park in Lakewood, not far from Lutheran Medical Center.

No one was around.

There were no cameras.

Lance wiped his prints off the vehicle and got in Del Rae's car. A half mile later he used Scotty's cell phone to call 911 and make an emergency report about an injured man in a car in the park. Then he wiped his prints off the phone and threw it out the window into a small creek. Thirty seconds later they heard sirens heading for the park.

On the drive home Lance was silent.

His thoughts were on the two women.

They'd pay for this.

But he needed to be careful.

They were a lot more dangerous than he thought.

What was their problem, anyway?

IN THE AFTERNOON he loaded up the Wrangler with an eight foot stepladder, a toolbox, a battery powered drill, several boxes of assorted screws, a digital recorder, cameras, wires and all the rest. Then he slipped into his Dick Zipp suit and made the trek once again to the old farmhouse.

Tracy Patterson was gone.

Tashna Sharapova was chained on the mattress in her place.

Unconscious.

Beautiful.

The lawyer already chopped off her hair and threw it in the corner on top of Rain St. John's and Tracy Patterson's. Why had he done it already instead of waiting until he came back to kill her? Maybe to avoid getting stray strands on his clothes then. Or maybe to save time later so he could concentrate on the real work. Whatever the reason, the sight brought a smile to Lance's face.

It meant the lawyer was committed.

Lance wasn't sure where the lawyer would kill her. If it was up to him, he'd do it in the bedroom, right there on the mattress, without even unchaining her.

So he hid two cameras in that room.

Then, just to be safe, one went into every other room.

They were motion activated and powered by battery packs. Their signals got transmitted to an expensive digital recorder that accepted up to sixteen simultaneous inputs. Each input wrote directly to a hard drive. They could then be downloaded to DVDs.

It took Lance three hours to hook everything up and get it totally hidden.

He wasn't too worried about the lawyer dropping by since he'd be rubbing elbows with the cops all day and playing the role of the concerned husband desperately trying to get his poor wife back.

When he was done the whole system was invisible.

And operated in total silence, being digital.

He checked it meticulously to be absolutely sure it operated perfectly and then got out of there. Tashna Sharapova never regained consciousness or saw him. Not that it would make any difference in any event.

She'd be dead by midnight.

WHEN LUNDEEN GOT HOME, Del Rae jumped up and wrapped her legs around his hips. He cupped her ass and pulled her tight.

"He just called me," she said. "He's going to do it tonight."

"So it's a definite go?"

"A hundred percent definite," she said. "He wants me to be there with him, though."

Lance chewed on it.

Not sure if he'd let her.

"I think I need to be there," she said. "I don't want to do anything to give him second thoughts."

Lance frowned.

And realized she was right.

"Okay, but two things," he said. "First, be sure you don't participate in any way, shape or form. If he uses a gun, don't load it for him or hand it to him or do anything stupid like that."

"He's going to slit her throat," she said.

"He is?"

She nodded.

"With a box cutter," she said. "You can get them at any hardware store and they're easy to get rid of."

"You didn't buy it for him, did you?"

"No."

"Okay," he said. "Just be sure you don't touch it."

"I won't."

He kissed her.

"What's the second thing?" she asked.

"What do you mean?"

"You said *two things.*"

"Oh, right," he said. "The second thing is this—we only

have cameras set up inside the house, not outside. Be sure he kills her in the house. My guess is he'll do it in the bedroom right where she already is. That's where I put the most cameras so encourage that. And here's the third thing."

She smiled.

"You said two things."

He chuckled.

"I'm giving you a third one at no extra charge," he said. "Don't be in the room when he does it. I don't want the camera picking you up."

"Right."

"I'm serious," he said. "That's important. I can probably edit you out later if I have to, but I'd rather not have to find out. Plus, if I have to edit you out later, he's going to figure out why."

He paused.

"And here's the fourth thing," he said.

"Fourth?"

"We need light for the cameras," he said. "Be sure either you or him brings a flashlight. If he does it after dark, be sure you get it lit up. You don't need to point it directly in his face or anything like that. The cameras are sensitive but they're not miracle workers."

"Got you. What are you going to be doing while all this is going down?"

He carried her to the mattress, set her down on her back and straddled her.

"What am I going to be doing?" he repeated. "I'm going to be getting two women out of my life once and for all."

Chapter Fifty-Eight

Day Eight—May 12
Monday Afternoon

A FULL DAY OF LAW SCHOOL made Kayla Beck stronger. The learning added value to her life and kept her momentum moving in the right direction. It brought her one step closer to her long-term goals and helped put all this other stuff in perspective. Also, this morning she learned something about herself—she wasn't the running kind.

No Greyhound buses for her.

Aspen was right.

Things were getting close to the end.

Kayla had the strength.

She knew that now.

When her last class ended at 3:30, she drove down to Colfax and picked up her new Taurus .357Mag revolver, together with five boxes of ammunition. The weapon brought mixed emotions.

It could save her.

Or doom her.

The secret was to use it if she needed to and not use it if she didn't.

She set the gun on the seat, wound over to the 6th Avenue freeway and headed west with the sun in her eyes and the radio turned to a country-western station playing an old Shania Twain song, "That Don't Impress Me Much." Traffic got thick and moved slowly.

Normally she hated rush hour.

For wasting her life.

But today it didn't grate her. Instead, it felt more like a protective barrier where she couldn't be hurt. She set the gun on her lap, feeling its weight, getting strength from it. She needed to shoot it and get comfortable with its action. And get her marksmanship back up to where it was in high school.

She called Aspen.

No answer.

SHE HOPED TO FIND ASPEN AT THE HOTEL. Instead, the room was empty and lifeless. Aspen's knife and one pair of Bushnell binoculars were gone.

Not good.

The woman shouldn't be screwing around with anything too deep on her own. If they'd learned anything in the last week or so, it was that.

Kayla called her again.

No answer again.

Come on.

Déjà vu.

She left a message, loaded the gun and set it on the toilet. Then she got the shower to temperature and stepped inside. It felt good but didn't relax her. When she stepped out, Aspen still wasn't there.

Kayla called her again.

No answer.

Maybe Aspen's battery died.

KAYLA OPENED HER BOOKS and tried to get a jump on her assignments, absorbing only half of what she should, but not knowing what else to do. Then she drove to Wendy's, bought two combos and brought them back to the hotel room.

Aspen still hadn't shown up.

And still didn't answer her phone.

Kayla turned on the TV and paced, gun in hand, while her imagination made up horrible little scenarios with Aspen as the star player.

When the streetlights kicked on and Aspen still hadn't shown up, Kayla stepped into the night and headed for her car.

Chapter Fifty-Nine

Day Eight—May 12
Monday Morning

IN THE HEART OF DENVER'S FINANCIAL DISTRICT, Bryson
Coventry walked through the five-story lobby of an office building, holding a half-empty disposable cup of coffee in his left
hand. Car-sized pieces of modern art stuck on the walls as if
thrown there at high speed. At the elevator banks he groaned.
Lots of business types already waited there, carrying leather
briefcases, getting ready to pack it in and face the front.

Naturally.

He wasn't in the mood to be a sardine.

Or breathe other people's fumes.

So he headed over to the stairwell and walked up. The first
fifteen floors were tolerable. Then his legs caught on fire. By the
20th Floor, elevators didn't seem like such a bad idea. By the 25th
Floor, they seemed like a miracle invention. Finally he arrived at
the 27th Floor, which was the lowest of the three floors that
housed the law firm of Davis, Holland & Owens, P.C.

He walked into the reception area and stopped in his tracks.

Shocked.

No less than ten original Edgar Payne oils hung on the walls. He'd seen the man's work in magazines but had never been in the presence of an original.

The receptionist, a cute redhead, looked at him.

He knew he should walk over.

But instead he headed to the nearest piece, a California seascape laid with a loose, impressionistic brush. Then he looked in her direction and said, "Edgar Payne."

"Glad to meet you," she said.

"No. I'm not Edgar Payne. These paintings are by Edgar Payne."

"Oh."

"This one alone is worth more than my house," he added.

She looked doubtful but said, "They're sort of cool."

Sort of cool.

Well put.

Ten minutes later Coventry was escorted by a nicely dressed elderly woman to the law office of Robert Sharapova, Esq.

SHARAPOVA TURNED OUT TO BE A LOT YOUNGER than Coventry envisioned. He couldn't have been more than thirty-seven or thirty-eight, an unlikely age given the size of his corner office and his obvious stature in the firm.

He looked like he knew his way around the weight room, too.

He spent a lot of time outside, judging by his tan, maybe on the tennis court or on a sailboat. He looked too full of energy to waste time on a golf course.

His hair was thick and on the wild side.

He had a solid, square, manly face, with piercing blue eyes.

Coventry didn't know if he'd be able to take him in a fair fight. For some reason, the man reminded Coventry of a cat in the jungle.

Built for survival.

The hunter, not the hunted.

"Quite the art gallery you have going out there," Coventry said, extending his hand.

Sharapova shook it.

"My wife's," Sharapova said.

"Oh yeah?"

"Every one of them," he said.

"She's got a good eye," Coventry said. "Payne painted a lot of great pieces, but cranked out his share of duds, too. I didn't see any of those. Just out of curiosity, what are pieces like that going for these days?"

"Average? One-fifty or thereabouts," Sharapova said.

"Unbelievable."

More than a numbers-matching 1967 big block Corvette, Coventry thought, pulling up an image of the stinger and side pipes.

Sharapova motioned Coventry to a chair in front of his desk and said, "I hope you don't think I'm insensitive because I came to work. I need to be in familiar settings, otherwise I'll go nuts."

Coventry understood.

"I want you to know how much I appreciate you coming down here," Sharapova said. Then he put a serious tone in his voice. "Tell me where we're at."

COVENTRY HAD ALREADY TOLD HIM SOME OF THE BASICS last night but now laid in the details. A woman named Rain St.

John disappeared first, abducted from Bannock Street. She showed up unconscious in the car of Tracy Patterson, who subsequently showed up in Tashna's BMW. Both had been raped.

"So if the guy stays true to form, Tashna will turn up in someone else's car after he rapes her," Sharapova said.

Coventry shrugged.

"That's certainly possible," he said.

He must not have had too much sunshine in his voice because Sharapova said, "But you think otherwise."

Coventry couldn't deny it.

"We don't know enough about the guy to tell why he let the first two women live," he said. "You seem like the kind of guy who can handle the truth, so I'm going to give it to you. I've been talking to an FBI profiler by the name of Leanne Sanders about this case. In her opinion—and I agree—this guy is a lot more than just your basic sexual predator. He's a half step away from murder. This is a serious situation. We may or may not get her back alive."

Sharapova nodded in appreciation of the candor.

He walked over to the window, stared at the skyline, and then turned to Coventry.

"If it takes money—a reward or ransom, whatever—"

"I'll keep that in mind, but I don't think we're dealing with a money issue," Coventry said. "Did Tashna have any enemies?"

Sharapova answered immediately.

"No, never. Why?"

"No reason, just curious."

Sharapova pounded his fist on the desk. "I want to get my hands around this guy's neck so bad that you can't even believe it."

Coventry knew the feeling.

And told him so.

"If this guy rapes her," he added, "his dick's coming off with a chain saw. It may take some time, but it'll definitely happen, sooner or later. That's just between you and me."

Coventry studied him.

"There's one more thing," he said. "The guy has a set of rules that he gives to the women. One of the rules is that if they disobey any of the rules then they die."

The lawyer cocked his head.

"Tashna's not a tough woman," he said. "She's more of an inside person than an outside one. But I have to believe she has enough guts to do what it takes to get through this. If there are rules, and she understands that she has to obey them to survive, I think she'll find a way."

Coventry nodded.

Then gave Sharapova the bad news. "There's one more thing. Even if the woman obeys the rules, the rules say that the guy still flips a coin to determine if she lives or dies."

The shock on Sharapova's face was palpable.

The lawyer swept a pile of papers off his desk and scowled.

"So best case scenario is that she gets raped and then has a fifty-fifty chance of living?"

"We're not positive that he really flips a coin," Coventry said. "He could just be screwing with their minds. We don't know."

They talked for another ten minutes. When Coventry stood up to leave, he said, "Think positive."

"You'll keep me in the loop?"

"Absolutely."

"She doesn't deserve this," Sharapova said. "I'm going to personally hunt this guy to the ends of the earth and cut his balls off."

Chapter Sixty

Day Eight—May 12
Monday Night

AFTER DARK, DEL RAE CALLED just as Lance Lundeen got back to the loft from a five-mile run. He pulled an ice-cold bottle of Gatorade from the fridge as he answered.

"Guess where I'm at?"

He took a long swallow, draining half the bottle, and said, "Tell me."

"Sitting in a King Soopers parking lot," she said. "The lawyer's going to be here in five minutes. Then we're going to take a drive."

Lance snapped his fingers.

"Whose car you taking?"

"Mine."

He frowned. "Just remember what we talked about," he said. "The cameras need light. Stay out of the picture. Don't participate. Wear gloves so you don't leave any prints."

"I remember."

"Come over afterwards," he said. "Can you do that?"

"I think so," she said. "The lawyer will have to get back

278

home and be a worried husband."

"Good."

"He met with some homicide detective this morning named Bryson Coventry," she added. "Apparently this detective warned him that the guy who took Tashna might very well kill her and that he's way more than just a sexual predator. So the lawyer's feeling pretty good about the whole thing right now."

"Excellent."

She chuckled.

"What?" he asked.

"Nothing—just the irony that this detective actually ended up giving the lawyer a higher comfort level. I could just imagine the look on his face if he ever found out."

Lance laughed.

"Maybe we should call him from Monte Carlo some day and let him know."

AFTER DARK, LANCE LUNDEEN STEPPED into the stairwell where no one could see him—if they were watching—and slipped into black jeans and a dark blue sweatshirt. Then he silently snaked down the fire escape to ground level and skirted his way around the northern edge of the railroad yard.

The cool night air fingered its way into his clothes.

It felt good.

He hugged the shadows of the railcars, which were now nothing more than deep dark silhouettes, slightly blacker than the sky but not by much.

His feet moved with a catlike silence.

Not even remotely detectible, especially with the freeway noise blowing this way.

This was a total shot in the dark, figuratively and literally. But he needed to do it, not only for himself but for Scotty Marks. Del Rae had called the hospital from a public phone this afternoon in an attempt to get information on Scotty's condition. They wouldn't release anything to her. However, she gleamed enough to confirm that Scotty was in fact a patient, meaning he wasn't dead.

The women would pay.

Who were they?

What did they want?

Why were they stalking him?

He continued to move through the shadows. From this location, at the north edge of the yard, he couldn't see into his windows, meaning that anyone spying on him wouldn't be around here.

He cut south, to where they'd be.

The chilly night air felt healthy in his lungs.

Crisp and fresh.

RIGHT ABOUT NOW THE LAWYER WOULD BE SLITTING his wife's pretty little throat with a box cutter. It was too bad that Del Rae had to be there to witness it. Sure, she'd end up with enough money to paper the sky, but something like that could still leave a mental scar.

She was a good woman.

A perfect woman, actually.

Mature.

Stable.

Beautiful.

Not to mention that she honestly and truly loved him.

Deep down where it counted.

He slipped his left hand into his pants pocket and felt the tiny jewelry box, the box he'd been carrying around for the last three weeks. Inside that box was a flawless, 2-carat diamond in a contemporary gold setting.

He'd give it to Del Rae when the time was right.

Which would be soon.

Very soon.

Maybe even tonight.

He smiled.

Then he turned his attention back to the night, just in time to hear something swish through the air.

His head immediately exploded in colors.

And he felt blood in his ear before his body hit the ground.

He'd been hit with an object.

Hard.

Chapter Sixty-One

Day Eight—May 12
Monday Night

FROM THE HOTEL, KAYLA BECK drove to Mitch Mitchell's house first since it was so close. She didn't spot Aspen's car in any of the likely parking places. Then against her better judgment she made sure the car doors were locked and drove down the man's street.

No lights came from inside his house.

Not a one.

So she headed over to Lance Lundeen's place, with the gun on the seat next to her, fully loaded. On the way she called Aspen.

Still no answer.

Then, bingo.

On an industrial side street on the west side of the railroad yard she spotted Aspen's vehicle in the same place they'd parked before. She pulled up behind it, killed the engine, grabbed the gun and stepped into the night. The freeway noise was louder than usual.

No one was around.

Aspen's car was locked.

There wasn't much light, but there was enough that Kayla could see into Aspen's vehicle and not spot a phone.

She exhaled.

Then she headed towards the railroad yard.

No lights came from Lance Lundeen's loft.

She searched the area and called softly, but got no response. Minute after minute passed and still there was no sign of Aspen. Where was she?

Kayla doubled back to Aspen's car.

It was still there.

Aspen must have gone inside Lundeen's building.

Kayla swallowed.

Then headed in that direction.

Gripping the gun with a tight, sweaty hand.

Chapter Sixty-Two

Day Eight—May 12
Monday Night

THE RED '67 CORVETTE SAT IN THE GARAGE with the nose pointed towards the street. Bryson Coventry opened the garage door, climbed behind the wheel, popped the top of a Bud Light and sat there, staring into the night through the windshield and trying to shake the frustration of the day.

The frustration involving Tashna Sharapova.

The hunt had been unproductive.

In fact, *unproductive* was too mild.

Non-event would be closer to the truth.

He knew a few things. She was at some abandoned hideaway out in the sticks where the coyotes lived. She was drugged and chained on a mattress. She had been, or soon would be, raped. Her hair had been chopped off. She had rules to follow. The guy drove a rusty vehicle, one that sat high, most likely an SUV or a truck.

He knew one more thing, too.

She had only two days, assuming the guy stayed consistent.

And Coventry had totally wasted one of them.

He wasn't a step closer to finding her now than he was last night when he first responded to her abduction.

Not even half a step.

He took another swallow of beer just as his cell rang. He pulled it out, didn't recognize the number but answered it anyway. Rain's voice came through.

"Hey, it's me. What are you doing?"

"Sitting here alone in the dark and trying to think of a way to get brilliant."

"You want some company?"

He did.

And gave her directions.

She showed up twenty minutes later, found him in the garage and slipped into the passenger seat with a chilled bottle of white wine.

"Nice car," she said. "Yours?"

He nodded.

"Temporarily," he said. "No one ever really owns a car like this. You just save it for the next guy. Right now I'm the next guy."

She kissed him—something between *Hello* and *I'm going to screw your brains out later.*

"I'm not going to be any fun tonight," he warned. "It's been a long day."

"You mean Tashna Sharapova?"

"Right."

"No leads?"

"Not a one," he said. "I may as well have played checkers all day. It turns out there were no surveillance cameras that shined on the museum parking lot. We interviewed everyone at the board meeting and no one saw a thing. They all just got in their fancy little cars and drove home."

"She'll turn up somewhere tomorrow," Rain said.

Coventry grunted.

That's what he was afraid of.

"I'm in a total slump," he said. "I got a bunch of other cases too that are just as dead in the water."

"Which ones?"

He drained the rest of the beer and then crushed the can in his hand. "There's a law student named Marilyn Poppenberg. We found her down by some railroad tracks, bound in blue rope, with a screwdriver pounded into her ear. So far we don't have a clue."

"That's sick," Rain said.

"Unfortunately there's a lot of that going around," Coventry said. Then, of course, there was the razorblade killer—another case going nowhere—but he didn't feel like getting into it. "If you ever get taken again, just pray I'm not the one who's supposed to find you."

She squeezed his hand.

"I wouldn't want anyone else."

He thought about kissing her but his cell phone rang.

WHEN HE ANSWERED NO ONE WAS THERE. Instead the phone clunked as if it had been dropped to the ground. Then he heard a woman's voice, but it came from a distance and he couldn't make out the words.

She sounded panicked.

Scuffling sounds came through.

Then everything faded and finally stopped altogether.

"Someone's in trouble," he said.

"Who?"

He looked at the display. It said, *Private Number.*

"I don't know."

Chapter Sixty-Three

Day Eight—May 12
Monday Night

THE EXPLOSION ON THE SIDE OF HIS HEAD felt like it came from a two-by-four. That was the one and only thought that had time to enter Lance Lundeen's brain before he dropped to the ground.

He expected to pass out.

But didn't.

Then he muscled his bulk up, rubbed blood out of his eyes and ran after the dark silhouette that was escaping into the night. His arms flailed wildly and his feet pounded the ground with heavy thuds. He forced his knees higher and picked up speed.

Then he was on her.

He had her on the ground.

And pounded her in the head again and again.

Until she stopped moving.

He didn't know if he'd killed her or not.

And didn't care.

He stood over her and put a hand to his head. The wound

288

was deep. He'd need stitches. But if it was going to kill him it would have done it by now. He reached down, pulled the woman up by her hair, flung her over his shoulder and carried her limp body back to the building.

He took her to the mechanical room on the ground floor, where they'd be away from prying eyes, and examined her enough to ascertain that she was alive and that she was the same woman who'd bashed him in the head with the beer bottle.

The one who'd been stalking him.

The one who screwed up Scotty Marks.

He slammed the door shut, locked it from the outside and then took the elevator up to the loft. He kept the main lights off, just in case anyone else happened to be out there watching, and then showered the blood off.

Déjà vu.

In the stairwell he examined the wound, using a flashlight and hand mirror. It was a three-inch gash on the side of his head, where it would be insanely tough to stitch. It still bled but not as much, thanks to the pressure he'd been applying. For a heartbeat he thought about stitching it up himself but couldn't figure out how he'd do it and decided to wait for Del Rae.

He set the mirror on a step and walked down to the mechanical room to see if the woman had woken up yet.

SHE LAID THERE, A LIMP RAGGEDY ANN DOLL, still unconscious. He got a wet towel and dabbed the dirt and blood off her face. Her lip had a good-sized cut but wasn't bleeding.

A search of her pockets turned up no wallet or identification, only a set of car keys.

He stripped her clothes off.

Just so she'd be even more freaked out when she woke.

Then he locked the door behind him and headed outside into the dark with her car keys in hand. She must have parked somewhere on the west side of the railroad yard. No doubt her purse was in the vehicle. Inside it he'd find all the information he needed.

He had to be careful, though, and not leave any blood DNA in her car, just in case he decided later that he needed to kill her.

After a long search he finally spotted a car where there shouldn't be one—two cars, in fact. He inched his way over, staying in the thick of the shadows.

He stopped about thirty yards short.

Good thing, too.

He spotted someone sitting behind the wheel of the second car.

A woman.

No doubt the same woman he captured before.

The one who stabbed him in the back with a pencil.

Good.

Perfect.

This was his chance to return the favor.

What was the best way to capture her?

No doubt she was waiting for her buddy to show up. The big question is whether she had the car doors locked. Assume she does. He retreated farther into the shadows and looked around for something to smash the window with, finally finding a steel pole about five feet long.

Then he circled around so he could sneak up on her from behind.

The freeway noise blew in.

Masking all his little sounds.

He worked his way through the dark with a racing heart until he got right up to the back of the car. He crouched there, swallowed hard, and then got in position to lunge.

He would smash the window.

Then grab her by the hair before she could turn the ignition.

Chapter Sixty-Four

Day Eight—May 12
Monday Night

KAYLA BECK SAT BEHIND THE STEERING WHEEL of the rental in the middle of a dark world with the gun in her lap, wondering what to do next. As far as she could tell, Aspen hadn't entered the building. The window by the fire escape, where they slipped in last time, was now locked shut. Nor had she found any other means of entry. Plus, even if Aspen had found a way in, she would have gotten out of there long before now.

So where was she?

Then it dawned on her.

Aspen must be on the east side of the building. She parked over here by the railroad yard to look in his windows but Lundeen wasn't home. So she headed over to the other side of the building to check him out when he came back.

Kayla cranked over the engine, put the car in reverse and almost stomped on the gas before she acknowledged that the pressure building up in her bladder had suddenly reached critical mass. She shifted the car back into park, left the engine running and stepped into the night.

Carrying the gun.

Not needing it.

But liking the feel.

She almost squatted down right next to the rear wheel but then detected a slight rustle behind the car, no doubt a mouse or something, and headed over to an even darker area across the street.

She relieved herself.

There.

Much better.

She got back into the vehicle and drove over to the east side of the building.

She parked in a remote spot, probably farther away than she needed to, but not wanting to take any chances. She doubled back on foot, expecting to find Aspen behind the dumpster.

Or the electrical shed.

But she wasn't there.

Or anywhere else for that matter.

Kayla started to hoof it back to the rental when headlights suddenly appeared. She scurried into the shadows barely in time to avoid detection. The vehicle passed her and pulled up to the base of Lance Lundeen's building. The headlights died and a dark figure stepped out—a large figure with a mane of hair, unmistakably Lundeen. A minute later the garage door opened, the vehicle pulled in and the door closed.

Kayla watched the building for a few minutes, didn't detect anything of interest, and then worked her way back to the rental. She drove back over to Aspen's car on the west side of the railroad yard.

Strange.

Very strange.

Aspen's vehicle wasn't there anymore.

Kayla parked on the side of the road and dialed Aspen's phone.

No answer.

Aspen must have gone back to the hotel.

Kayla headed that way.

When she arrived, the room was dark and empty. Aspen wasn't there and didn't show up during the next half hour as Kayla paced back and forth in front of the TV. She must have left Lundeen's to stake out Mitch Mitchell.

Why would she be doing all this on her own? Was she trying to protect Kayla from the danger?

Well screw that.

They were a team.

They were in this together.

All the way.

Kayla stormed out of the hotel, got back in her car, slammed the door and squealed out of the parking lot.

Heading to Mitch Mitchell's house.

Chapter Sixty-Five

BRYSON COVENTRY DIDN'T HANG UP. Instead he kept the cell phone connection alive, on the off chance that the caller's phone would pick up sounds that might tell him where the call came from—traffic or airplanes or whatever.

He half expected to hear coyotes.

Meaning the call had come from Tashna Sharapova. But how could she possibly have his cell phone number?

She couldn't.

But her captor could.

Maybe he'd placed the call, just to rub the whole thing in Coventry's face. He told Rain, "Be right back," and then stepped into the house, pulled a fresh beer from the fridge, and called Shalifa Netherwood and Kate Katona from his house phone to see if they were okay.

They were.

When he got back to the Corvette he was surprised how good it felt to have Rain waiting for him. So far he hadn't shown her much of a good time but she didn't seem antsy or on the verge of leaving. She appeared to be content to be around him.

Very nice.

They stared out the windshield into the night and talked. Humidity crept into the air and a deep thunder crackled over the mountains, rolling this way.

It turned out that Rain had a sister named Dawn who needed a kidney transplant. She was on a list but needed to come up with $250,000 cash to actually get the operation. Rain was saving up to help her.

That explained the $50,000 he found in her closet.

He checked the battery of his cell phone to be sure it wasn't about to die. It was two-third's full; good enough for the time being.

Every minute or so he put the phone to his ear and concentrated.

So far no sounds came through.

Not a one.

Then the weather moved in; just a drizzle at first, followed by a heavy rain that pounded straight down.

"So have you christened this thing properly, yet?" Rain asked, referring to the car.

Coventry had a pretty good idea what she was talking about, but wasn't positive.

"You mean the back seat?"

She put her hand on his crotch and rubbed. "What do you think I mean?"

He chuckled.

"It's too small," he said.

She stepped out of the car and got into the back.

"Let's find out," she said.

Coventry considered it. It would be tight but not impossible. Apparently she wasn't about to take no for an answer because her pants and thong were already coming off.

"Come on," she said. "I want you to think of me every time you get in here."

He climbed back.

She straddled him.

Then she rocked back and forth, slowly at first, but with an ever-increasing tempo. Her breathing grew deeper and deeper as she worked herself into more and more of an animal frenzy. Then she flung her head wildly and made a sound that Coventry had never heard before. She continued gyrating for another minute and then collapsed on his chest.

"Yeah," she said.

Coventry agreed.

And held her tight to prove it.

SUDDENLY THEY WERE BOTH STARVED and headed for the kitchen. On the way, Coventry put the cell phone to his ear. The line had gone dead.

He pictured the other phone sitting in a puddle of water.

Killed by the storm.

Meaning the call had come from an outside location.

The phone had still been working when the storm first reached Coventry's house. That meant that the call originated from somewhere east of here. Because that's the direction the storm was moving.

And not just east, but east and close.

Because the storm had reached it at some point in the last fifteen minutes.

Chapter Sixty-Six

Day Eight—May 12
Monday Night

AFTER LANCE LUNDEEN GOT THE WOMAN'S CAR hidden safely inside his garage, he grabbed her purse and the papers from her glove box and carried them into the stairwell where no one would see him. There he shined a flashlight on them.

Inside the purse he found cash.

Lots of cash.

Almost five thousand dollars according to a quick count.

Plus a number of platinum credit cards.

The woman certainly wasn't hurting for money.

She turned out to be someone named Nicole Aspen White from Santa Fe. He didn't recognize the name and had never been to Santa Fe. In fact, he didn't even know anyone from there.

Now he knew some stuff, but not nearly as much as he needed. He still had no clue why she was stalking him. Or who her friend was, the one he almost snatched earlier this evening until she stepped out of her car to piss—holding a gun.

The lucky little thing.

HE STUFFED THE MONEY IN HIS POCKET.

Then he left the purse and papers where they were and headed for the mechanical room. The woman was still unconscious. He carried her up to the loft, kept the lights off, set up a tri-fold screen so she'd be hidden from any prying eyes that might come from the outside, and laid her face down on the floor.

He tied her wrists together behind her back.

Then tied her ankles together.

Then looped her wrists to her ankles with a third rope.

A classic hogtie position.

Throughout it all she didn't move a muscle or open her eyes. The gash on his head bled again from all the movement and strain. He stepped back into the shower, washed the blood out of his hair, and then sat on the floor and applied pressure to the wound with a warm, wet towel.

For what seemed like a long time.

He wondered why Del Rae hadn't called yet.

Strange.

She should have.

When the bleeding stopped he eased down onto the mattress and closed his eyes. Almost immediately the world disappeared.

THE NEXT THING HE KNEW, THE WOMAN GROANED and pulled him out of a pitch-black sleep. His head throbbed and he instinctively put his hand to it. The wound must have opened again because dried blood caked his hair.

Lots of blood.

Maybe the injury was more serious than he thought.

He muscled his bulk off the mattress, walked over to the bathroom naked and took a piss.

Then he headed over to the woman and shined a flashlight in her face.

She looked at him.

Defiantly.

So he pulled her hands to the side and slapped her ass as hard as he could and said, "That's for the two-by-four." When she screamed he said, "Shut up or I'll gag you."

She must have sensed seriousness in his voice.

Because she immediately grew silent.

He slapped her again.

Even harder this time.

She gasped but said nothing.

"Now, *Nicole Aspen White*, you're going to tell me what you're up to and I'm going to decide whether you live or die."

Before he could say anything else the phone rang.

Probably Del Rae.

No doubt to tell him that the lawyer had killed his wife exactly as planned and that she'd be over in a half hour to screw his brains out.

He answered.

The voice that came through had so much stress laced in it that it took him a moment to process the fact that it actually was Del Rae.

"We got problems," she said. "Big problems."

Chapter Sixty-Seven

Day Eight—May 12
Monday Night

TWO MINUTES AFTER KAYLA BECK GOT IN THE CAR, black rain fell out of a mean sky. She turned on the wipers, an automatic reaction, and drove to the service road for the rock quarry on the west side of Mitch Mitchell's neighborhood, where she and Aspen parked before.

Aspen's car wasn't there.

She smacked her hand on the dash.

Now what?

She killed the lights, then the engine, and sat behind the wheel thinking, while a heavy sky pummeled the roof. She pulled her phone out to call Aspen for the umpteenth time.

But got no signal.

No doubt because of the storm.

Come on.

Where are you?

She closed her eyes and listened to the weather, with the weight of the day suddenly pressing down. Then she realized something. She'd run out of the hotel room so fast that she forgot the gun. The realization forced her eyes open. What she saw she could hardly believe.

HEADLIGHTS REFLECTED FROM THE REARVIEW MIRROR into her face.

She turned her head.

A car approached from behind, jerking with twitchy motions on the bumpy gravel road. She looked ahead, at the quarry, to see if there were any signs of life.

There weren't.

Nor should there be.

No one mined at night.

What to do?

She cranked over the starter and the engine fired up. She wanted to leave the headlights off but the world was too black for that. She turned them on and floored it.

The car behind her sped up.

She swallowed.

She hoped that a light-bar would turn on, meaning the car was a cop simply checking out a suspicious vehicle. She'd have a story ready by the time he got to her. But no light-bar appeared. Nor would the car be kids looking for a place to party. They'd avoid other cars, not chase them.

It had to be Mitchell.

He or his neighbor must have been keeping an eye on the area—waiting for them to show back up. She shouldn't have stopped once she found out that Aspen's car wasn't here. She should have immediately turned around and left.

Lightning flashed.

All this was because she was just too stupid for her own

good.

The other car closed in.

She sped up.

The tires slipped in the mud and gravel, on the edge of a spinout. But she kept her foot on the gas. It did no good. The other car reduced the gap. Then she remembered that Mitchell drove a pickup, probably a four-wheel drive.

She wouldn't stand a chance.

How could she be so stupid to forget the gun?

The quarry loomed in front of her.

A lightning bolt ripped across the sky, illuminating large pyramids of gravel and several giant front-end loaders. The other car was right on her tail now.

Then it rammed her.

The back end of her vehicle spun around, slammed into a deep waterhole with a giant splash, and jerked to a violent stop. When she floored the gas pedal the wheels spun and threw water but got no bite.

She put it in reverse and floored it.

Still no traction.

Not even close.

The other vehicle slid to a stop.

She opened the door and ran.

Chapter Sixty-Eight

Day Nine—May 13
Tuesday Morning

BRYSON COVENTRY PULLED HIMSELF OUT OF BED at 5:00 a.m. on Tuesday morning, intent on squeezing every possible hour out of the day in hopes of getting to Tashna Sharapova before it was too late. He showered downstairs so he wouldn't wake Rain, gave her a soft kiss while she slept and then put a note on the kitchen table officially reserving her for tonight.

When he got to headquarters the lights were already on.

More important, the coffee pot was full.

Nice.

Very nice.

He poured a cup as Shalifa Netherwood walked into the room and set a white bag next to the pot.

"Are those donuts?" he asked.

She pulled one out and took a bite.

White cake with chocolate frosting.

His absolute, all-time favorite.

"No, they're these new miniature salads," she said. "Very good for you."

"Well, I better have one then," he said. "You know what a health freak I am."

"Yes I do."

He took a bite.

Delicious.

"Best salad I ever tasted," he said. "I'm going to marry you some day. I hope you know that."

She rolled her eyes.

"I'll take that as a threat."

"Thanks for being here," he said. "I really appreciate it."

"I had a feeling you'd be in early."

He frowned.

True, he was there early, but not because he was busting with brilliant ideas.

Or even non-brilliant ones.

HE FILLED HER IN WITH ALL THE DETAILS about the mysterious phone call last night and she agreed to run it to ground, just in case it was somehow connected to Tashna Sharapova. She got busy working the phone and fax and a short time later handed him a piece of paper with a phone number and said, "The call came from Nicole Aspen White."

Coventry looked at the phone number and recognized it as Aspen's.

"Are you sure?"

She was and asked, "Is that your Aspen?"

Coventry nodded and said, "I didn't know her first name was Nicole."

"I like Aspen better," Shalifa said.

Coventry did too.

"She might not have been in trouble," Shalifa said. "She might have been pissed because you blew her off for Rain St. John."

Coventry raised an eyebrow.

"You think? I don't follow."

"She may have just called you and then threw the phone on the ground and walked away; something in the nature of a statement, if you will."

He pictured it and grunted.

"See," he said. "That just supports my theory that guys can never win. No matter what we do, we lose."

Then he called Aspen.

Her phone didn't respond.

"Do me a favor and see if we have the phone number of her friend anywhere in the file, that law student. What was her name?"

"Kayla something."

"Right, Kayla Beck, the one with the Mustang. See if she knows where Aspen is and if she's okay," he said. "If you can't find her number have someone drop by her apartment." He pulled another donut from the bag and took a bite. "Oh," he said, "one more thing. See if Aspen's phone company can get us an approximate location of the call. They should know what tower picked up her signal. I'm guessing it was in Lakewood or western Denver."

She raised an eyebrow.

"Why do you say that?"

He told her about his storm-killed-the-phone theory.

She said, "So, you're face down in a mud puddle right now."

He nodded.

"If I'm right."

"What does that tell you?"

He grunted.

SHORTLY AFTER EIGHT O'CLOCK Robert Sharapova called and wanted to know if Coventry had any new leads. "No, I wish I did but I don't," Coventry admitted.

"Let's get a reward out for information," the lawyer said. "Not ransom money for her return, but money for information that leads to her return. Maybe someone knows where the guy is and will rat him out."

Coventry considered it.

"Let me think about it," he said. "The problem is that every idiot in the world ends up calling and then we end up spending all our time chasing down false leads. We usually don't do something like that until down the road, when we have more time."

The lawyer hesitated.

Coventry sensed friction.

"You're the boss," the lawyer said. "Just remember I'm here to help any way I can."

Coventry thanked him, hung up and looked at Shalifa.

"That was the husband," he said. "He wants to write a check and get her back."

"How much?"

"He didn't say."

"Do it," she said.

"Why?"

"Because if you don't and she ends up dead, he has something to blame you with," she said. "I can already hear it. *If only they'd put out the reward like I told him to, blah blah blah.*"

Coventry shrugged.

"I could care less about that," he said. "He can blame me all he wants after the fact. But I don't see the reward as the best angle right now and don't have time to get sidetracked by it today. If I ever get to the point where I start molding an investigation to cover my behind instead of getting to the bottom of things, shoot me."

She laughed.

"I'm serious," he said. "Right here in the forehead."

She nodded.

"Just because you're mentioning it for the first time now doesn't mean I haven't thought of it already," she said.

He grinned.

The oversized industrial clock on the wall, the one with the twitchy second hand, said 8:18 a.m. "If the guy's going to kill her, it will be by this time tonight," Coventry said

"So what are we going to do?"

"I don't know but we better do it fast."

FIFTEEN MINUTES LATER the chief—Forrest Tanner—walked in and creased every wrinkle in his sixty-year-old face. "Put out a reward for information in the Tashna Sharapova case," he said. "Fifty thousand."

Coventry explained his theory.

The chief listened patiently and said, "I'll get you extra help to man the phones and keep you out of it unless something looks incredibly good," he said. "That way it won't get in your way and no one's head will end up rolling down the street and dropping into a gutter if the woman turns up dead."

Coventry stared at him.

"Have you ever had your head roll down the street and fall

into a gutter?" the chief asked.

"No."

"Trust me. It's no fun."

Coventry didn't really care if it was any fun or not.

Right now he could only think of Tashna Sharapova.

She wasn't having any fun.

He was pretty sure of that.

HE POURED ANOTHER CUP OF COFFEE and then flopped down into his chair.

Then it came to him.

Something he hadn't thought of before.

He grabbed Shalifa's arm.

"Come on," he said.

Ten seconds later they were halfway down the hall.

"Hold it" Coventry said, turning around. In two heartbeats he returned with a donut and fresh cup of coffee. "Okay, let's go."

Chapter Sixty-Nine

Day Nine—May 13
Tuesday Morning

WHEN DEL RAE FINALLY SHOWED UP, it was four in the morning and she looked like she'd been dragged around by the storm all night. Her hair was tangled and matted, her makeup was long gone, and her clothes were wrinkled. The cuffs of her jeans were caked with mud.

Lance Lundeen put her in a bear hug and pulled her tight.

"What happened?"

"In a minute," she said. "Fix me a drink first."

By the time Lance got the rum and coke out, Del Rae had already stripped and turned on the shower. He brought the drink over as she felt the temperature of the water and handed it to her as she stepped into the spray. She downed it in one long swallow, said "Another one, please."

Lance cocked his head.

"Well someone had quite the night," he said.

"You're not even going to believe it."

Five minutes later she stepped out, toweled off and slipped into one of Lance's long-sleeve shirts. Her hair hung wet, soaking the cotton wherever it touched.

They ended up sitting on the mattress in the dark, she with another rum and coke in hand, he with a beer.

"Better?" Lance asked.

She nodded and took a sip.

"So what happened?"

"Coyotes," she said.

He wrinkled his forehead.

"Coyotes?"

"Yeah, they look like dogs except they live in the wild."

He knew it was a joke and he was supposed to laugh but he couldn't. He needed to know what happened and how much trouble they were in.

Then she told him the story.

EVERYTHING WAS GOING GOOD RIGHT UNTIL THE END. She was driving and the lawyer was in the passenger seat. They were heading to the abandoned house with the radio off. The lawyer twisted the box cutter in his hands, anxious to get it over with. The wipers were on full speed, fighting a heavy storm that had pounded them for the last twenty minutes. They made it all the way to the dead-end road and were halfway down it, not more than a mile from the hideaway, when it happened.

A small deer ran out in front of them.

Approaching from the left.

A baby deer.

Probably not more than a week or two old.

Del Rae knew better than to jerk the wheel or slam on the brakes. She slowed as much as she could without losing control and by the time they got to the animal it was almost across the road.

She veered to the left.

Just to be absolutely sure she didn't clip it.

Suddenly a pack of coyotes ran directly in front of her.

Chasing the deer.

There must have been six or seven of them.

She hit a bunch of them.

Maybe all of them.

"You wouldn't think it, but it was like running into a brick wall," she said. "One jumped right before we got to it and ended up coming straight into the windshield, shattering it. The others didn't jump and got caught by the front end. The radiator ended up punctured and we were dead in the water."

"Ouch."

"With no ride out, the lawyer wasn't about to slit anyone's throat, and I don't blame him," she said. "The big problem we had at that point was getting the car out of there before daybreak. I didn't want to call a tow truck company from the area because they might put two and two together after Tashna's body eventually gets found. So I called one from Golden. Sharapova removed the plates before the guy showed up. Then I had it towed to my house. That took forever."

Lundeen shook his head.

"Of course it rained like a bastard the whole time," she added.

"Of course."

"Then we had another problem, namely that we couldn't let the tow truck driver see Sharapova, since his face would eventually be on the news mourning for his wife," she said. "He can't be connected with that area in any way, shape or form. So he hid while the car was getting hooked up and waited there for over two hours. Then I had to drive back out with my other car and pick him up."

Lance was impressed.

"You handled it good," he said.

She shrugged.

"Anyway, we're back on schedule for tonight."

"So he's still holding the course?"

"More than ever," she said. "On the way back I let him drive and gave him the blowjob of the century, just to be sure he didn't start having second thoughts."

Lance detected a hesitation in her voice.

"What?" he asked.

She held his hand.

"I called the hospital again this afternoon," she said. "Scotty Marks died. I didn't want to tell you over the phone."

Lance swallowed what was left in the can and crushed it in his hand.

His thoughts turned to Nicole Aspen White.

Chapter Seventy

Day Nine—May 13
Tuesday Morning

KAYLA BECK DIDN'T GET BACK TO THE HOTEL until two in the morning but was more than content just to get back at all. She felt and looked like a drowned rat—an exhausted drowned rat, so exhausted that she fell asleep as soon as her body dropped on the bed. She didn't move a muscle until the first rays of light crept into the room. Then she sat bolt upright and looked at the clock. She hadn't gotten more than a few hours sleep but that would have to do. She'd rest in her next life.

Aspen's side of the bed was empty.

Kayla muscled to a standing position, rubbed her eyes as she walked to the window, pulled the curtain back and peeked out.

Aspen's car wasn't in the parking lot.

She took a quick shower, threw on jeans and a T-shirt and headed out into the world on foot.

Walking north.

Towards the rock quarry.

IN HINDSIGHT, SHE HANDLED LAST NIGHT remarkably well. When her vehicle got stuck and she ran into the storm, she made the fatal mistake of forgetting to grab her purse. Luckily Mitch Mitchell had been too stupid or too adrenalin-filled to check her car before chasing her. Instead he got right on her tail so he wouldn't lose her in the dark.

He was a fast little freak.

She had to give him that.

It took a full half mile but she finally got far enough ahead to lose him in the dark. Then she doubled back and grabbed her purse and cell phone. A flash of brilliance told her to check his truck.

The door was unlocked.

The keys were in the ignition.

She fired it up, slammed it into drive and got out of there. A half hour later she parked it at a bus stop on the edge of Denver where it would be sure to get towed. She threw the keys down a gutter, took a bus back to Golden and then hiked the remaining mile to the hotel.

All in the rain.

No, not rain—*storm*.

Her biggest worry was that Mitchell had been smart enough to write down her license plate number and would trace it.

Anyway, that was last night.

Now it was morning.

SHE HEARD THE RUMBLE OF THE MINING OPERATIONS a full half mile away. As the amount of gravel in the road diminished, her shoes got more and more caked with mud. By the time the front-end loaders and fabricated buildings came into view, she was a mess.

She got to where she thought her car should be but didn't see it. Then she spotted it next to a metal building. Someone must have pulled it out this morning so it wouldn't be in the way.

Ouch.

Even from here she could tell it was trashed.

The freak must have taken a rock or stick or iron bar or something to it after Kayla took off in his truck.

Every window was shattered.

A red pickup truck came out of nowhere and pulled alongside her, slowing down so it wouldn't throw mud. A window opened and the tanned, leathery face of a man in his fifties appeared. "It looks like one of us is lost. And it's probably not me since I've worked here for ten years," he said.

She felt the corner of her mouth turn up ever so slightly.

"Then it must be me," she said.

"That'd be my guess."

"That's my car over there," she said, pointing.

"Hop in."

On the way she told him the story. She and her boyfriend drank a little too much last night and went down the wrong road and somehow ended up here. They got stuck in the mud and had a fight. She took off on foot. It looks like he trashed the car after she left.

"Dump him," the man said.

"That might be good advice," she said.

"Trust me, it is."

Luckily the vehicle was still drivable. She offered him twenty dollars for whoever it was that pulled it out of the mud this morning. He declined.

HER CELL PHONE RANG as she parked the car and walked into the hotel room. She answered it as fast as she could, hoping against hope it was Aspen.

It wasn't.

It was the man with the scrambler.

"You've been a bad girl," he said.

She hung up and threw the phone against the wall.

FIVE MINUTES LATER IT RANG AGAIN—surprisingly unbroken. She almost ripped it in two but answered instead.

A man's voice came through.

Not scrambled this time.

"Do you know who this is?"

She recognized the voice but couldn't place it.

"Are you the one who just called?"

"Just called? No—"

Suddenly she recognized the voice.

"Lance Lundeen," she said.

"Very good," Lundeen said. "Now listen carefully because what you say and do are going to tell whether things go very good, or very bad, for your pretty little friend."

Chapter Seventy-One

Day Nine—May 13
Tuesday Morning

BRYSON COVENTRY AND SHALIFA NETHERWOOD got the two live victims—Rain St. John and Tracy Patterson—in the same room and had them go over their captures, hoping they'd feed off each other and collectively remember something they hadn't told him before. Coventry didn't want much; just a scraggly little piece of information, one more seemingly irrelevant piece of the puzzle, no matter how small.

But he didn't even get that.

And found himself back at square one.

Mid-morning Shalifa Netherwood strolled over, eased into a chair and propped her feet on his desk. "Aspen White's phone company just got back to me," she said. "They were able to identify the location where she made the call to you last night and gave me some GPS coordinates. They said the call probably originated from within a hundred yards of there. Apparently it's not too far from here, on the west edge of Denver near the Lakewood border."

Coventry nodded and processed the information.

Tashna Sharapova was the top priority today.

He didn't need a distraction.

But Aspen White still didn't answer her phone.

And he had no idea what to do next on the Sharapova matter.

The need for motion and activity washed over him. He stood up and said, "Let's go find that phone."

Shalifa got up and fell into step.

THEY WALKED PAST THE ELEVATORS and hiked down the stairwell three floors to the parking garage, then wove through the streets with the slow version of "Hotel California" on the radio. They ended up on the west edge of the city where they entered a frayed industrial zone.

Fifteen miles to the west, clouds were already building over the mountains.

"More rain coming," Coventry said.

Shalifa looked at him. "I'll take your word for it, now that you're a professional at being in the middle of the rain."

Coventry chuckled.

Pretty sure what she was referring to.

"You're not speaking of rain as in rain the weather, are you?"

"No."

"You're speaking of rain as in Rain the person."

She nodded.

"Very good."

"And by *the middle of the rain*, you're referring to—"

"—right, you being in the center of the storm, so to speak."

He chuckled.

Then cocked his head.

"What do you think of her? Do you like her, or what?"

"You're asking the wrong person."

"Why?"

"She's too gorgeous," Shalifa said. "Women like me don't like to be in the same room as women like her. We feel like Raggedy Ann dolls."

"Give me a break."

"I'm serious."

"Are you fishing for a compliment?"

She grinned. "Maybe—why?—you got one?"

"I might have a spare one sitting around somewhere. But I'm not going to give it to you because it wouldn't mean anything after you fished for it."

"Just out of curiosity, what would it be, if I hadn't fished for it?"

"It would be something like, *You can hold your own in any room, no matter who else is in there—including Rain.*"

She smiled.

"Sorry I missed that one."

"Next time don't fish for it," he said. "Just wait for it to jump out of the water and land in the boat."

WHEN THE GPS LED THEM TO A RAILROAD YARD, Coventry felt a knot in his stomach. The razorblade killer—the one Dr. Leanne Sanders wanted so badly—put his latest victim in a boxcar. Then there was Marilyn Poppenberg, the law student, found dead next to railroad tracks down by Santa Fe Boulevard, bound in blue rope with a screwdriver in her ear.

Now this.

Trains.

Trains.

Trains.

They parked as close to the yard as they could and then headed over on foot.

"I got a bad feeling," Coventry said.

"Meaning what?"

"Meaning I'm not going to be too surprised if we find more than her phone."

"Meaning what? Her body?"

He nodded.

It took over an hour, but they finally found Aspen White's cell phone, buried in a puddle of water. Coventry put on gloves, picked it up by the antenna and placed it in an evidence bag. Then he stuck a pen in the ground to mark the spot.

Weird.

They were surrounded by tracks and cars.

"What would Aspen be doing around here?" he asked.

Shalifa cocked her head.

"Nothing," she said. "Someone must have forced her here."

Coventry couldn't disagree.

And frowned.

"Okay," he said. "We need to get as many people as we can down here and start searching for her. Can you get that in motion?"

"Are you serious?"

He was.

Dead serious.

Then he turned and walked down the tracks.

"Where are you going?" she shouted.

"To find the yardmaster," he hollered back. "I don't want any cars leaving this place until we look inside."

"They're not going to like that," she said.

"Too bad, because I don't really care."

AS COVENTRY HIKED UP THE TRACKS, his phone rang and the voice of Dr. Leanne Sanders came through. "Remember before, when I said there were a couple of those Mustang owners who I interviewed and wouldn't mind knowing more about, if I had unlimited time and money?"

He remembered.

"Well, I found a little spare time and threw it their way," she said. "One of those guys is starting to get very interesting. A guy named Todd Underdown. I'm heading to Denver to dig deeper and thought you deserved a warning."

"Good, because I have all kinds of stuff I need to bounce off you. Are you going to stay at my place?"

"That depends," she said. "Do you have a squeeze hanging around?"

"Well, sort of, I suppose."

Leanne chuckled.

"In that case I'll pass," she said. "I can't sleep when you have someone screaming."

He laughed.

"She's not a screamer," he said.

"Give me a break, Coventry," she said. "With you they're all screamers."

COVENTRY TOLD HER ABOUT THE LATEST DEVELOPMENT involving Aspen White and the search they were about to undertake.

"Another tie to trains," he noted.

"So I see."

"Meaning an awful lot of coincidences or a connection," he said.

"I agree," she said. "And here's a juicy little fact you might be interested in. Todd Underdown was a switcher for Burlington Northern for ten years."

Coventry raked his hair back with his fingers.

"Is he still?"

"No. That was up in Cheyenne. He flunked one too many drug tests, got fired, and moved to Denver about six months ago."

Chapter Seventy-Two

Day Nine—May 13
Tuesday Morning

LANCE LUNDEEN WOKE AT 10:00 A.M. on Tuesday morning feeling like a new man. Good thing, too, because today would be critical on a number of fronts and he needed to be at his absolute best. He washed the sleep out of his eyes, brushed his teeth, slipped into his jogging shorts and stepped outside, shirtless.

A cloudless blue Colorado sky floated overhead.

He tossed his hair to the side and pointed his face to the sun.

The rays landed hot and bright.

Nice.

He stretched first and then jogged around the edge of the building towards the railroad yard. Some days his body felt good. Others it felt great. This was one of those great days.

A hundred yards into the run his muscles loosened up. He picked up the pace and his lungs hardly noticed.

A total stud.

He had no idea how far he would run—maybe five miles, maybe ten. Whatever it took to get to that point where his body screamed for him to stop.

HE FELT PRETTY GOOD ABOUT LAST NIGHT. After Del Rae left, he paid a little visit to his lovely little captive—Aspen White—and didn't leave until he broke her down and got the information he wanted.

No more screwing around.

Luckily she realized that.

Because he would have killed her.

For Scotty Marks' sake if nothing else.

AS HE JOGGED FARTHER INTO THE RAILROAD YARD and swung around a string of boxcars, he could hardly believe his eyes.

Cops.

Lots of cops.

From out of nowhere a man wearing jeans and a gray sport coat intercepted him.

"Hey, buddy, this place is off limits," the man said.

It was the man himself more than the words that brought Lundeen to a stop. His first thought was that the guy could hold his own in a street fight. He had a scrapper look to him; the kind of guy who wouldn't get derailed by pain. He had an incredible face and there was something wild about his eyes. The guy reminded Lundeen a little of himself, except on a smaller scale. As tough as he looked, Lundeen could still crush him. It would take some time and Lundeen would get his fair share of pain, but the ultimate result was inescapable.

Lundeen flicked his mane and asked, "What's going on?"

"This is a crime scene," the man said. "You need to go out the same way you came in."

"A crime scene? What's going on?"

Lundeen regretted the question as soon as it left his mouth. He should have turned and disappeared. Now the man was studying him.

"You live around here, right?" the man asked.

Lundeen was impressed. The man had realized that Lundeen hadn't broken a sweat, meaning he hadn't been at it long. Another runner would notice something like that; a couch potato wouldn't. Lundeen knew better than to lie but decided to keep it vague.

"Yeah," he said, turning. "Good luck with whatever it is you're doing."

"Hold on a minute," the man said.

Lundeen stopped.

His heart raced.

"Where do you live?"

Lundeen pointed at his building and said, "There."

"There?"

"Right."

"It looks like an old abandoned warehouse or something."

Lundeen nodded.

"They made furniture there twenty years ago," he said. "I bought it for cheaper than a house."

The man looked impressed.

Then he pulled a printout of a driver's license and showed it to Lundeen.

"Have you ever seen this woman? Her name is Aspen White."

Lance took the paper and studied it.

Then shook his head.

"No. Wish I had, though. She's a hot little ticket."

The man agreed.

Then he asked, "Did you happen to notice anything suspicious around here last night by any chance?"

Lundeen paused as if giving it ample thought.

"I don't even remember looking out this way last night," he said. "I don't have any blinds or curtains, so my windows get black at night. They turn into mirrors, basically."

"You didn't hear anything?"

"Freeway noise. Why? What's going on?"

The man turned.

"Nothing. Thanks for everything," he said over his shoulder.

Chapter Seventy-Three

Day Nine—May 13
Tuesday Morning

AFTER KAYLA BECK FINISHED TALKING with Lance Lundeen and shut the phone, she couldn't breathe. It seemed that no matter how deeply she inhaled she couldn't get enough air into her lungs. She told herself that she was okay, that this was just some kind of panic attack, but nothing like this had ever happened before.

She was starting to break down.

She could feel it.

When the phone rang again she jumped and then stared at it. The hotel suddenly seemed cold and lifeless—evil, almost. She left the phone where it was, walked out the door and drove to her apartment. She entered tentatively and saw no obvious evidence of intrusion or break in.

The aroma of dried rain greeted her.

It came from the old brown couch—the one she found by the side of the curb more than a year ago and hauled over here in a friend's pickup. She inhaled deeply, getting a good whiff of the couch, and suddenly her lungs worked fine.

Air.

Sweet air.

She had a Property Law class scheduled for one o'clock this afternoon. But she wouldn't make it. That's when she would either be surrendering herself to Lance Lundeen or meeting with the police.

She didn't know which yet.

Her watch said 10:30.

Tick, tick, tick.

There was no way she'd be able to sort this all out in the next couple of hours, even if her brain cleared up enough to rationally process information.

Surprisingly she didn't worry about herself.

Her anxiety all centered on Aspen.

The woman's life was in her hands.

For some reason her thoughts fell back to that earlier conversation, when she and Aspen were talking about the fact that Aspen had saved Kayla's life twice and Kayla had only saved Aspen's once.

And that she owed Aspen one.

It had been a conversation in jest and the corner of Kayla's mouth went up just a touch as she recalled it. But now, in the witching hour, she realized that it had been much more.

She *did* owe Aspen one.

So, the big question was this—did she have a better chance of helping Aspen if she surrendered herself to Lance Lundeen or if she went to the police?

SHE HARDLY DRANK AT ALL and never in the morning, or alone. But she filled a water glass with white wine, slumped into the couch and took a long swallow.

The next few hours would be critical.

She knew she had to keep one thing in mind.

Aspen killed the drifter.

The guy in the boxcar.

She shot him in the face with Kayla's gun.

They spoke about it several times afterwards. Aspen's thoughts on the matter were unbending and consistent: the police could *never* know about that, no matter what. Aspen would rather die than go to prison.

Suddenly someone knocked on the door.

It was at that moment that she realized that everything important was back at the hotel.

The gun.

The knife.

Her first thought was to run into the bedroom and hide. But instead she peeked out the curtain and saw a man, an attractive man, wearing jeans and a sport coat.

When she opened the door the man handed her a card and said, "You're not answering your phone."

She didn't look at the card.

She didn't have to.

"You're Bryson Coventry," she said.

The man nodded. "Guilty. How do you know?"

"Aspen told me about your eyes, plus I saw you on the news," she said. "Come in."

As Coventry eased into the couch, Kayla spotted the glass of wine and pushed it behind a stack of books. Coventry's attention focused on the kitchen, as if searching for something.

"What are you looking for?"

"Nothing."

She chuckled, headed that way and pulled the coffeemaker out of a cabinet. "Aspen told me about your addiction," she said.

Coventry was impressed.

"What else did she tell you?"

Kayla frowned.

"She fell for you, you know. That first day," she said. "She's a good person, so it's your loss."

Coventry said nothing.

Then looked her in the eyes.

"She's missing. You know that, right?"

Kayla's first instinct was to lie but she didn't.

"I've had a bad feeling about her since last night," she said.

"Her cell phone records show she got a lot of calls from you last night," Coventry said. "A lot of calls that she never answered. So tell me the story. Where did she go last night? Why were you calling her every ten seconds? What happened to her?"

Over the next ten minutes Coventry told her why he thought Aspen was in trouble, and about the search being conducted at the railroad yard even as they spoke. Kayla filled Coventry full of coffee and patiently explained that she didn't know a thing, other than she and Aspen were supposed to get together last night but Aspen never showed up and didn't answer her phone.

Coventry didn't believe her.

She could see it in his eyes.

She didn't care.

She had Lance Lundeen to worry about.

WHEN COVENTRY LEFT, Kayla drove back to the hotel, but in the Mustang this time. She stuffed the gun and knife in her backpack and headed to where she was supposed to meet Lance Lundeen.

On the way her cell phone rang and Bryson Coventry's voice came through. "I forgot to ask you something," he said. "Two things, actually. Did you know Marilyn Poppenberg? She was a law student at D.U., same as you."

"Yes."

A pause on the other end.

"She got killed."

"I heard."

"I'm going to want to talk to you about her," he said. "Maybe tomorrow."

"Sure. If you think it will help."

"The other thing is this," he said. "I'm investigating the death of a drifter. He got shot in the face on the north edge of Denver, in an industrial area, almost two weeks ago. Surveillance cameras down the road picked up the image of a first-generation Ford Mustang. We thought the driver of that vehicle might have seen something. You own a 1967 Mustang. When I came to talk to you, you weren't home. But Aspen was. She said you were with her all that night. Would you agree with that statement?"

"I don't know what night you're talking about exactly," Kayla said. "But I haven't been in an industrial area for a long time. And don't know anything about a dead drifter."

"Okay," Coventry said. "Just thought I'd ask."

"No problem. Anything else?"

A pause on the other end.

She sensed that Coventry was about to say something.

Something important.

But whatever it was, he held back.

"I'll be in touch," he said. "You have my card if you need it."

FIVE MINUTES AFTER SHE HUNG UP she almost called him back.

But she didn't.

Instead she pulled the gun out of her backpack, set it on the seat where she could see it, and continued driving to the place she was supposed to meet Lance Lundeen.

Chapter Seventy-Four

Day Nine—May 13
Tuesday Morning

FROM KAYLA BECK'S APARTMENT, Bryson Coventry swung by the 7-Eleven on Simms and bought a thermos of coffee, some kind of new banana nut blend—good stuff, his immediate new favorite. Then he pointed the Tundra east on 6th Avenue and flicked through the radio stations until he landed on Robert Palmer's "Addicted to Love." Back at the railroad yard the search was still in progress. He kicked an empty beer can as he walked, finally spotting Shalifa Netherwood hopping out of a boxcar. He handed her a disposable cup.

She took a sip and said, "Banana. No Aspen yet."

Coventry frowned.

"Kayla Beck knows something but she's not talking," he said.

"She does? What?"

"I don't know and right now I don't have time to find out. I absolutely have to get refocused on Tashna Sharapova." His watch said 11:23 a.m. "Starting this minute."

"So what's the plan?"

He kicked the dirt.

"Wish I knew."

Suddenly his cell phone rang.

IT TURNED OUT TO BE JENA VERNON from Channel 8. The sound of her voice pulled up a memory of tickling her down by the river in eleventh grade.

"I did something that you need to know about," Jena said.

That didn't sound good.

"What?"

"I stopped by Robert Sharapova's law office this morning to see if he'd give me an interview about his missing wife," she said. "He did. We're going to air it starting at noon."

Coventry frowned.

This was his fault.

He wasn't staying close enough to the case to keep it under control.

"What did he say?"

"Well, he basically just wants the guy to know that he took someone important, and that if anything happens to Tashna, there are going to be serious repercussions."

"Don't air it," Coventry said.

"Why?"

"The last thing we want to do is scare the guy," Coventry said. "He might be planning to drop her off somewhere alive. But if he feels there's too much heat, he might decide he can't risk her being alive as a potential witness. Or he can't risk driving around with her. He might just slit her throat, dump her in the woods and head to Mexico. Is this making sense?"

"Sort of," she said. "But the guy already has to understand

there's a lot of heat. I don't see how this changes things."

"Trust me, it does," Coventry said. "Lots of people aren't afraid of the police. They got rights. We don't strap them to a chair and torture them. But if a rich guy with a personal vendetta is after you, it's a whole different ballgame." He took a sip of coffee. "Can you derail it?"

"You really want me to?"

"I'd consider it a personal favor."

She hesitated and then said, "Let me get back to you. If I do, though, you owe me one."

"Fine."

"Breakfast," she said.

"Fine, breakfast."

"And I'm not talking about breakfast-breakfast," she said. "I'm talking about morning-after breakfast."

He chuckled.

"Be careful," he said. "I might just call your bluff one of these days."

HE LEFT SHALIFA IN CHARGE OF THE SEARCH at the railroad yard and went to the office, bumping into Kate Katona at the coffee pot. "Lot's of people out there would like to put fifty grand in their pocket," Katona said.

He looked at her.

And tried to not get distracted by her world-class chest.

"Getting a lot of calls?" he questioned.

"Too many," she said. "All duds so far, as near as I can tell."

Coventry hugged her on the shoulder.

"Thanks for being the gatekeeper," he said. "What's going on with the Marilyn Poppenberg case? Anything?"

She shook her head.

"I'm dead in the water."

"Welcome to the club." He slurped the coffee. "You heard that we're searching a railroad yard, right?"

She had.

"Another tie to trains," he said. "I'm starting to wonder if all this stuff isn't connected somehow."

"What do you mean by *all this stuff*?"

"You know—the dead drifter in the boxcar, Marilyn Poppenberg next to the tracks, and now this new woman, Aspen White."

She scratched her head.

"How could they be connected?"

"I don't know, but a law student by the name of Kayla Beck is the common denominator," he said. "She has a first-generation Ford Mustang and we have videotape of that type of car at the area where the drifter got killed. She's friends with Aspen White who is now apparently missing. And I just found out today that she knows Marilyn Poppenberg."

Katona licked her lips.

"She knows Poppenberg?"

"Apparently," Coventry said. "But I haven't peeled her back on that yet, so I don't know how deep it goes or whether it means anything."

"You want me to do it?"

He shrugged.

"Sure, if you have time later," he said. "But it's more important right now to stay focused on these reward calls that are coming in. We need to do what we can in the next few hours for Tashna Sharapova."

He clinked his coffee cup against hers.

Then headed for the door.

"Where you going?" she asked.

"To have a quick talk with Robert Sharapova before he screws things up even more. Then I'll be back."

Chapter Seventy-Five

Day Nine—May 13
Tuesday Morning

LANCE LUNDEEN TOOK A POSITION at the edge of a window and watched the activity in the railroad yard through binoculars, amazed at the intensity of the hunt. It all related to Aspen White. What he couldn't figure out is how they traced her there.

He needed to get her out of the building.

And her car, too.

He threw the binoculars on the mattress, picked up a pair of drumsticks and twisted them in his fingers as he paced back and forth.

The more he thought about it the more he became convinced that he should get the woman out of there now instead of waiting for nightfall. Kayla Beck knew he had her. If she called the cops and tipped them off, he was dead.

He ran down to the mechanical room and unlocked the door.

Aspen White lay hogtied on the floor.

Awake now.

Staring at him with serious, watery eyes.

"Please untie me," she said. "My arms are killing me. I won't do anything. I promise."

"Okay," he said. "Just give me a minute."

Instead of untying her, he injected her in the ass and watched her struggle until she slipped into unconsciousness. Then he put her in the trunk of her car, opened the garage door and looked around before pulling out.

He saw no cops.

Or other vehicles.

A chill ran up his spine.

If one single cop managed to spot her car and pull him over to investigate, his entire life was over. He quickly replayed the decision and decided it was the right one in spite of the risks.

He shifted the car into drive and headed out.

HE HADN'T GONE MORE THAN A HUNDRED YARDS when another vehicle came down the road towards him. Lundeen recognized the driver as the well-dressed black woman from the railroad yard.

No doubt a detective.

Great.

He threw on the sunglasses and baseball cap, then brought his hand up and scratched his forehead as she passed. By some miracle she didn't turn and chase him.

She kept going.

Paying him no attention, actually.

So beautiful.

He pulled off the hat and slapped it against the dash.

Oh yeah, baby.

One for the good guys.

But then something not so good happened. The woman pulled up to the base of his building and stopped.

Lundeen stepped on the gas.

And disappeared around the corner.

Chapter Seventy-Six

Day Nine—May 13
Tuesday Afternoon

AT THE SOUTH EDGE OF RED ROCKS PARK there's a large parking lot that backs up to the enormous rock formations. Kayla Beck parked at the appointed place—next to a scraggly pinon pine at the corner of the lot—and killed the engine. The gun was loaded with the safety off, tucked under the front seat. The knife was under her ass.

She watched the entry to the lot.

Waiting for Lance Lundeen to drive in.

But he didn't show.

Not at one o'clock.

Not at five after.

Not at ten after.

She turned on the radio. A country-western song came on, one she'd never heard before. Then the man suddenly appeared next to the car, opened the door and pulled her out by the hair. The knife came into view as her body came off the seat.

He shook his head with disgust.

"It's amazing," he said, "fifty thousand country songs, every one of them about pickup trucks and cheating hearts, and every one of them sounds just a little different. Almost the eighth wonder of the world, when you really stop and think about it." He pulled the keys out of the ignition and asked, "You wearing a wire?"

"No."

He led her into the rocks until they were well hidden from prying eyes. He put her in a standing spread-eagle position, with her hands against the stone, and felt every nook and cranny of her body until he convinced himself she wasn't wired.

She said nothing.

He twisted her around, pulled her over to a boulder, sat her down and stood in front of her.

"Where's Aspen?" she asked.

"She's safe so long as you don't do anything stupid," he said. "The main thing right now is that the three of us come to an understanding."

"What kind of understanding?"

"The kind that means that you two get out of my life."

Kayla nodded.

Sure.

No problem.

"Done," she said. "Let Aspen go. You'll never hear from either one of us again, guaranteed."

Lance chuckled.

"If only it were that simple. Aspen told me everything, including the fact that you two planned to blackmail me into killing some skinhead named Mitch Mitchell," he said. "The truth is that I might actually oblige you if he turns out to be who you say he is."

ASPEN WHITE, IT TURNED OUT, HAD TOLD Lance Lundeen just about everything. He knew the story almost as well as Kayla did. Some guy was running around the country abducting women, sticking them in desolate places with only a bottle of water and a razorblade, then bringing yet another woman into the game as a rescuer. Aspen got stuffed in a boxcar to die but Kayla rescued her. In the process Aspen got raped by a drifter and shot him in the face with Kayla's gun.

Then a fellow classmate of Kayla's by the name of Marilyn Poppenberg turned up dead—naked, bound with blue rope and stabbed through the ear with a screwdriver.

Found at a railroad yard.

Another tie to trains.

Another tie to Kayla's law school.

It was too much of a coincidence to not be connected.

Kayla knew that Poppenberg had been investigating cases where defendants escaped justice because the cops got their evidence through an illegal search. She and Aspen found that two of the potential targets of Poppenberg's investigation lived in Denver—namely Mitch Mitchell and Lance Lundeen.

They started investigating both men.

That's why they were in Lundeen's loft.

They didn't find any evidence that Lundeen was the razor-blade killer—in fact, just the opposite. But in the process they found out about his trailer and discovered pictures of two women who had recently been abducted and were in the news. They were going to use this as leverage to force Lundeen to kill Mitch Mitchell once they confirmed that Mitchell was in fact the razorblade killer.

Lance kicked a stone.

"You two have been busy little beavers," he said.

Kayla stared at him.

"How'd you get Aspen to tell you?"

He shook his head.

"That's not important."

SUDDENLY HER CELL PHONE RANG.

The sound came from the front pocket of her jeans.

"Take it out," Lundeen said.

She did and looked at the number.

Unknown.

"I think it's him," she said.

"Who?"

"The guy."

Lundeen pulled his hair back, put his ear next to hers and said, "Answer it."

She flicked open the phone and brought it up where they could both listen. A voice came through, a scrambled voice, the same scrambled voice as all the previous times. "You've been a bad girl, Kayla Beck, a very bad girl. You know what that means, don't you?"

"Leave me alone,'" she said. "I'm out of your games."

"There is no out, Kayla. You know that."

She hung up.

"Is that him?" Lundeen asked.

"Yes," she said.

He paced for several moments and then said, "I don't like this guy. Hit redial and see who answers."

She did.

The phone rang.

"No one's answering," she said.

"Let it ring."

Then suddenly someone answered.

A woman.

"Who is this?" Kayla asked.

The phone turned out to be a payphone on the 16th Street Mall in downtown Denver. The woman who answered just happened to be walking past as it rang. She didn't see who used the phone last. There were lots of people in the area, probably more than a hundred within sight. Some of them had shaved heads.

"Thanks," Kayla said. "I really appreciate it."

"Are you okay?"

"Yeah, fine."

"You sound stressed. Are you sure you're okay?"

"I'm fine. Thanks again."

When she hung up, Lundeen said, "If you really want all this to end, I have a plan—a win-win for all of us. It's going to take some guts though, on your end of the equation." He looked her straight in the eyes. "Is that going to be a problem?"

She held his eyes.

"No."

Chapter Seventy-Seven

Day Nine—May 13
Tuesday Afternoon

IF THE CLIMB TO ROBERT SHARAPOVA'S LAW OFFICE was painful, the meeting at the end of the climb was even more so. The lawyer saw no harm in threatening the man who took his wife. Moreover, he wasn't overly pleased with the fact that Coventry still didn't have a clue where she was or who had her.

He'd be talking to the chief.

That was for sure.

Coventry put his tail between his legs and felt so tired, frustrated and pressed for time that he slowed down at the elevators and seriously thought about pushing the button. Then he hurried into the stairwell and bounded down the steps two at a time. Somewhere around the 15th Floor, Jena Vernon called and said she wasn't able to derail the interview.

It would air on the evening news.

"I really tried," she said. "You need to know that."

"I know," he assured her.

"I'm sorry," she added. "I really am."

"I know. Don't worry about it."

He exited the building on the Broadway side.

An RTD bus rolled past and threw a cloud of diesel fumes at him. His first thought was to hold his breath and step back but instead he walked through it.

Thinking about what the lawyer said.

And admitting that the man was right.

Coventry *should* know more than he did.

Then Shalifa Netherwood called and said that they still hadn't found Aspen White. "We checked every car in the yard," she said. "Also, I drove over to that building to the east, where that Tarzan guy lives, to see if he happened to have any security cameras that might have picked up something. He wasn't home, but I walked around the building and didn't spot any. Right now I can't think of anything else to do. So unless you tell me otherwise, I'm going to wrap it up here."

Coventry frowned.

"Go ahead," he said. "Be sure to tell everyone thanks for me. Oh, and hey, find out if any cars got pulled out of there before we started searching."

"Will do," she said. "By the way, all the TV stations got wind of things and showed up."

"That figures."

HE GOT BACK TO THE OFFICE and then went nowhere, literally and figuratively, except for the usual ping-pong trips to the coffee pot and the restroom.

Precious time slipped away.

More followed.

No brilliant ideas dropped out of the sky and fell on him.

Then Dr. Leanne Sanders called and said she'd be landing at

DIA in about forty-five minutes. Should she drop by the office or stay out of his way?

"I'll pick you up," he said.

On the drive to the airport his phone rang. It turned out to be the last person on the face of the earth he expected to hear from.

NAMELY ASPEN WHITE.

"Kayla Beck says you're looking for me," Aspen said. "What's going on?"

She sounded tired.

But otherwise fine.

"You're okay?"

"Of course I am," she said. "Why wouldn't I be?"

Coventry told her about the call he received last night and the fact that they traced her phone to the railroad yard this morning. She explained that she left her cell phone sitting on the sink of a ladies room last night.

"Why would someone call me with it?" Coventry questioned.

"They probably didn't mean to," she said. "I had your number programmed on speed dial—number eight, if you care. They must have hit the button."

"So you're fine?"

"I wouldn't go that far," she said. "You did blow me off, in case you forgot."

Coventry almost responded but hit the brakes instead.

Slowing the Tundra down barely in time to avoid riding up the taillights of a Porsche.

"I didn't blow you off," he said.

"Prove it," she said. "Take me to dinner tonight."

He almost said no.

But then saw it as an opportunity.

An opportunity to find out what Kayla Beck—Little Miss Common Denominator—was up to.

"Deal," he said.

"Good," she said. "It's supposed to rain tonight."

Coventry didn't know that.

But it didn't surprise him.

"Do you remember what happened the last time it rained?" she asked.

His thoughts flashed.

With such speed and vivid imagery that he could almost hear the storm.

And feel her body pressed against him.

And taste her lips.

"I remember," he said.

He felt her hesitate.

"What?" he asked.

"Nothing," she said.

"Okay."

Then she said, "That meant something to me. In case that means anything to you."

As soon as he hung up he remembered something.

He had already promised to take Rain to dinner tonight.

TWENTY MINUTES LATER he stood under the white peaked roof of DIA and waited for Dr. Leanne Sanders to emerge from the masses. When she did, Coventry was never so glad to see anyone in his life. He put her in a bear hug and spun her around to prove it.

"Thanks for picking me up," she said. "I'll buy you dinner to make up for it."

Coventry chuckled.

"What?" she asked.

"Nothing, I'll tell you later. Right now I'm dead in the water on the Tashna Sharapova case and I need your insight."

"My insight?"

He nodded.

"How about my hindsight? That seems to work a whole lot better than my insight."

He knew he should grin but didn't.

"She's going to die tonight if I can't think of a way to get my engine in gear," he said.

She looked at him hard.

"I've never seen you like this before."

Chapter Seventy-Eight

Day Nine—May 13
Tuesday Afternoon

LANCE LUNDEEN BOOSTED Aspen White and Kayla Beck into the boxcar, then climbed up and closed the door, leaving it cracked just enough to allow a sliver of light. This is where Aspen got chained and where the drifter took a bullet to the face. Lance wanted to see the place for himself, just to be sure they weren't lying to him. Plus they needed a private place to talk.

The sky crackled with distant thunder.

Aspen seemed apprehensive.

As if the place freaked her out.

Kayla too, even though she had her gun in hand—a showing of good faith on Lundeen's part.

"Do you believe me now?" Aspen questioned.

He did.

"So what's this master plan you keep talking about?" Kayla asked.

Lance dropped to the floor and leaned against the steel siding of the car. "First things first," he said. "For this to work it's important that we trust each other, so I want to clear up a few misconceptions you may have about me. My name used to be Gordon Andrews. One night, four years ago, I'm heading to a party in the hills outside L.A., minding my own business and perfectly sober, when the cops pull me over. They said I had a busted taillight and wrote me a ticket, which was fine, I didn't care. Then without any justification whatsoever they made me take a roadside sobriety test. You ever had one of those?"

Aspen nodded.

"Once," she said. "They're hard to pass, even sober."

He nodded.

That was true.

"I passed, of course, but wasn't too subtle about what I thought of the whole thing. In hindsight, I think they were trying to piss me off on purpose so they'd have a reason to escalate things."

"To escalate things? Why?"

"Because it was all part of their plan to get a reason to search the car," he said.

"What do you mean?"

"What I mean is, the next thing they did is ask if they could search the car. I told them no. They said, *Why, are you hiding something?* I said no. They said, *In that case, you won't mind if we have a quick look around.* They made me lay on the ground while they searched the car. Guess what they found?"

Kayla Beck looked at him and said, "They found a dead woman in the trunk—naked and bound in blue rope."

Lance nodded and exhaled.

"Just like Marilyn Poppenberg," Kayla added.

"DON'T RUSH TO JUDGMENT," Lance warned. "I was a lot

more shocked than they were. I recognized the woman vaguely but couldn't place her. She turned out to be someone named Carolyn Malone. I was charged with first degree murder and got assigned to a public defender who kept telling me to take a plea—namely life in prison but no death penalty. In an act of desperation I cashed in every penny I had and retained a private defense attorney, a woman named Alex Ringer. That turned out to be the best decision of my life."

"Obviously," Aspen said. "You're here."

He nodded.

"She filed a motion to exclude the evidence based on the argument that the police conducted an unreasonable search of the car, in violation of the Fourth Amendment. The D.A. opposed the motion and we all sat back and waited for it to come to a hearing. Meanwhile, my attorney dug around and uncovered some very interesting facts. It turned out that the dead woman—Carolyn Malone—had an ugly breakup a month earlier with her boyfriend, a man named Johnnie Poindexter. Even more interestingly, Johnnie Poindexter turned out to be the son of a detective in the L.A. vice department."

"So you were set up?" Aspen asked. "Is that what you're saying?"

"Absolutely," he said. "I think they targeted me at a nightclub named Midnight because it turned out that the dead woman used to go there too. That's probably where I'd seen her. As far as I can figure, they planted the body in my car and expected me to go down at the hands of an incompetent public defender."

"Wow."

Lance nodded.

"Anyway," he said, "my attorney had a private talk with the

prosecuting D.A. and they cut a deal. She wouldn't go public with the theory that I was set up if they cut me loose. They agreed but asked that we all go forward with the exclusionary hearing. That way, if they lost there, they could save face and in effect tell everyone they had the killer but he got off on a technicality."

"Wow."

"Right, wow," Lance said. "I shouldn't have agreed to go along with that part of the deal, in hindsight. But I was too scared not to. Anyway, we won the hearing and the D.A. dropped the case, but I was still branded as a killer. I got out of Dodge, changed my name and started a new life in Denver."

He studied the women.

To be sure they understood what he was saying.

Aspen did.

But he couldn't read Kayla Beck.

Then Kayla said, "So how is it that Marilyn Poppenberg ends up dead in Denver, after you move here, bound with blue rope? Are you telling us that's just another great big coincidence in your life?"

HE STOOD UP AND LOOKED OUTSIDE.

No one was around.

Low charcoal-gray storm cells rolled overhead and brought the thunder closer.

"You already figured out what happened to Marilyn Poppenberg," he said. "You have it all connected except the last two dots." He looked at her and smiled. "Why don't you try to connect them while I step outside to use the facilities. Let's see if you're smart enough to be a lawyer."

Chapter Seventy-Nine

Day Nine—May 13
Tuesday Afternoon

AFTER THE MEETING AT THE BOXCAR, Kayla Beck headed to law school, partly to catch her four o'clock Environmental Law class, but mostly to be in a normal environment where she could think. Up front, behind a podium, Professor Buckley droned on about the Endangered Species Act in that nasal monotone of his, proving once again that he was the most boring person on the face of the earth—as if anyone within ten miles had any doubts.

A thrill a minute, he wasn't.

But the class was packed.

Because he was the easiest grader on the face of the earth; show up with a warm body and walk away with at least a B-plus. Kayla paid enough attention to take notes but focused on a deeper question.

Namely whether she would help Lance Lundeen and Aspen White kill Mitch Mitchell.

Tonight.

Or tomorrow.

Soon, in any event.

SHE HAD TO PAT HERSELF ON THE BACK for at least being smart enough to connect the dots regarding Marilyn Poppenberg. As far as she could figure, Poppenberg had been investigating both Mitch Mitchell and Lance Lundeen. Chances are that one of them found out about it, perceived her as a threat and took her out.

At first Kayla thought it had been Lundeen.

Because Poppenberg had been bound in blue rope.

The same as the woman in Lundeen's trunk.

But now, in hindsight, Lundeen didn't even use blue rope once, much less twice. Plus, even if he had used it the first time, why would he be so obvious as to use it again?

He wouldn't.

But someone trying to frame him would.

So what happened is this. Mitch Mitchell spotted Poppenberg following him. He laid a trap and caught her—just like he tried to catch Kayla, twice in fact. He squeezed her until he found out what she was up to. She confessed that she was investigating both him and Lance Lundeen. He pressed her for information about Lundeen and learned about the blue rope.

Then he killed her.

Using Lance Lundeen's signature.

To frame him.

MARILYN POPPENBERG DISAPPEARED ON TUESDAY, May 6th, sometime after eight o'clock in the evening when her last class ended. According to the newspaper article the following day, her body was discovered later that evening.

The big question Kayla now had is whether Lance Lundeen had an alibi for that time period. So when her Environmental Law class ended, she called Lundeen from the payphone next to the restrooms at the end of the first floor.

"Nothing personal," she said, "but I was just curious what you were doing on the evening of May 6th."

Lance laughed.

"Does this relate to Marilyn Poppenberg?"

"Guilty," Kayla said.

"You're trying to find out if I have an alibi?"

"Maybe just a little."

"Woman, you need to relax and trust me," he said.

"I do," she said. "I just need to convince myself all I can. Lawyers call it due diligence."

"Whatever," Lance said. "Let's see—May 6th."

"That's a Tuesday."

"Let me think," Lance said. "I don't keep a calendar or anything like that."

"I understand."

"Bingo," he said. "Now I remember. We were getting ready to do a photo shoot. I had a bunch of models from MODELLE scheduled to show up at noon the next day. That evening, Scotty Marks was down on the second floor constructing a set. I took a lady friend to a long dinner that evening at Marlowe's, down on the 16th Street Mall. We got there about 7:30 and left about 9:00. Hold on a minute."

She heard walking.

Then papers shuffling.

"Okay," he said. "I found the credit-card receipt. It's dated May 6th at 8:52 p.m. I'm showing it to Aspen."

Suddenly Aspen's voice came through.

"Are you having second thoughts?" Aspen asked.

"No."

"Good. The credit-card receipt is just like he says," Aspen said. "It's dated May 6th at 8:52 p.m."

When Lance came back on the line, Kayla asked, "Then what did you do, after that?"

He laughed.

"You really aren't a very trusting, soul, are you?" he asked. "*Then, after that,* we came back to my place. My lady friend read a book and I did an inventory of my darkroom supplies, in preparation of the shoot. I ordered a bunch of stuff that night, both online and by phone. I should be able to get you email printouts or receipts or something to prove it if you really want to take it that far. In fact, hold on a minute."

Aspen's voice came through again.

"Okay," Aspen said. "We're pulling up his emails from May 6th. Here's one at 9:45 p.m.—from Lance to a place called Photo Discounts, ordering some stuff." A pause. "All right, here's another one—10:23 p.m., to a place called Quality Photo Products, ordering color paper." Another pause. "We got five more, running through midnight."

Lance came back on the phone.

"You feel better now?" he asked.

"Sorry," she said. "I'm a jerk."

Lance chuckled.

"No you're not," he said. "You can look at all this stuff yourself."

"No, that's okay."

"I want you to," he said. "I want you to be comfortable with the fact that I had nothing to do with Marilyn Poppenberg, because that is the honest-to-God truth. So are you still in, or what?"

She didn't hesitate.

"I was never out."

"Good," he said. "Nine o'clock tonight. My place."

"Don't worry, I'll be there."

Chapter Eighty

Day Nine—May 13
Tuesday Afternoon

ON THE DRIVE TO HEADQUARTERS FROM DIA, Bryson
Coventry told Dr. Leanne Sanders everything he knew about the
Tashna Sharapova case, hoping she would be able to point him
to that one critical rock he hadn't had the foresight to look under yet—the one that had the map to where Tashna was being
held. When Coventry finally stopped flapping his lips, the profiler frowned and admitted that no neon lights were flashing
inside her head.

"Maybe something will come to me later," she said.

Coventry looked at his watch.

4:32 p.m.

"It's already later," he said. "If she isn't dead by now she will
be by midnight. I can feel it in my bones."

He got quiet—partly to pay more attention to staying out of
the way of the maniac I-70 drivers, but mostly to give Leanne
some quiet time to digest the information.

Then Forrest Tanner—the chief—called.

And spoke in a serious, concerned voice.

He wanted to know the story behind the manhunt that Coventry commissioned this morning at the railroad yard. After Coventry explained, the chief made a few points. First, Coventry was the head of the homicide unit, emphasis on *homicide*. Second, not only did the situation this morning not involve a homicide, in hindsight it didn't even involve a missing person. Third, did Coventry have some kind of personal relationship going with this non-missing woman?

Coventry couldn't lie.

"We've had a few private moments," he said.

He didn't see the need to volunteer anything about dinner tonight.

"Bryson," the chief said. "We both know you're the best hunter this place has, or may ever have for that matter. If my daughter turned up missing and I could only have one person look for her, it would be you. But this deal this morning concerns me in a big way. You need to know that."

When Coventry hung up he must have had a look on his face because Leanne said, "Problems?"

An 18-wheeler rode Coventry's bumper.

He wasn't in the mood to care.

"That was the chief," he said. "His basic theory is that my dick got in the way of my brain this morning and caused a bunch of lost man hours."

"People hours," she said.

"The truth is, that's not what happened," Coventry said. "But I can see why he'd think it. Now I have to buy him lunch and straighten things out."

She laughed.

"What?" he asked.

"You referred to yourself and used the word *buy*—as in the

act of buying or purchasing—both in the same sentence," she said.

He grinned.

"I did?"

She nodded.

"See what stress will do to you?" he said.

"I always knew it could have an effect," she said, "but never anything like this."

FROM I-70 THEY TOOK I-25 SOUTH into downtown, getting sucked into increasingly thicker stop-and-go traffic. "Rush hour," Coventry said. "One of the world's great misnomers. So tell me about this guy on your radar screen. What's his name again?"

"Todd Underdown."

"Right, him."

"He might be something, he might not," she said. "Right now he has three strikes against him. One, he owns an old Ford Mustang, like the one in the vicinity of the boxcar that night. Two, he worked for BN for several years, another tie to trains. And three, he was in Oregon at the same time as one of the killings. Some poor girl got chained and left to rot on the rocks down by the ocean and ended up using the razorblade."

"Poor thing," Coventry said.

"If I can just catch this one guy, my whole time with the bureau will have been worth it," she said.

Coventry understood.

"So what's your plan?"

"Get some decent photos of him for starters," she said. "Then grab his garbage and process it for prints and DNA and see where that goes. If things start adding up I'll go for a phone tap and all the rest."

"If there's anything I can do—"

She nodded.

Appreciative.

"There is one small thing," she said.

"No problem. Name it."

"You can be the one to go through the garbage."

Coventry chuckled.

"You have an evil streak in you. Do you know that?"

COVENTRY DROPPED THE PROFILER OFF at the downtown Marriott and then pointed the Tundra towards the Rock Rest on South Golden Road to meet Aspen for dinner.

Not wanting to be late.

He got there before her, took a booth at the edge of an empty dance floor and ordered a Bud Light. The dim lighting washed the wooden beams and walls with a warm intimate glow. The sky had been rumbling for the last half hour and finally started to drop water.

The beer felt good in his gut.

Too good.

A couple of young women walked over to a jukebox, put in a bill and got a country song out. Coventry never heard it before but liked it within the first few bars. The women whispered something to each other, laughed, and then walked over to his booth and slid in.

"She's Mandy," one of them said, pointing to the other one.

"And she's not," the other one said.

Coventry grinned.

"This is really weird because we have the same name," he said. "I'm not-Mandy too."

Mandy looked at Coventry, then to her girlfriend, and said, "So how am I going to tell you two apart, having the same name and everything?"

Coventry chuckled.

"She's the cute one," he said.

Coventry bought them beers and learned they were seniors at the Colorado School of Mines, celebrating the fact that they made it through an engineering exam alive this afternoon. The third song on the jukebox turned out to be a slow one.

Mandy grabbed Coventry's hand, pulled him onto the dance floor, put her arms around his neck and pushed her stomach to his.

"I love this song," she said.

"So I see."

WHEN THEY GOT BACK TO THE TABLE, Coventry's phone rang. He expected it to be Aspen telling him she was running a little late. Instead it turned out to be Tracy Patterson, victim number two, the one who got dumped in Tashna Sharapova's BMW at the museum parking lot.

"Bryson," she said. "You told me to call you if I thought of anything no matter how small it was."

Right.

He did.

"This is probably nothing," she said. "But I was watching the evening news and saw Tashna Sharapova's husband on it."

Coventry winced.

He'd forgotten about that.

"Right," he said.

"Well, he seemed familiar to me, as if I'd seen him some-place before," she said.

"Where?"

"I don't know."

"Was he following you or something?"

She laughed.

"No, nothing like that," she said. "I just remember seeing him somewhere, but not in a weird or threatening way."

Coventry processed the information.

And didn't find it particularly helpful.

"Okay," he said. "You did the right thing, calling me. I'm glad you did. If you remember where you saw him, let me know."

He hung up just in time to see Aspen walk in.

She stopped to get her bearings.

Then spotted him.

With Mandy and not-Mandy.

And Bud.

She immediately turned and huffed out.

Chapter Eighty-One

Day Nine—May 13
Tuesday Night

AFTER NIGHTFALL, DRESSED IN BLACK, Lance Lundeen and the two women—Aspen White and Kayla Beck—crept through the dark fields behind Mitch Mitchell's street. They carried flashlights but kept them off.

They didn't speak.

A dog barked but it was a ways off, a block at least, probably more. The ground squished under their feet, still soaked from the rain. Cold water worked its way into their tennis shoes. The wind blew and thunder rolled through the clouds, warning of even more weather. Kayla carried the only gun. Lance and Aspen each had knives, but Lance didn't care that much if he had one or not.

He had his hands.

Mitch Mitchell's truck wasn't parked in the driveway.

All his windows were dark.

Perfect.

They crept around to his back door, stopped and put on latex gloves. Lance put his face to the window and saw no signs of life.

He knocked.

No sound of movement came from inside.

Lance pulled off his sweatshirt, wrapped it in his fist and punched the window. The busting of the glass sounded deafening.

No alarms went off.

Lance reached through the opening, unlocked the door and stepped inside. The women followed. They closed all the window coverings before turning on their flashlights. Then Kayla kept a lookout through the front window while Aspen and Lance started to take the place apart.

They pulled drawers out, dumped them on the floor and shuffled the mess with their feet.

They didn't care if Mitchell knew they had been there.

"It's starting to rain again," Kayla said.

Lundeen didn't care.

"Just keep watching," he said.

"It's dead quiet out there."

"Good."

They rifled through one thing after another.

And found nothing.

THEN ASPEN SHOUTED SOMETHING from the bedroom. Lundeen ran in and saw a pile of papers on the bed, looking as if they'd been dumped out of a file folder. Aspen was on her knees, shuffling through them.

"Found this in the closet," she said.

"What is it?"

Then he saw.

Two sections of newspaper, folded open to articles about Marilyn Poppenberg's murder.

Mementos.

His jaw dropped.

He knew in his heart that the little freak had set him up, but didn't expect to actually find evidence.

"This guy's dead," he said.

Aspen handed him a set of printed pages, stapled together. "Does this look familiar?" she asked.

Lance recognized it immediately.

It was a printout of the court's decision in his California case, ruling that the search of his car had been unconstitutional. Part of the text was highlighted in yellow marker. When Lundeen read that section the veins in his neck bulged. It was the part of the decision stating that the woman had been found naked and bound in blue rope.

"You were definitely framed," Aspen said.

Lundeen shook his head in disbelief.

"This guy is so dead," he said.

"Look at the bottom," Aspen said. "This was printed off the Internet on May 6th, which is the day Poppenberg got killed. I can just picture the poor woman tied up and getting closer and closer to death while the little scumbag squeezed her for information on how to locate the case."

"To be absolutely sure about the blue rope," Lundeen said.

"Exactly."

Aspen took the papers out to Kayla and said, "Look at this."

Then things got even more interesting.

They found blue rope in a bag in the closet.

About forty feet in length.

Cut at one end.

The leftover part that Mitchell hadn't needed for Poppen-berg.

BEHIND THE HOUSE SAT A WOODEN STRUCTURE, probably a one-car garage at one point but now looking more like a storage shed. There they found a small trunk stuffed in the corner, hidden behind a cache of rakes and shovels.

Inside that trunk they found three steel neck collars, several sections of chain, a dozen or so Master padlocks, three boxes of razorblades, a voice scramble and a two-foot high stack of newspaper articles and Internet printouts regarding various women.

"Oh my God," Aspen said. "He's definitely the one."

"Unbelievable," Lance said.

Aspen grabbed one of the collars and took it into the house to show Kayla.

"This isn't exactly like the one used on you," Kayla noted.

"Right," Aspen said. "I know that. But here's something I didn't tell you before, because there was no need to, really. But the collar used on me was slightly different than the ones used on the other woman—the one's I was sent to rescue. This collar, on the other hand, is *exactly* like those other ones."

"So he's unquestionably the one," Kayla said.

Aspen nodded.

Lance couldn't get the rage down.

"I say we just stay here and kill him as soon as he gets home."

"Agreed," Aspen said.

"Me too," Kayla said.

Chapter Eighty-Two

Day Nine—May 13
Tuesday Night

KAYLA BECK SAT ON MITCH MITCHELL'S COUCH with a flashlight in hand and forced herself to go through the stack of gruesome papers retrieved from the trunk. Aspen stood at the window, keeping a lookout. Lance Lundeen paced back and forth with an animal intensity, tossing an eight-inch serrated knife from one hand to the other.

The papers painted a ghastly picture of at least eight dead women and several others who disappeared.

Most of the articles had photographs of the women.

They were all attractive.

One was almost in Aspen's league—model quality.

"He likes them pretty," Kayla said. "That's for sure."

Aspen grunted.

Then she asked the question that was on all their minds. "So how are we going to do it?"

Kayla set the papers down and turned off the flashlight.

They decided that all three of them would play a material role in the murder. That was the only way they could all trust one another.

"After we do this we take it to our graves," Kayla said. "None of us ever tells anyone about it. Not even in twenty years. Not ever. I need that assurance to go on."

Lance nodded.

"That's the deal," he said.

"Same here," Aspen added.

"That's the only way we'll all be able to sleep at night," Kayla added.

True.

"So how are we going to do it?" Aspen asked again.

NO ONE SPOKE.

Then Lance Lundeen stopped pacing and said, "I have two ideas."

"Shoot."

"One is this," he said. "We kill him with his own blue rope. We wrap it twice around his neck. I get on one end and you two get on the other end. Then we pull until he stops breathing."

Aspen considered it and then said, "He deserves worse."

Lance chuckled.

"What's your second idea?" Aspen questioned.

"The second idea is this," he said. "He's got a set of steak knives in the kitchen. We get him immobile—tie him down or I'll sit on him or something. Then we all stab him in the chest at the same time, at the count of three."

Aspen didn't hesitate. "That's the way," she said.

"You like that?"

"After what he did? Yeah, I like it a lot."

They both turned to Kayla.

"What about you?" Lance asked. "Does that sit okay with you?"

Actually it was a little more horrific than Kayla preferred.

But Aspen and Lundeen were clearly set on it.

And she needed to get this behind her.

"That's fine," she said.

"Are you sure?" Lundeen asked. "You don't sound sure."

"I'm sure," she said. "I'm just not going to enjoy it."

"We need to *all* participate," Lance reminded her. "That's the deal. That's the only way we can all be sure that no one has second thoughts after the fact."

"I said I'm in," Kayla said. "Stop worrying about it."

Lundeen studied her.

"This isn't just about us," he said. "It's about all those poor women he killed too. Not to mention the ones in the future. Don't forget about them. And don't forget about your law school friend Marilyn Poppenberg."

Suddenly Aspen said, "Headlights!"

AS SOON AS MITCH MITCHELL WALKED THROUGH the front door, before he could even get his hand to the light switch, Lance Lundeen punched him in the nose.

So hard that the cartilage snapped.

Then Lundeen dragged the little freak into the center of the room and straddled him.

Aspen shined a flashlight into his eyes.

The man started to say something and Lundeen smacked him across the face.

"Shut your mouth!"

The man almost said something but thought better of it.

"Now listen to me carefully," Lundeen said. "Are you listening?"

"Yes."

"I'm going to ask you a question. I'm only going to ask it one time," he said. "You're going to answer that question truthfully. If you lie to me, things are going to get very painful for you—very painful. Do you understand what I'm saying?"

"Yes."

"So painful that you'd do anything in the world to make that pain stop," Lundeen added. *"But it won't stop.* If you make me start the pain, it won't stop. There won't be anything you can do or say to make it stop. Do you fully understand what I'm telling you?"

"Yes."

"That pain's going to come in a lot of different ways," Lundeen said. "Some of it will come from pliers. Some of it will come from a razorblade. Some of it will come from matches. And a lot of it will come from ways that I haven't even begun to think of yet. Do you understand what I'm saying?"

"Yes."

"I hope so," Lundeen said. "Because if you think I'm exaggerating, you're going to learn a very hard lesson and go to a very insane place."

"I understand."

"Okay," he said. "Here's your question. Did you kill Marilyn Poppenberg?"

No answer.

Then the man cried.

And muttered, "Yes."

Barely audible.

"Did you say yes?"

"Yes."

"Did you bind her in blue rope and dump her by the railroad tracks?"

"Yes."

"Did you bind her in blue rope so it would look like someone else did it?"

"Yes."

"Are you telling me the truth right now?"

"Yes."

THE IMAGE OF MARILYN POPPENBERG DEAD in the night, tied up like a sack of garbage, rushed into Kayla's brain.

And snapped.

She kicked the man on the side of the head.

He immediately screamed and thrashed.

Lance said, "Get the knives!"

Suddenly they all had knives in their hands. Lundeen continued to pin the man under his weight. Aspen got on one side and Kayla got on the other.

All three of them raised their knives.

Lundeen looked at Aspen. "Are you ready?"

"Yes!"

He looked at Kayla. "Are you ready?"

"Yes."

"Okay," he said. "On the count of three."

Thunder crackled directly overhead.

So close that the house shook.

"One—two—three!"

Chapter Eighty-Three

Day Nine—May 13
Tuesday Night

BRYSON COVENTRY LEARNED A FEW THINGS about Aspen White during their dinner at the Rock Rest, after he got her calmed down and scooted Mandy and not-Mandy out of the booth. The main thing he learned was that she wasn't about to let him learn anything about her.

Or Kayla Beck.

He learned something else when she twisted her hair into a ponytail and her blouse rode up. Namely that she had a lot of stitches on the side of her stomach—crude stitches, the *take a swig of vodka and we'll do it right here in the kitchen* kind; no doubt the medical emergency that kept her from calling Friday night.

He didn't mention them.

She glanced at her watch repeatedly throughout the meal, keeping most of the chat directed at the manhunt Coventry commissioned this morning, telling him that it was so romantic. Then at exactly seven o'clock she kissed him on the lips and said she had to run.

He almost followed her.

But didn't.

Instead he paid the bill, left a hefty tip and walked out to the Tundra in the rain. He liked the sound of the storm on the roof of the truck and decided to just sit there for a minute. He closed his eyes and tasted Aspen's kiss.

Then he opened his eyes and focused on the water running down the windshield. Something had been nagging at him for the last hour. Namely the call from Tracy Patterson, telling him that she'd seen Robert Sharapova somewhere before.

For some reason Coventry had the same feeling.

Not that it meant anything.

After all, the man was a prominent lawyer. No doubt he'd been on the news a number of times. Plus Coventry spent his share of time in the courthouse and could have seen him there.

Then a wild thought entered his head.

He immediately called Tracy Patterson.

She didn't answer.

Of course.

HE FIRED UP THE ENGINE, jammed the transmission into drive and stepped on the gas. He got caught at a red light, slowed, looked around and then went through it. Two heartbeats later he got Shalifa Netherwood on the phone.

"It's me, the pain in your posterior," he said.

"Bryson?"

"Right."

"What's wrong? Where are you?"

"Listen," he said. "You know what Tashna Sharapova's husband looks like, don't you?"

"You mean the lawyer?"

"Right. Robert Sharapova."

"I saw him on the news earlier today," she said. "But that's it."

"Would you recognize him if you saw him?"

A pause.

"Probably, why?"

"Do me a favor. Go down to headquarters, can you do that?"

"I suppose so if it's important. Why?"

"The Tashna Sharapova file is on my desk," he said. "Find the DVDs labeled Camel's Breath—they're the bar's surveillance tapes from the night when Tracy Patterson was there and got taken. See if you can find the lawyer in the crowd."

"He won't be there," she said.

"Why?"

"Because he already said he was out of town that weekend," she said. "Remember?"

"He could be lying," Coventry said. "Tracy Patterson called me earlier this evening and said she saw him somewhere. I'm thinking that she saw him there at the bar that night but doesn't recall it very well because she was so drunk. After she called and mentioned it, I started to have the same feeling, like I'd seen him somewhere before. I'm wondering if I saw him in the surveillance tapes and that's why he seems familiar to me."

"Okay," she said. "I'm heading down. Are you going to meet me there?"

"No, there's no time. I'm on my way to his house," he said. "Call me as soon as you have something. And thanks. I owe you one."

"One?"

"Love you," he said.

TWENTY-TWO MINUTES LATER HE DROVE slowly down the lawyer's street. Inside the house a light went off and a different one went on.

Good.

The man was home.

Coventry parked at the far end of the block, turned off the headlights and killed the engine.

The storm immediately grew louder.

He licked his lips.

And tasted Aspen's kiss.

He sat in the storm for a long time, barely able to see the lawyer's house through the downpour. Rain called to tell him she missed him and wanted him to come over. Her voice reminded him of their prior conversation, the one where she told him that the man who abducted her was stronger than Coventry.

A lot stronger.

The lawyer didn't fit that bill.

Meaning Coventry was probably wasting his time.

Yet again.

Then Tracy Patterson returned his call and told him that she had no specific recollection of seeing the lawyer at the Camel's Breath, but could have.

Not good.

Not good at all.

Finally Shalifa Netherwood phoned.

"If he's in the crowd, I can't find him," she said.

Coventry slumped in the seat.

"You sure?"

"Well, the cameras are on the ceiling so the angle's not good, and I went through it using fast forward," she said. "But I still think I would have been able to tell."

Coventry thanked her and hung up.

Two heartbeats later headlights pulled out of the lawyer's driveway and headed in the opposite direction. Robert Sharapova was on the move. Coventry could feel it.

He called Shalifa back.

"I need to impose upon you to do one more thing," he said.

"You know what time it is—right?"

He did.

Late.

"Drive down to the Camel's Breath and show the bartenders pictures of the lawyer," he said. "See if they recognize him."

A pause.

Then she said, "I'll do it but only because you're the one asking. I have to say, though, that I've never seen anyone chase something so vague with such intensity."

He grunted.

"I learned how to do this when I was twenty-one. Trying to catch women in bars. Same exact thing."

Chapter Eighty-Four

Day Nine—May 13
Tuesday Night

AFTER THEY STABBED MITCH MITCHELL TO DEATH, they left only one knife sticking in his chest to make it look like the work of a single person. The other two weapons got thrown into the open space more than a half mile from the house as they walked. They took off their gloves at the car, turning them inside out as a precaution against tracking blood into the vehicle. The gloves then went into a brown paper bag which in turn went into the trunk.

Then they took the 6th Avenue freeway east.

Passing Union/Simms, Kipling, Wadsworth, Sheridan and Federal.

Driving through the storm with the wipers on high.

Dangerously close to hydroplaning.

To Lance Lundeen's place.

To regroup.

As soon as they got there, Lundeen put on a fresh pair of latex gloves and washed the other three pairs thoroughly in the kitchen sink. Then he cut them into little pieces, threw the pieces into the brown paper bag, and then drove for a good two miles until he found a desolate industrial dumpster.

In they went.

On the drive back, he tried to decide how upset he was at Kayla Beck for not thoroughly stabbing Mitchell. Her knife had barely penetrated the man's flesh, in stark contrast to his knife and Aspen's, both of which sank down to the handle and drew solid pools of blood.

Kayla Beck wasn't fully vested in the kill.

That presented a problem.

WHEN HE GOT HOME, the two women were on the couch, feeling no pain. A bottle of white wine sat on the floor, almost empty. He grabbed a Bud Light, downed it at the refrigerator in one long swallow, then grabbed another and sat on the floor by the women's feet.

"I've been thinking about it," he said "I don't see how we could have covered our tracks any better."

Aspen and Kayla agreed.

"In hindsight, we should have worn hairnets, but there's nothing we can do about that now."

Aspen grunted.

"The cops aren't going to be looking too hard," she said. "It's going to be obvious that he was the one who killed Marilyn Poppenberg. Their attitude is going to be *good riddance.*"

"Not entirely," Kayla said.

"What do you mean?"

"What I mean is, they're going to figure out he's the razor-blade killer," she said. "Because there are so many victims in-volved, and because the guy's crossed so many state lines, I'm sure the FBI is working the case."

"They are," Aspen said.

"They'll show up and go through that place with a micro-scope," Kayla added.

Aspen laughed.

"Who cares? They won't connect us in a million years."

Then Kayla looked at Aspen.

"What do you mean—*They are?*" she asked.

Aspen looked confused.

"When I said, *The FBI is working the case*, you said, *They are*," Kayla said. "As if you know that for a fact."

Aspen rolled her eyes.

"Well, I do know it for a fact," she said.

"How?"

"From the newspaper articles at Mitchell's house," she said. "The FBI is mentioned."

Kayla didn't seem as if she remembered that but said, "Oh, okay."

"And because I've personally talked to them," Aspen added.

Both Kayla and Lundeen looked at her with confusion.

She said nothing else.

But must have felt the pressure of their eyes and said, "Okay, as long as we got this whole thing behind us, I should probably come clean with a few tiny little things."

Chapter Eighty-Five

Day Nine—May 13
Tuesday Night

WITH THAT, ASPEN TOLD A STORY that Lundeen could hardly believe. Aspen had a sister—a younger, married sister named Drew Young—who lived in an eastern suburb of Cleveland called Mentor On The Lake. She had been a victim of the razorblade killer.

"Eighteen months and twenty-one days ago."

The FBI got involved in the investigation, particularly a profiler by the name of Dr. Leanne Sanders, who took a special interest in the case. Aspen had several meetings with the profiler, who was kind enough to keep her in the loop.

Aspen learned about the other victims.

And how the perpetrator operated.

Unfortunately the trail grew cold.

The profiler and everyone else moved on to more pressing matters. Aspen called the profiler a number of times and even showed up at her office once in an attempt to jump-start the investigation.

That did no good.

"We're basically dead in the water until there's fresh blood," the profiler said.

But no fresh blood showed up.

Either the perpetrator had gone dormant or no one was finding the bodies. Either way, the investigation came to a solid standstill.

Then the guy started calling the profiler and taunting her, maybe because he found out that she was so involved in the investigation. The profiler determined that the calls came from public payphones in Denver. She told Aspen about them.

But everything stopped again.

"Then I came up with a plan," Aspen said. "I decided to make my own fresh blood and get the case back on everyone's radar screen."

"What do you mean—*make your own fresh blood?*" Kayla questioned.

Lundeen didn't like the tone of Kayla's voice.

And sensed trouble.

"I DECIDED TO SET MYSELF UP AS THE NEXT VICTIM and make it look like the guy was back at it," she said. "I went out and bought a neck collar and chain and padlock and razorblade. I scouted around until I found the kind of place the guy would actually use, namely the old boxcar. Then I found you, Kayla."

Kayla's eyes flashed.

"What do you mean, you found me?"

"You were helping some woman change a tire," Aspen said. "You seemed like the kind of person who would rescue someone if given the chance. Then I had a male friend of mine call you with a scrambler."

"So the guy who called me wasn't real?"

Aspen shook her head.

"No. He's just a man I know who agreed to help me out."

"You had no right," Kayla said.

Aspen agreed.

"I know," she said. "It was absolutely wrong of me. I intruded on your life and scared you to death. I had no right to do that. But, in my own defense, I had to do something to stop this guy; and get him either behind bars or dead for what he did to Drew."

"You went way over the line," Kayla said.

"I agree. I absolutely agree."

"Do you have any idea what you've done?"

Aspen looked away.

"It wasn't supposed to get this complicated. It was supposed to be simple," she said. "You were supposed to come and rescue me. Sure, you'd be scared, but you really wouldn't be in any danger. At that point, after you rescued me, I would encourage you to call the police and then I would disappear, so no one would figure out that Drew's sister was involved. The FBI would get back on the case and hopefully think of something they hadn't thought of before. I didn't mean to screw up your life. I only intended it to be a couple of hours of inconvenience."

"That doesn't justify it," Kayla said.

Aspen agreed.

BUT THINGS WENT HORRIBLY WRONG.

The drifter showed up from out of nowhere and raped Aspen. She reciprocated by blowing his face off with Kayla's gun.

Then everything was suddenly messed up big time. They couldn't go to the police. Aspen was just about to head back to Santa Fe when Marilyn Poppenberg got killed and Kayla started coming up with ideas.

The women started following Mitch Mitchell and Lance Lundeen, figuring that one of them was the razorblade killer, but not knowing which.

"I couldn't do that investigation without you," Aspen said. "We were getting so close, but you were always on the verge of dropping out. So I had my friend continue to call you with the scrambler, to keep you scared enough to stay focused."

"I can't believe you did that!" Kayla said.

Then she sprang.

And got a fistful of Aspen's hair.

And pulled as hard as she could.

Aspen screamed, struck at Kayla's face with a fist, and both women fell to the floor in a tangled web.

Lundeen scrambled out of the way.

And let them go at it.

Two loose cannons.

Loose cannons that he couldn't afford to have in his life.

Chapter Eighty-Six

Day Nine—May 13
Tuesday Night

ROBERT SHARAPOVA PULLED HIS BMW into the parking lot of the 24-Hour Fitness in Lakewood and killed the engine. Coventry pulled to a stop a good hundred yards away but left the engine running, now knowing that he'd been wasting his time. The lawyer wasn't up to anything, he was just working out.

But Sharapova didn't get out.

Two minutes later another car pulled next to him. Sharapova got into the passenger seat and the vehicle pulled away.

Coventry hung back as far as he could and followed them east on the 6th Avenue freeway, north on I-25, and then northeast on I-76. Just as they took the Highway 85 exit and headed north, Shalifa Netherwood called.

Bar sounds filled the background.

"Chalk one up for your gut," she said. "You were right. A bartender down here by the name of Ryan Smith remembers seeing Sharapova at some point in the last week or two. He was with some incredibly beautiful woman, which is the reason he remembers him. They were dressed down and getting rip-roaring drunk."

"I knew it," Coventry said.

"It could have been the night that Tracy Patterson got abducted," she added. "He doesn't specifically remember, but did confirm he was working that night."

"I'm sure it was."

"So what are you thinking?"

"I'm thinking that the woman he was with wasn't just an escort or anything, she was a woman on the side, which is a good motive to get rid of the wife. His being there where Tracy Patterson got abducted is more than just a coincidence. He's in this thing up to his eyeballs."

"How?"

Before he could answer, the Tundra's right front tire exploded.

The vehicle jerked violently and left the road.

And smashed into something.

Hard.

With a deafening sound.

Chapter Eighty-Seven

Day Nine—May 13
Tuesday Night

COVENTRY WASN'T SURE HOW BAD HE WAS HURT. Blood rolled down his forehead and into his eyes. He squeezed it out and fumbled for the door handle, desperate to get out, just in case the gas tank had been punctured. The driver's door wouldn't open but the passenger one did.

He ran.

The storm pummeled down and soaked him immediately.

Cold and invasive.

A pain shot up his spine every time he twisted to the right, but wasn't anything that would kill him. He didn't see any fire coming from the vehicle, and when it didn't blow after a few moments, he ducked back inside and fumbled around until he found the cell phone.

Shalifa Netherwood was still on the line.

He told her to pick him up.

Immediately!

SHE SQUEALED TO A STOP NINETEEN MINUTES LATER in her personal vehicle, a dark blue 4-cylinder Honda. Coventry opened the passenger door, stuck his head inside but stayed where he was. "I'm not going to call for backup because the only way we'll ever find this guy is to sneak up on him," he said. "So if you don't want to go I have no problems with that."

"Just get in the car," she said.

As soon as he did, Shalifa floored it.

Heading north on Highway 85.

Into coyote country.

"So how do we find him?" Shalifa asked.

"I don't know," he said. "I haven't gotten that far yet. The only thing I'm sure of is that he's on his way to kill Tashna Sharapova."

"How do you know that?"

"I don't know. I just do."

The storm got even worse and the Honda's wipers couldn't keep up. The city was long gone and so were the city lights. Streetlights had long since disappeared.

"I can hardly see," Shalifa said.

"Don't slow down."

LIGHTS APPEARED AHEAD ON THE RIGHT.

A gas station.

Coventry instinctively looked at the Honda's gauge and found the needle pointing to half. Just as they were about to pass the station he shouted, "Stop!"

Shalifa slammed on the brakes and the vehicle fishtailed to a stop.

"Back up to the station," Coventry said.

She did.

He jumped out and ran inside. A kid about nineteen with greasy yellow hair stood behind the cash register. Three people stood in line. Everyone gasped when Coventry bounded in. He immediately remembered that his face was covered in blood.

"I'm a police officer," he said. "I'm looking for an abandoned house. Small—just a couple of rooms. It's probably been vacant for some time but the windows aren't broke. You can hear coyotes at night."

No one said a word.

"Coyotes are everywhere around here," the kid behind the counter said.

The others nodded.

Other than that, no one knew anything.

COVENTRY AND SHALIFA HEADED FARTHER NORTH. There weren't that many gas stations so they stopped at every one. No one knew anything about an abandoned building.

They came to a Sinclair station.

Just as the lights inside went out. The door was locked. Coventry banged on it until an old man wandered out of the back room and shouted that the place was closed.

Coventry flashed his badge and said, "I'm a police officer. Open up."

Three minutes later he hopped back into the Honda and said, "In two miles we're going to come to a gravel road and take it to the right."

Shalifa put the pedal to the floor.

Chapter Eighty-Eight

Day Nine—May 13
Tuesday Night

KAYLA BECK REGAINED CONSCIOUSNESS when her chest got so tight that she could hardly breathe. She was dangling at the end of a rope tied around her chest, under her arms, being lowered into darkness. She reached up, grabbed the rope above her head and pulled up as best she could to get the pressure off her chest. She kicked with her legs but that only made things worse.

The only light came from above, through a round manhole of some sort.

"Help me!"

The lowering continued.

Until she hit the bottom.

Then the other end of the rope dropped down on her head. She smelled coal and felt dust work its way into her lungs. Then someone shined a flashlight from above. She saw that she was in an underground chamber of some sort, a large deep chamber, about the size of four or five boxcars.

Aspen lay on the ground next to her.

Unconscious or dead.

Next to her was a blue bag.

"Glad you're awake. I wanted to at least say goodbye," a voice said from above.

She recognized it immediately.

Even through the echoing.

Lance Lundeen.

"What are you doing?"

He laughed.

"What does it look like I'm doing?" he said. "You'll find flashlights, razorblades and two bottles of water in that blue bag. Enjoy."

"Please don't do this," she said.

"By the way," he said. "There won't be a rescue. This is it. This is all you get. You two represent the end of an era. If you need something to think about, think about me sitting on a beach in the French Rivera drinking those little drinks with umbrellas in them."

"But why?" she asked. "I don't understand. I thought we had a deal."

"I did too," Lundeen said. "I was actually going to let you two live. But you didn't help kill Mitch Mitchell like you were supposed to."

"Yes I did."

"No you didn't!" he said. "You held back. That made you a loose cannon, someone who might eventually get a guilty conscious and go to the police. And then, when Aspen told us how she'd been playing you for a sucker all along, you became even more of a loose cannon. She wasn't anyone you'd go out of your way to protect any more. In fact, if I'm reading that little catfight right, you hate her stinking guts and I don't blame you."

"Lance, you got this all wrong," she said. "I'd never go to

the cops about anything, not in a million years. The only thing I want to do is go back to law school and forget that any of this ever happened. I'm going to take all this to my grave, just like we talked about."

He laughed.

"You got that right. Except sooner than you thought."

"Please, Lance, don't do this."

"THERE'S ONE MORE REASON why I can't have you running around alive," he said. "You're too smart."

Kayla didn't understand.

"What do you mean?"

"It means that sooner or later you'd figure out that Mitch Mitchell wasn't the razorblade killer," he said. "You'd figure out that I am. When that happens it's inevitable that you and Aspen will either go to the cops or try to kill me."

The words stunned her.

"What do you mean—*you are*?"

"Simple," he said. "Too simple, which is why you'd eventually connect the dots. I needed you and Aspen out of my life. Once you two got the razorblade killer out of your lives then you'd get out of mine. You figured it was either me or Mitch Mitchell. So I took all my stuff—my collars and chains and padlocks and all my newspaper clippings—and put them in Mitchell's garage while you were down at law school and your little friend Aspen was out having dinner somewhere."

"That was *your* stuff?"

"It was," he said. "In fact, Aspen recognized the authentic collar, the same exact kind that I used on her sister. The one Aspen bought to pull her little prank had been close to authentic but wasn't exactly the same. As soon as she saw the real one in Mitchell's trunk she knew immediately that he was the one."

"But you can't be the razorblade killer," Kayla said. "You never recognized me or Aspen."

"Of course I didn't," he said. "That's because that whole boxcar thing involving Aspen and you was nothing more than a charade that Aspen set up. I had nothing to do with it."

Kayla bowed her head.

He was right.

"I would have never figured that out," she said. "You should have just let it be."

"Sure you would have," he said. "And if not you, then the FBI. They'd do an investigation to be sure that Mitchell was the one who killed all the victims. Chances are they were going to find that Mitchell was here in Denver, at work or something, during one of the times that someone got killed in another state. That profiler would tell all this to Aspen, who would tell you. I'd be the only suspect left in your mind. Then you'd figure out that I must have used my own stuff to frame Mitchell."

Kayla said nothing.

He was right again.

"Do me a favor," he said. "When Aspen wakes up, tell her it was fun to kill her but it was even more fun to kill her stupid little sister."

He took several pictures.

Each one exploded with an insanely bright flash.

"For the scrapbook," he said.

The lid closed on the manhole.

And the world plunged into darkness, so black and absolute that Kayla might as well have been blind.

"Lance come back!"

He didn't.

And the sound of Kayla's own breathing suddenly terrified her.

Chapter Eighty-Nine

Day Nine—May 13
Tuesday Night

WHEN THEY CAME TO A DARK VEHICLE parked on the side of the road out there in the middle of nowhere, Coventry slapped his hand on the dashboard. "Oh yeah, baby!" Shalifa pulled up behind it and immediately killed the headlights.

Then they stepped outside, into the storm.

Weapons in hand.

They saw no farmhouse or lights.

They heard no sounds.

Coventry let the air out of both rear tires of the other vehicle. Then they walked up the road for a couple of hundred yards and came to an old abandoned bridge. The one the gas station guy told Coventry about.

"This is definitely the right place," he said. "The farmhouse should be over there somewhere."

They headed that way.

"A half mile or more," Coventry added. "That's what the guy said."

"I can't see a thing," Shalifa said.

Neither could Coventry.

Stupid rain.

Neither of them had a dry spot left.

Their clothes were cold and heavy.

Suddenly a bolt of lightning ripped across the sky, lighting up the world for only a fraction of a second, but long enough for them to spot the structure.

About two hundred yards away.

Totally creepy.

They picked up the pace, stumbling and repeatedly catching themselves. As they got closer a flicker of light bounced inside the structure.

"A flashlight," Shalifa said.

Coventry's heart raced.

"We need to proceed as if Tashna Sharapova is still alive," he said. "That means we need to be careful where we shoot. When we get there, you take the back and I'll take the front. Be careful."

"Wish I had a flashlight," Shalifa said.

"Be careful not to shoot me."

"That goes both ways."

COVENTRY POSITIONED HIMSELF AT THE FRONT DOOR as Shalifa disappeared around the side of the building. The doorknob wasn't locked. He turned it as quietly as he could and then slowly pushed the door open.

No reaction came.

No charging footsteps.

No gunfire.

He stepped inside.

A flashlight bounced off the walls of a rear room.

A woman sobbed, hardly audible over the pounding of the storm.

"Please, Robert, don't do this. I'll give you the money, every single penny—it's all yours, honest to God. If you kill me you're just going to end up in jail."

Smack!

"Shut up!"

Coventry took a step towards the room.

Then another.

And another.

Suddenly a bright light flashed.

And glass exploded.

Gunfire.

Shalifa Netherwood shouted, "I'm hit!"

Chapter Ninety

Day Nine—May 13
Tuesday Night

WHEN COVENTRY BOUNDED INTO THE ROOM, he wasn't prepared for what he saw. A woman—no doubt Tashna Sharapova—was lying on a ratty mattress, naked and tied with rope. Robert Sharapova was on his knees behind her with a fistful of hair in one hand and a box cutter in the other, pressed against the woman's throat. Shalifa Netherwood's body hung jackknifed through a window, her torso inside and her legs out. She didn't move. Her arms hung limp and blood dropped to the floor.

A woman stood next to Shalifa.

Holding a gun.

"Drop it!" Coventry said.

She almost did but Sharapova shouted, "No!"

Then he locked eyes with Coventry and said, "Drop the gun or I slit her throat." Sharapova looked at the woman with the weapon. "If he doesn't drop the gun by the time I count to three, shoot her again."

The woman swung around and trained her weapon at

Shalifa's back. Coventry held his hands up in surrender, quietly flipped the safety back on, then slowly stooped down and set his weapon on the floor.

"Now back up," Sharapova said.

Coventry obeyed.

"Get me his gun," Sharapova told the woman.

She did.

With Coventry's gun in hand, Sharapova stood up.

"Get in here," he ordered.

COVENTRY WALKED SLOWLY. If he charged, there was no way he could get to Sharapova before the man shot. The best he could hope for was the guy didn't have enough knowledge about guns or enough presence of mind to take the safety off.

Sharapova said, "Stop there!"

Coventry did.

"Very good," Sharapova said. "I'm sorry about this, but you understand that I can't leave any witnesses."

Coventry lunged.

The gun didn't fire.

Both men landed on the floor and the nerves in Coventry's back exploded. Then something burned his cheek. He immediately put his hand to it and felt blood.

Lots of blood.

Gushing.

And realized that Sharapova had slashed him with the box cutter.

Then Sharapova was up and running out of the room.

Coventry forced himself to his feet.

The woman with the gun stood there, frozen, not knowing

what to do. Coventry turned his head, as if he just saw someone come into the room, and when the woman did the same he pounced. But she dodged him and disappeared out the door as he struggled with the pain in his back.

Then Shalifa Netherwood's body fell into the room.

"Get 'em," she said.

"No. I'm not leaving you."

"Don't argue with me."

Coventry rolled her onto her back and ripped her blouse open. She wasn't wearing a vest. The bullet had gone all the way through the edge of her body, missing her heart and lungs. He untied Tashna Sharapova and put his cell phone in her hands.

"Call 911," he said. "Then keep pressure on her wounds. Can you do that?"

"Yes."

He looked at Shalifa again.

"Go," she said.

He picked up his gun and ran out the door.

SHARAPOVA HAD A LONG HEAD START but Coventry didn't care. He knew where the man was going.

To the car.

The car with the flat tires.

Coventry slowed to a walk so he wouldn't be out of breath when he got there. Lightning ripped across the sky and gave enough light to confirm that the man wasn't doubling back to the house.

When he got to the road the woman was nowhere to be seen but Sharapova was there, crouching next to the vehicle.

"Very clever," he said. "The tires. Give me your keys."

"I'd like to but they're in my partner's pocket," Coventry said. Then he bent down, unscrewed the cap of one of the Honda tires and started to let the air out. "By the time you get them these will all be flat. There's no escape. You may as well make it easy on yourself and give up now, before you get yourself in more trouble."

The man laughed.

"You cops are all the same," he said. "Dumb as dirt. You're going to die because of your own stupidity. How does it feel?"

Coventry didn't understand.

"What do you mean?"

"What I mean is, there were guns in that room when you ran out and you weren't smart enough to grab one before you bounded out the door. You have to admit, that was pretty stupid."

Coventry cocked his head.

The man must think that Coventry didn't have a weapon because he hadn't yelled "Freeze!" or told him to get on the ground.

"I suppose you're right," he said. "What can I say?"

Sharapova held up the box cutter and waved it back and forth.

"Like I said before. I can't have any witnesses."

Coventry could hardly breathe.

His body felt heavy from the loss of blood.

Then he said, "Put that thing down and I won't have to use it on you."

Sharapova laughed.

Coventry quietly slipped the safety back on.

Then Sharapova charged.

As he did, Coventry tossed his gun to the side.

FIVE MINUTES LATER, the last drop of blood that was going to drip out of Sharapova's neck did.

No one was there to watch.

Not even Coventry.

Who at that moment was applying pressure to Shalifa Netherwood's wounds and talking into a cell phone, giving directions to the paramedics.

A coyote barked.

Back by the road.

Then another.

In a matter of seconds a whole pack yelped and yapped.

And Coventry pulled up an image of sharp yellow teeth tearing the flesh off Robert Sharapova's body.

Chapter Ninety-One

Day Ten—May 14
Wednesday Afternoon

IT WAS THREE IN THE MORNING before Bryson Coventry arrived at the hospital to get the cut on his face, and the gash on the top of his head, stitched up. Both turned out to be a lot more serious than he thought.

"Do a hack job," Coventry told the doctor. "I need a couple of good scars."

The doctor chuckled and said, "Hack jobs cost extra."

The chief showed up, wrinkled his face and personally drove Coventry home. Coventry fell into bed and didn't open his eyes again until noon.

When he got to the office, the FBI profiler, Dr. Leanne Sanders, was using his desk and didn't notice as he walked in. He got a cup of coffee and sank into the chair in front of her.

"Meet Frankenstein," he said.

"This is so unfair," she said.

"What?"

"You still look good, even with five hundred stitches in your face."

He leaned towards her.

"To tell you the truth, I sort of like it. I took a couple of pictures. After it heals, I'm going to have it tattooed on."

He expected her to smile.

But instead she put a serious look on her face and said, "Are you up for some work today?"

"No, but I will be, after two more cups of this brown stuff."

She stood up.

"Bring them with you," she said. "We're wasting time."

THEY TOOK HER CAR, an Avis rental, and winded west through the city under a perfectly blue Colorado sky. On the way she explained where they were going.

A skinhead named Mitch Mitchell got stabbed to death last night in his crappy little house on the outskirts of Golden, not far from a rock quarry.

The Golden cops found lots of stuff by the body.

Neck collars.

Chains.

Blue rope.

And most importantly of all, lots of newspaper articles and Internet downloads about a number of victims—the victims of the razorblade killer. The word spread fast and worked its way to the FBI.

Leanne got the call about six this morning and went straight to the scene. The newspaper articles were all genuine. So was the stuff. Everything pointed to the fact that the guy was the razorblade killer.

"There's only one problem," she said. "He isn't the right guy."

"He isn't?"

"No."

"How do you know?"

"Because the guy we're looking for is big," she said. "We know that for a fact. This guy's a little twerp. Plus I've already been able to verify that the guy was reporting to work right here in Denver when some of the murders took place out of state."

Coventry scratched his head.

"Then how do you explain all the stuff?"

"My guess?"

"Right."

"He was set up. Now who would want to do that, other than the genuine article?"

"No one."

"Precisely."

"So who set him up?"

"I don't know, but we found a couple of very interesting fingerprints on one of the collars," she said. "They belong to a man named Gordon Andrews, from California. He got pulled over one night for a broken taillight and just happened to have a dead woman in the trunk of his car, bound in blue rope."

The words shocked Coventry.

"Like Marilyn Poppenberg," he said.

"Right," she said. "He got off on a technicality, moved to Denver and changed his name to Lance Lundeen."

THEY WERE APPROACHING THE RAILROAD YARD where Aspen White's cell phone had been found. Leanne pulled to the side of the road and killed the engine.

"Lundeen lives in that building over there," she said. "He's a big man. Six-three."

Coventry nodded.

"I know. I've met him. He looks like Tarzan."

"You have?"

Yes, he had.

And explained how.

Then he remembered his conversation with Rain, about the man who abducted her, and the fact that the man was stronger, in fact a lot stronger, than Coventry.

"One more thing," Leanne said. "The car out by the farmhouse last night where you had your little party is registered to one Del Rae Paris. Her phone records show lots of calls to and from our little friend over there, Mr. Lundeen."

"You figured all this out this morning?"

"I've been busting my behind for over seven hours," she said. "You don't even want to know how many markers I called in and how many blowjobs I owe."

Coventry chuckled.

Then frowned.

"So now what?" he questioned.

"Now we find out if Lance Lundeen is the person I've been hunting for the last four years."

"We have enough for a warrant," Coventry said.

"I'm not so sure," she said. "It's too complicated. I don't want to search his place, find everything we need, and then have some judge throw it all out after the fact. He walked on a technicality once. It's not going to happen again."

"So what are you proposing?"

"I'm proposing that we go knock on his door and hope that he says or does something to give us a reason to arrest him."

"That's your plan? Knock on his door?"

"Right."

Coventry frowned.

"If you're looking for an opportunity to kill him," he said, "don't do it."

She looked at him hard.

"I'm going to knock on his door. You can come with me or not, your choice."

Chapter Ninety-Two

Day Ten—May 14
Wednesday Afternoon

KAYLA BECK ACCEPTED ASPEN WHITE'S apology a long time ago and it wasn't an issue anymore. The manhole thirty feet above them was unreachable. There wasn't a single thing in the tomb they could stand on. There was nothing above for the ropes to hook to. The surfaces were totally smooth.

They were sealed tight and had come to accept it.

They huddled in the corner and held each other in the dark.

Talking about people they knew and things they did when they were kids. Trying to keep their minds off the fact that every breath they took robbed the air of that much more oxygen.

"At least we have the razorblades," Kayla said.

Aspen agreed.

"I can't go by suffocation."

"Me either."

"We'll do it at the same time."

"Okay."

Chapter Ninety-Three

Day Ten—May 14
Wednesday Afternoon

WHEN THEY KNOCKED on Lance Lundeen's door, and rang the buzzer ten times, no one answered. Leanne headed for the fire escape and said, "I'm going in."

"Are you nuts?" Coventry said. "We're better off with a dubious warrant than an illegal entry."

"Del Rae Paris has already tipped him off," Leanne said. "If he's on the run and gets too much of a head start, and ends up falling back into his old habits a month down the road, I'm not going to be able to live with myself."

Coventry considered it.

"I can't have the blood on my hands," she added. "I just can't."

Coventry studied her.

"We're wasting time," she added.

They headed up the fire escape, broke a window on the second floor and climbed in.

No sounds came from inside.

Something that looked like a large spider web hung from the

412

ceiling at the far end of the room. They walked up a stairway to the next level and found it equally vacant. Then they headed up to the top floor.

That's where the living quarters were.

They did a quick sweep.

The roof too.

The man wasn't there.

"He's already on the run," Leanne said.

They searched the place, gently, putting everything back exactly as they found it. The man was clearly a photography nut.

"He's got souvenir photos around here somewhere," Leanne said. "That's what we need to be looking for."

Behind the dark room they found another room.

Filled with hundreds of drawers.

Drawers filled with photographs and negatives.

Leanne searched while Coventry stood guard outside.

Two hours later she shouted, "Bingo!"

COVENTRY RAN IN and found Leanne pulling a stack of photographs out of a bottom drawer.

Hundreds of eight-by-ten color photographs.

Depicting a dozen or so different women.

Wearing collars.

He looked over her shoulder as she rifled through them.

When they came to the last seven or eight in the stack, Coventry couldn't believe his eyes and grabbed them out of Leanne's hand.

"This is Aspen White and Kayla Beck," he said.

Leanne studied the pictures harder.

"This is Nicole White," she said. "I know her. She's the sister of one of the victims. Drew Young."

Nicole?

Then Coventry remembered that Aspen's first name was actually Nicole.

Nicole.

Aspen.

Whatever.

In the photo, she laid on the ground.

Either unconscious or dead.

Kayla Beck was looking up at the camera.

With fear etched on her face.

"I just had dinner with her last night," Coventry said.

Chapter Ninety-Four

Day Eleven—May 15
Thursday Evening

KAYLA BECK AND ASPEN WHITE slit their wrists at the same time and then laid down on their backs and held hands. Kayla felt the life seeping out of her.

It felt right.

It felt good.

It was time.

In the darkness above, she saw a round tunnel of light and said, "I'm going to heaven."

"Me too," Aspen said.

"They're calling for me."

"I hear them."

"I'll meet you up there."

"You want to be roommates?"

"Sure. That'll be nice."

Chapter Ninety-Five

Day Twelve—May 16
Friday Morning

BRYSON COVENTRY SLEPT IN FRIDAY MORNING, not caring for a change that he had wasted part of the day. Then he threw on sweatpants and headed outside for a jog under a stunning blue Colorado sky. By some miracle he didn't break a leg when he dropped down into the tomb yesterday. He didn't even sprain an ankle, in fact.

He showered.

And then headed east on the 6th Avenue freeway, stopping at the 7-Eleven on Simms for a thermos of coffee.

Jan and Dean's "Surf City" spilled out of cheap speakers.

Coventry hung around in the store and drank coffee until the song ended. He was just about to leave when he spotted roses. He bought three and then headed to the hospital.

He gave one to Shalifa Netherwood.

And one to Kayla Beck.

Then walked down to Aspen White's room. She was awake and reading a book called *Bangkok Laws.*

"How'd you find us?" she asked.

416

He shook his head. "In a nutshell, Lundeen took pictures of the two of you which we were lucky enough to find. The place you were in is pretty unique and we were able to figure out that it was part of an old mining operation. Some of the professors at the Colorado School of Mines helped us pinpoint it. If he had stuck you in plain old 55-gallon drums we wouldn't have had a chance."

"I want their names," she said. "So I can thank them."

Coventry nodded.

"They'd like that."

"What happened to Lundeen?"

Coventry frowned.

"He's on the run. Him and Del Rae Paris," Coventry said. "We'll get them, though. It's just a matter of time."

She nodded.

"How's Rain?"

Coventry frowned.

"It turned out that Lundeen's phone records showed calls going back and forth between him and Rain," he said.

"Did you ask her about them?"

Coventry nodded.

"I did."

"What'd she say?"

"She said she loved me and wanted to know if I loved her."

"What'd you say?"

"I said I did," Coventry said.

"Was that the truth?"

He nodded.

"Then she told me a story and asked if I loved her enough to give her a 24-hour head start."

"What'd you say?"

"I told her I did."

"Then what happened?"

"She kissed me goodbye and left," he said. "That conversation was thirty-six hours ago. You're the only person I've told so far."

"So this is our secret?"

He nodded and said, "If you don't mind."

SHE DARTED HER EYES AS IF MAKING A DECISION and then said, "Can I tell you something totally off the record?"

"Of course."

"When I told you before that I fell in love with you right off the bat, I wasn't playing around."

"I know."

"We had a connection," she said.

"I know."

"We still do."

He nodded.

"I know."

"So I have a hypothetical question for you," she said. "Suppose, just for the sake of argument, that I was chained in a boxcar and a drifter came in and raped me and then I shot him in the face. Is that the kind of thing that would get in the way of you having feelings for me?"

He pondered it.

It was different than Rain's situation.

Rain played along with Lundeen's charade for a worthy cause, namely to get $50,000 to help her sister with a kidney transplant. If that had been all there was to it, Coventry could have overlooked it. But Rain kept quiet the whole time Coventry was trying to save Tashna Sharapova, which was something he couldn't overlook.

Not in a hundred years.

He locked eyes with Aspen.

True, she had killed someone.

But in the heat of passion.

And someone who had it coming.

"I can understand how that could happen," he said. "I'm not in a position to criticize."

She took his hand.

Tears rolled down her cheeks.

"Does that mean you're going to take me out to supper again?"

He smiled.

"It certainly looks that way, doesn't it?"

She squeezed his hand.

"With dessert this time?"

He squeezed back.

And smiled.

"Dessert's my favorite part."

About The Author

Jim Michael Hansen, Esq., is a Colorado attorney. With over twenty years of high quality legal experience, he represents a wide variety of entities and individuals in civil matters, with an emphasis on civil litigation, employment law and OSHA.

JimHansenLawFirm.com.

Visit Jim's Website

For information on all the *Laws* thrillers, including upcoming titles, please visit Jim's website. Jim loves to hear from readers. Please feel free to send him an email.

JimHansenBooks.com

Email Jim@JimHansenBooks.com